BLOOMSBURY
GOOD READING GUIDE
TO CRIME FICTION

BLOOMSBURY
GOOD READING GUIDE
TO CRIME FICTION

This edition edited by
Nick Rennison

Original Authors
Kenneth and Valerie McLeish

BLOOMSBURY

First published in 2003 by
Bloomsbury Publishing Plc
38 Soho Square
London W1D 3HB

www.bloomsburymagazine.com
Bloomsbury's website offers booklovers the chance to participate in the literary life online. Its features include a magazine archive, advice for reading groups, a research centre and a writers' almanac. Most books mentioned in the *Bloomsbury Good Reading Guide to Crime Fiction*, where still in print, may be purchased through the website.

The moral right of the author has been asserted.

A CIP entry for this book is available from the British Library.

ISBN 0 7475 6089 7

10 9 8 7 6 5 4 3 2 1

Typeset by Hewer Text Ltd, Edinburgh
Printed and bound in Great Britain by Clays Ltd, St Ives plc

CONTENTS

INTRODUCTION

When and where did crime fiction begin? A few students of the genre, eager to provide it with a respectably lengthy pedigree, have traced its sources back to stories in biblical and Ancient Greek literature, but this is special pleading. More convincingly, the critic and crime writer Julian Symons cited William Godwin's 1794 novel *Caleb Williams* as the first true crime novel. But crime fiction really began in the middle decades of the nineteenth century and it began in America, England and France.

In America, in the 1840s, Edgar Allan Poe became the founding father of detective fiction with the three short stories in which the brilliantly ratiocinative Dupin solves apparently insoluble mysteries. In England in the 1860s Wilkie Collins wrote *The Woman in White* and *The Moonstone*, novels which hinge on the working out of a crime mystery. And *The Moonstone* introduces in Sergeant Cuff the first of what have been, in the 140 years since, innumerable police protagonists. Collins may have been influenced by the short-lived French novelist Emile Gaboriau (1833–1873) who, also in the 1860s, published a number of books (for example, *The Lerouge Affair*) which use themes and motifs still recognizable in crime fiction today. Together, the American, the Englishman and the Frenchman set patterns which have lasted until the present day.

The next leap forward came, of course, with Doyle's creation of Sherlock Holmes. With Holmes, unashamedly based on elements of Poe's portrait of Dupin, the detective story achieved a popularity that it has never lost. Doyle had countless imitators and by the end of the second decade of the twentieth century, the 'Golden Age' of English crime fiction was set to dawn. Agatha Christie published her first novel, *The Mysterious Affair at Styles*, in 1920 and other women writers – Dorothy L. Sayers, Margery Allingham, Ngaio Marsh – made their debuts in the course of the next decade or so.

In the USA, in the 1920s, there were writers (S. S. Van Dine, for example) who were happy to produce their own American versions of the mannered and often eccentric mysteries that were so popular in Britain. Side by side with these, however, were the growing numbers of American writers who were creating – often in the pages of the so-called 'pulp' magazines like *Black Mask* – an indigenous form of crime writing that owed nothing to models from across the Atlantic. Dashiell Hammett and other lesser talents, in the words of Raymond Chandler, 'gave murder back to the people who commit it for reasons, not just to provide a corpse'. Hard-boiled or '*noir*' fiction was born.

In some ways these two main strands of crime fiction – the elaborate puzzles of the classic English detective story and the hard-boiled crime that developed in the pulp magazines – have continued to this day. There have been many crossovers and many novelists who have successfully used elements of both but there is a tradition that links Christie and Marsh with writers like P. D. James and Peter Lovesey just as there is a line that can be drawn from Hammett and Chandler to modern American novelists such as James Ellroy and Elmore Leonard.

The other main strand of crime writing – what is usually termed the psychological thriller – began in the 1930s and can be traced to the novels Anthony Berkeley Cox wrote under the pseudonym Francis Iles. Here the emphasis is not on the solution of a puzzle (in Iles's *Malice Aforethought* there is no doubt who committed the murder) nor on the gritty realism of city life. The interest of the books lies in the slow unravelling of the psyche of the protagonist(s). The psychological thriller has attracted the talents of some of the best writers in the genre, from Iles through Patricia Highsmith to contemporary novelists like Ruth Rendell, Minette Walters and Nicci French.

So, this is the territory that this guide takes as its subject. What other criteria have been used to choose the 200-plus authors who feature here. Any guide to crime fiction that failed to acknowledge the giants of the genre would be a poor one indeed, and Doyle, Christie and Dashiell Hammett and some twenty to thirty others fell into this category. In selecting the other crime novelists, I was influenced by a mixture of criteria. First, of course, quality. I wanted all the writers I picked to be skilled exponents of their craft. Secondly, I wanted the writers chosen to have a body of work that was, by and large, readily available in bookshops and on library shelves. Not every book in the guide is currently in print – that would have been far too restricting – but I have tried to remember that, while it's easy enough for me to recommend a book or a writer as 'brilliant' or 'unmissable', it's very annoying for readers if that brilliant writer or unmissable book is impossible to obtain.

Thirdly, I wanted to reflect the enormous range of writing that gets classified as 'crime fiction'. It is sometimes assumed, by those who know little of the genre, that crime fiction is all much of a muchness. Fans are aware that nothing could be further from the truth. There are as many different types of writing in the crime genre as there are in 'mainstream' or 'literary' fiction: the historical crime novels of Ellis Peters, set in medieval Shrewsbury; the dark, hard-boiled epics of James Ellroy; the frenetic, surreal capers of Carl Hiaasen; the sophisticated Golden Age mysteries of Margery Allingham; the psychological thrillers of Ruth Rendell writing under her pseudonym of Barbara Vine; the so-called 'tartan *noir*' of the Scottish writer Ian Rankin; the 'Alphabet' series by Sue Grafton featuring her female detective Kinsey Millhone. There are dozens of different ways in which writers can work within the broad church of crime fiction. I wanted the guide to be as inclusive as it could be.

One of the great debates among enthusiasts of the crime genre – at least, among those who enjoy such ultimately undecidable questions – is where to set the boundaries between 'crime fiction' and 'thrillers'. My own approach has been simple, perhaps even simplistic. If a book focuses on the commission of a crime (murder, fraud, theft etc.) and much of the interest in its plot depends on discovering who committed that crime and why, I have considered it for inclusion in the guide. If a book focuses on international politics and/or espionage, then I have omitted it. Thus John Grisham and John Le Carré both write books that could be called thrillers. The plots of Grisham's books hinge on the law and the commission of crime and, therefore, I have given him an entry in the guide. The interest in Le Carré's books centres on the morally ambivalent world of espionage and, therefore, I have excluded him from the guide.

There are more than 200 novelists included in this guide but it would have been easy enough to include at least as many again without in any way compromising the quality of the writing covered. Crime fiction remains one of the most popular of genres. Each year thousands of crime novels are published in the UK and the USA and hundreds of skilled practitioners work in the genre. Space alone has meant that I have had to ignore some writers to whom I would have liked to have given an entry, although I have tried to use the read ons at the end of each entry and the Read on a Theme menus as a means of broadening the range of novelists the guide covers. Users of the guide will, almost inevitably, find that one or two of their favourite writers are absent from its pages. However, I confidently hope that everyone who consults the guide will find in it both reminders of old favourites and pointers to new discoveries and that they will gain a renewed awareness of just how varied and enjoyable the genre is.

HOW TO USE THIS BOOK

Each of the author entries in this guide contains some or all of the following four elements:

1 a paragraph describing the author's work in general terms, sometimes by featuring a selection of books
2 a more detailed description of one book by the author
3 a listing, selected or complete, of the author's other books
4 a list of suggested 'read ons'. These use the symbols ● for another book by the same author and ▶ for books by other authors.

Throughout the guide the symbol ▷ before a name means that that author has his or her own entry.

In addition there are a number of 'Read on a Theme' menus dotted throughout the guide which take a particular subject (the art world, gay and lesbian detectives, Greece, medieval mystery, serial killers etc.) and provide a list of up to a dozen books on that theme.

At the end of the book there are two appendices – one which lists detectives and other investigators and their creators who appear in the main entries and one which lists the winners of the most prestigious award for crime writing in Britain, the CWA Gold Dagger, and winners of the Edgar Award in the United States.

ACKNOWLEDGEMENTS

This book could not have been completed without the generous assistance of two people. Valerie McLeish, with her late husband Kenneth, compiled the first edition of the guide. I have used some of the original entries almost verbatim because they were so well written – concise, witty and knowledgeable – that it seemed unnecessary to do otherwise. Valerie has also contributed many suggestions about writers who were not included in the first edition and I am very grateful for all her kind help. Richard Shephard is a fount of knowledge about American crime fiction. He supplied me with much information about writers about whom I knew little and more than a dozen of the entries are so dependent on what he wrote that they are, in effect, his work. Again, I am enormously grateful for his willingness to share his knowledge with me.

At Bloomsbury Kathy Rooney, Nicky Thompson and Gordon Kerr were consistently supportive of the project and all supplied ideas and suggestions that have been incorporated in the final text. Caroline Ball has proved the kind of copy editor that all authors should have. Her skill and patience as she turned the often chaotic manuscript I supplied into a form in which it could be delivered to the printers are much appreciated.

Finally, I would like to thank Steve Andrews, Paul Baggaley, Paula Croxon, John Magrath, Ion Mills and Linda Pattenden. All these people have, over the years, done for me what this guide hopes to do for others – pointed out rewarding and enjoyable crime novels which I would otherwise have missed.

A

AIRD, Catherine (born 1930)
British novelist

Catherine Aird's gentle mysteries, set in the imaginary English county of West Calleshire, are old-fashioned in the best sense of the term. They hark back to the golden age of ▷ Christie and ▷ Ngaio Marsh in their carefully structured, labyrinthine plotting and in their scrupulous planting of clues for the reader to follow towards a solution. All but one of her novels feature the phlegmatic and methodical Inspector Sloan whose investigations are helped, and occasionally hindered, by his more ebullient colleague, Detective Constable Crosby. The mysteries take place in traditional territory for English crime fiction – small villages, country houses – and the supporting cast of characters is always enjoyably packed with eccentrics and oddballs.

LITTLE KNELL (2001)
An Egyptian mummy-case donated to the local museum turns out to contain the body of a young woman who has met her end not thousands of years ago on the banks of the Nile but a week earlier and in Calleshire. As Sloan pursues the mysteries of the young woman's identity and the whereabouts of the missing mummy, the trail takes him and the reader through a maze of misdirection and false leads to a satisfyingly neat conclusion.

The Inspector Sloan novels include Henrietta Who?, Parting Breath, Some Die Eloquent, The Body Politic, A Going Concern, After Effects, Injury Time, Stiff News, Little Knell *and* Amendment of Life.

> **READ ON**

▶ ▷ Ngaio Marsh, *A Man Lay Dead*; ▷ Dorothy Simpson, *Once Too Often*; Veronica Stallwood, *Oxford Shadows*; June Thomson, *No Flowers by Request.*

ALLINGHAM, Margery (1905–1966)
British novelist and short story writer

Allingham is one of the most enjoyable of all English 'Golden Age' writers. Her characters are wonderfully bizarre, and she has a deep love for the cobbles and back alleys of a long-demolished 'village' London. Her detective, Albert Campion, conceals the obligatory razor-sharp intelligence of the detective beneath a vacuous, silly-ass manner and he is at home in stories that range from Buchanish adventure (*Sweet Danger, Traitor's Purse*) to stylish farce (*The Fashion in Shrouds, The Beckoning Lady*).

MORE WORK FOR THE UNDERTAKER (1949)

Someone is murdering the few survivors of the Palinode family in their rabbit warren of lodgings in Apron Street, London. What has Jas Bowels, proprietor of Reliable Interments, to do with it? Above all, can Mr Campion unravel the mystery in time to prevent someone else being forced to 'go up Apron Street' (whatever that sinister phrase might mean)?

Allingham's other books include Coroner's Pidgin, Police at the Funeral, Look to the Lady, The Tiger in the Smoke *and the short story collections* Mr Campion and Others, Take Two at Bedtime *and* The Return of Mr Campion *(which also contains non-Campion tales). After Allingham's death, her husband P. Young-man Carter wrote two further Campion novels, one of which,* Mr Campion's Farthing, *is up to his wife's most sparkling standard.*

READ ON ▷

● *Flowers for the Judge* (set in a seedy 1930s London publisher's office, and involving a priceless, but unprintably pornographic manuscript); *Hide My Eyes.*
▶ ▷ Michael Innes, *The Daffodil Affair*; ▷ Edmund Crispin, *The Case of the Gilded Fly*; ▷ P. D. James, *A Taste for Death.*

APOSTOLOU, Anna, see Paul DOHERTY

ARJOUNI, Jakob (born 1964)
German novelist

Arjouni's protagonist in his novels, Kemal Kayankaya, is in the long tradition of private eyes established by ▷ Hammett's Sam Spade and ▷ Chandler's Philip Marlowe. His personal life is shambolic and he drinks too much. He pokes his nose into corruption in high places and refuses to ignore the smell. His persistent determination to get to the truth earns him beatings and death threats that he ignores. He has his own, quixotic old-fashioned code of honour. In some ways, Kayankaya and the plots in which he is involved are formulaic and predictable. What makes the books intriguingly different and gives them a real edge is that Kayankaya is a Turkish-born private detective, living and working in modern Frankfurt. Genuine racial tensions and social problems lie behind Arjouni's work and give it a bite that it would not otherwise have.

The three Kayankaya novels are Happy Birthday, Turk, More Beer *and* One Man, One Murder.

READ ON ▷

▶ ▷ Henning Mankell, *Faceless Killers*; ▷ Daniel Pennac, *The Fairy Gunmother* (very different in style from Arjouni but also concerned with multi-ethnic modern Europe); Mike Phillips, *Blood Rights*; Barbara Nadel, *Deep Waters.*

READ ON A THEME: THE ART OF CRIME
(painters, sculptors, forgers, murderers . . .)

Lionel Davidson, *The Chelsea Murders*
▷ Michael Innes, *Private View*
Nicholas Kilmer, *O, Sacred Head*
▷ Laurie King, *A Grave Talent*
▷ Charlotte MacLeod, *The Resurrection Man*
▷ Ngaio Marsh, *Artists in Crime*
▷ Iain Pears, *Death and Restoration*
Arturo Perez-Reverte, *The Flanders Panel*
Douglas Skeggs, *The Triumph of Bacchus*
▷ Charles Willeford, *The Burnt Orange Heresy*

B

BALDACCI, David (born 1960)
US novelist

Like ▷ John Grisham, Baldacci is a lawyer turned novelist. Like Grisham his virtues lie not in the depth and subtlety of his prose and characterization but his ability to seize your attention on the first page and not let go until his story, with all its twists and turns, is complete. This was evident in his first novel, *Absolute Power* (in which a burglar witnesses the US President's involvement in murder and becomes the target of a secret service manhunt), and has been clearly demonstrated in five more best-selling books. Like Grisham, who wrote *A Painted House*, an account of a boy growing up in the 1950s, Baldacci has recently turned away from crime thrillers to publish *Wish You Well*, a coming-of-age tale of two children sent to live with their great-grandmother. Fans of both writers will have been relieved to discover that these were temporary diversions and that both have since returned to the style with which they are most comfortable.

LAST MAN STANDING (2002)
The hero of Baldacci's book is Web London, a member of an elite FBI team, who is the only survivor of a drug-dealer's ambush that killed many of his colleagues. Tormented by guilt, he is also desperate to know why he was the only one who was allowed to walk away from the ambush. The only other person seen leaving the alleyway where the killings took place was a young boy and London sets out to track him down. *Last Man Standing* takes no prizes for originality of plot but Baldacci succeeds in cranking up the tension as his hero fights to survive and learn the truth.

David Baldacci's other novels are Total Control, The Winner, The Simple Truth, Saving Faith *and* Wish You Well.

> **READ ON**

▶ ▷ **John Grisham,** *The Firm*; ▷ **Lee Child,** *Echo Burning*; ▷ **James Patterson,** *Along Came a Spider*; **Brad Meltzer,** *The Tenth Justice*.

BARNARD, Robert (born 1936)
British novelist

Barnard's crime stories are as cunningly plotted as ▷ Agatha Christie's, but without a great detective: the mysteries are solved either by his likeable London policeman Perry Trethowan or by members of the local force. He is particularly good at suggesting atmosphere, whether a great house riven by family feuding, the streets of a seedy Soho, or the 'typical English village' so familiar to Christie fans. His characters are sometimes stereotypes – his cockneys tend to say 'Cor blimey' a lot – but offer a rich and lethal mixture of personalities.

Robert Barnard's more than thirty novels include Death on the High Cs, Death in a Cold Climate, A Corpse in a Gilded Cage, Bodies, Death and the Chaste Apprentice, A Scandal in Belgravia, The Masters of the House, The Corpse at Haworth Tandoori, A Murder in Mayfair *and* Unholy Dying.
   Under the name Bernard Bastable he has published several mysteries ingeniously set in an alternative historical reality in which Mozart stayed in England after his childhood visit, lived on into old age and took up sleuthing in 1820. These are To Die Like a Gentleman, Dead, Mr Mozart *and* Too Many Notes, Mr Mozart.

READ ON ▷

▶ to the Trethowan books: ▷ **Elizabeth George,** *Well-Schooled in Murder*; ▷ **Reginald Hill,** *Bones and Silence*; ▷ **Ruth Rendell,** *Kissing the Gunner's Daughter*.
▶ to the Bernard Bastable books: ▷ **Kate Ross,** *Whom the Gods Love*; Lillian de la Torre, *The Detections of Dr Sam Johnson*.

BARNES, Linda (born 1949)
US novelist

Linda Barnes's engaging and funny crime novels are set in Boston, Massachusetts, where her six-foot-tall redhead heroine Carlotta Carlyle doubles up as a private investigator and, when cases are hard to come by, cab driver. Although Carlotta is the focus, the novels are more like ensemble pieces since there are plenty of opportunities for other recurring characters to make their presences felt – her boss at the cab company, Sam Gianelli, her 'little sister' Paolina and her former partner in the police force, Lieutenant Mooney. One of the strengths of the series is the way it shows the developing and changing relationships of these characters. Gutsy and sassy female private investigators have become ten a penny in recent years but Carlotta Carlyle remains one of the most consistently entertaining.

COYOTE (1990)
Carlotta's latest client speaks poor English but her message is clear. A corpse has been found clutching an immigrant's green card. It's hers and she wants Carlotta to help her get it back. The trail leads into the dark world of illegal immigration and those who make their money out of exploiting the would-be immigrants. And, somehow, Carlotta's 'little sister', streetwise Paolina, is involved.

The other Carlotta Carlyle books are A Trouble of Fools, The Snake Tattoo, Steel Guitar, Snapshot, Hardware, Cold Case, Flashpoint *and* The Big Dig. *Linda Barnes has also written a number of novels (e.g.* Bitter Finish *and* Dead Heat*) featuring Michael Spraggue, an actor and amateur private investigator.*

READ ON ▷

▶ ▷ **Karen Kijewski,** *Alley Kat Blues*; ▷ **Marcia Muller,** *Listen to the Silence*.

BASTABLE, Bernard, see Robert BARNARD

BENTLEY, E(dmund) C(lerihew) (1875–1956)
British novelist, critic and essayist

A journalist, critic and friend of ▷ G. K. Chesterton, Bentley invented the detective Philip Trent, a languid painter-about-town with a fine line in nonsense badinage. Bentley's best-known book, *Trent's Last Case* (1913), was begun as a spoof of the crime fiction of the time (Trent breaks every unwritten law, including falling in love with the chief suspect and getting his solution wrong), but is also a genuinely satisfying mystery. It has a tortuous plot but the clues are fairly placed, obvious to everyone but Trent. Bentley's other Trent books are the novel *Trent's Own Case* (in which Trent's investigations lead him to conclude that he committed the crime himself) and the short story collection *Trent Intervenes*.

READ ON ▷

▶ ▷ **S. S. Van Dine,** *The Scarab Murder Case*; **Anthony Berkeley,** *Dead Mrs Stratton*; **Ronald Knox,** *The Viaduct Murder.*

BERGMAN, Andrew (born 1945)
US novelist

Bergman's Jack Levine novels began as parodies of the private eye novels of ▷ Hammett and ▷ Chandler, and are crammed with wisecracks and one-liners. But they are also suspenseful, craftily plotted mysteries, as atmospheric as any of his models'. In *The Big Kiss-off of 1944* Levine is sucked into the corrupt politics of the 1944 US presidential election and in *Hollywood and Levine* he investigates a murder in the Hollywood of Bogart, Cagney and any other tough guys and gals you care to mention. Bergman recently returned to the character after a gap of a quarter of a century in *Tender is Levine*.

READ ON ▷

▶ ▷ **Stuart M. Kaminsky,** *High Midnight*; **George Baxt,** *The Dorothy Parker Murder Case* **(set in the 1920s rather than the 1940s but with similar, wisecracking dialogue); Max Allan Collins,** *Angel in Black.*

BERKELEY, Anthony, see Francis ILES

READ ON A THEME: **BLACK DETECTIVES**
   John Ball, *In the Heat of the Night*
   Grace F. Edwards, *No Time to Die*
   Barbara Hambly, *A Free Man of Color* (historical mystery set in nineteenth-century New Orleans)
   Gar Anthony Haywood, *When Last Seen Alive*
▷ Reginald Hill, *Blood Sympathy*
▷ Chester Himes, *Cotton Comes to Harlem*

Alexander McCall Smith, *The No. 1 Ladies' Detective Agency*
▷ Walter Mosley, *Devil in a Blue Dress*
Gary Phillips, *Only the Wicked*
Mike Phillips, *Point of Darkness*

BLAKE, Nicholas (1904–1972)
Irish novelist

Nicholas Blake was the pseudonym used by the poet C. Day Lewis for his crime fiction. He wrote 20 detective novels, many of them featuring the amiable amateur sleuth Nigel Strangeways. The books are in true British 'Golden Age' crime style. Wherever Strangeways goes – on a Greek cruise, to a London publishing house, to the Ministry of Information at the end of the Second World War – gruesome murder is committed, and Strangeways solves it by patiently getting acquainted with a large group of eccentric and extraordinary people. The books are leisurely, full of literary quotation and inconsequential banter: like many English upper-class detectives, Strangeways loves concealing his education – or showing it off – by talking frivolous nonsense.

The Strangeways novels are A Question of Proof *(the first, published in 1935 when Day Lewis was a master at Cheltenham College)*, Thou Shell of Death, There's Trouble Brewing, The Beast Must Die, The Smiler with the Knife, Malice in Wonderland, The Case of the Abominable Snowman, Minute for Murder, Head of a Traveller, The Dreadful Hollow, The Whisper in the Gloom, End of Chapter, The Widow's Cruise, The Worm of Death, The Sad Variety *and* The Morning After Death. *His non-Strangeways books are* A Tangled Web, A Penknife in My Heart, The Deadly Joker *and* The Private Wound *(his last crime novel, published in 1968, the year Lewis was appointed Poet Laureate).*

READ ON ▷

▶ ▷ **Margery Allingham, *Flowers for the Judge*;** ▷ **Edmund Crispin, *Holy Disorders*;**
▷ **Michael Innes, *The Weight of the Evidence*.**

BLINCOE, Nicholas (born 1966)
British novelist

Although his most recent novel, *White Mice*, an excursion into the emptily glamorous world of fashion, cannot be described as a crime novel, Nicholas Blincoe had, in his first few books, shown that he was one of the most exciting and provocative of young British crime writers. *Acid Casuals*, in which a transsexual returns to the Manchester club scene intent on the murder of her old boss, was sometimes irritating in its self-conscious, hipper-than-thou modishness but was full of violent energy and black comedy. This was followed by *Jello Salad*, an over-the-top cocktail of sex, drugs and murder set in a not very convincing Soho underworld, and *Manchester Slingback*, a darker, more consciously realistic attempt to evoke the vanished Eighties scene in Manchester through a story of murder and revenge. *The Dope Priest*, Blincoe's most ambitious work to date, is a thriller about dope-smuggling and international espionage in the Middle East.

READ ON >

▶ Jake Arnott, *The Long Firm*; ▷ Christopher Brookmyre, *One Fine Day in the Middle of the Night*; Graeme Gordon, *Bayswater Bodycount*.

BLOCK, Lawrence (born 1938)
US novelist

Block is one of the most remarkably prolific and versatile of American crime writers. He is best known for three series. The Matt Scudder novels are traditional private eye books, featuring a boozy (and later AA-attending) ex-cop, working the meaner streets of New York. The Bernie Rhodenbarr books are crime capers about a New York bookshop owner who is a burglar in his spare time. The Evan Tanner novels are self-consciously far-fetched comedy thrillers involving a man who, because of a bizarre accident, needs no sleep and fills the time he gains by acquiring the sort of knowledge that inevitably lands him in trouble. Block has also written splendid ▷ Rex Stout spoofs, including the magnificently titled *The Topless Tulip Caper*, published books under the pseudonym of Paul Kavanagh, and completed a novel by ▷ Cornell Woolrich, *Into the Night*, left unfinished at Woolrich's death.

The Matt Scudder novels include The Sins of the Fathers, Eight Million Ways to Die, When the Sacred Ginmill Closes, A Dance at the Slaughterhouse, The Devil Knows You're Dead, Even the Wicked, Everybody Dies *and* Hope to Die. *The Bernie Rhodenbarr books, which all have the word 'Burglar' in the title, include* Burglars Can't Be Choosers, The Burglar Who Liked to Quote Kipling, The Burglar Who Thought He was Bogart, The Burglar in the Library *and* The Burglar in the Rye. *The best of the Evan Tanner novels are the first two,* The Thief Who Couldn't Sleep *and* The Cancelled Czech.

READ ON >

● *When the Sacred Ginmill Closes* (Matt Scudder makes the transition from drink to sobriety while tackling one of the most difficult cases of his career).
▶ to the Bernie Rhodenbarr books: ▷ Donald Westlake, *The Hot Rock*.
▶ to the Matt Scudder novels: ▷ Loren D. Estleman, *The Midnight Man*; Jonathan Valin, *Day of Wrath*; ▷ Michael Connelly, *A Darkness More Than Night*.

READ ON A THEME: BOATS AND SHIPS

Donald Bain, *Murder on the QE2*
▷ John Dickson Carr, *The Blind Barber*
▷ Freeman Wills Crofts, *The Loss of the 'Jane Vosper'*
▷ Stephen Dobyns, *A Boat Off the Coast*
Sam Llewellyn, *Dead Reckoning*
▷ Peter Lovesey, *The False Inspector Dew*
▷ Ngaio Marsh, *Singing in the Shrouds*
C. P. Snow, *Death Under Sail*

BONFIGLIOLI, Kyril (1929–1983)
British novelist

After graduating from Oxford, Kyril Bonfiglioli spent much of his working life as an art, antiques and book dealer. Although he always had a strong interest in genre fiction – he was editor of a science fiction magazine in the mid-Sixties and published a number of sci-fi short stories – it was not until the 1970s that he published the three short crime novels (*Don't Point That Thing at Me*, *Something Nasty in the Woodshed* and *After You With the Pistol*) for which he is remembered. Collectively known as The Mortdecai Trilogy, the books introduced the world to the Hon. Charles Mortdecai and his manservant Jock, a kind of warped and much more worldly version of Jeeves and Wooster. Mortdecai is, like his creator, an art dealer. He is also a gloriously amoral hedonist – a shameless connoisseur of the pleasures of the flesh, from gourmet food washed down with lashings of fine wines and spirits to the allure of the beautiful of both sexes. Though an epicure in matters of food and drink and the finer things in life, Mortdecai is less fastidious in his professional work and, like ▷ Jonathan Gash's Lovejoy, his pursuit of art and antiques leads well him well off the straight and narrow and into dealings with some very shady characters indeed. He and the loyally thuggish Jock prove more than a match for anybody in lack of scruple and conscience and usually manage to stay one jump ahead of the competition (and the law), even when murder is involved. Throughout the trilogy Bonfiglioli has his tongue permanently positioned in his cheek and the books are filled with brilliant one-liners, Wodehousian flights of language and comic set-pieces. They can be irritating – Bonfiglioli was at the back of the queue when politically correct attitudes to gender were being handed out – but, at their best, the Mortdecai books are brilliantly funny and unlike anything else in English crime fiction.

As a late addition to the trilogy *The Great Mortdecai Moustache Mystery*, a book completed by Craig Brown from a manuscript and notes Bonfiglioli left unfinished at his death, was published in 1997.

> READ ON

▶ ▷ Jonathan Gash, *The Rich and the Profane*; ▷ Peter Guttridge, *Two to Tango*.

BRAMAH, Ernest (1868–1942)
British novelist and short story writer

Bramah is not a well-known writer today but during his lifetime he was famous for the creation of two characters. One was Kai Lung, a travelling storyteller in Imperial China, who appeared in several volumes of gentle, pseudo-Oriental tales. The other, of more interest to the devotee of crime fiction, was Max Carrados. Carrados is a blind, rich amateur detective who works out mysteries in his study, while his partner, the enquiry agent Louis Carlyle, does the legwork. Their relationship is akin to that of ▷ Rex Stout's Nero Wolfe and Archie Goodwin, and Bramah is worth mentioning in the same breath as Stout both for the ingenuity of his mysteries and the elegance and wit of his style. The Carrados short stories are collected in *Max Carrados*, *The Eyes of Max Carrados*, *The Specimen Case* and *Max Carrados Mysteries*. *The Bravo of London* is a full-length Carrados novel.

READ ON ▷

▶ ▷ **G. K. Chesterton,** *The Innocence of Father Brown*; ▷ **Rex Stout,** *Justice Ends at Home.*

BRAUN, Lilian Jackson (born 1916)
US novelist

The Cat Who . . . series, for which Lilian Jackson Braun is best known, consists of lightweight, undemanding stories in which the journalist Qwill Qwilleran stumbles across murder and mystery in the mythical Moose County and its main city, Pickax. Aided and abetted by his two Siamese cats, Koko and Yum-Yum, whose feline intelligence and gifts are always integral to the mystery, Qwilleran ambles genially towards a solution. The books are whimsical and lighthearted – harsh critics would call them twee – but Braun is unobtrusively skilful in spinning out her yarns. The significant details and clues are slipped neatly into the frothy narratives and Braun's engaging and offbeat sense of humour help to carry the reader along.

THE CAT WHO KNEW SHAKESPEARE (1988)
The mystery in this book in the series centres on the death of Senior Goodwinter, owner of the *Pickax Picayune* newspaper. It appears to be an accident but Qwilleran and the cats suspect foul play. Clues may exist in the copy of Shakespeare that Koko pulls from the shelf for Qwilleran to read. As so often in Lilian Jackson Braun's books, however, the pleasure lies in the gentle characterization and the Moose County setting as much as in the mystery.

The other Cat Who . . . *novels include* The Cat Who Played Brahms, The Cat Who Ate Danish Modern, The Cat Who Knew a Cardinal, The Cat Who Came to Breakfast, The Cat Who Tailed a Thief, The Cat Who Robbed a Bank, The Cat Who Smelled a Rat *and* The Cat Who Went Up a Creek.

READ ON ▷

▶ **Marian Babson,** *The Cat Next Door*; **Rita Mae Brown,** *Claws and Effect*; **Carole Nelson Douglas,** *Cat in a Midnight Choir*; **Sheila Rousseau Murphy,** *Cat on the Edge.*

BRETT, Simon (born 1945)
British novelist

Brett's Charles Paris comedy mysteries are set in the worlds of theatre, television, film and radio. Paris is a (deservedly) unsuccessful actor, one of that large pool of 'pros' who keep up appearance while hoping for small parts to turn up. Occasionally they do – as do the murders Paris investigates. Brett has a different 'backstage' setting for each book: the Edinburgh Festival (*So Much Blood*), the BBC (*Dead Side of the Mike*), a production of *Twelfth Night* (*Sicken and So Die*).

Brett has also written books in two other series – one set in Fethering, a village in the Sussex Downs, and the other featuring Mrs Pargeter, a mystery-solving, rich widow of a man whose profession is never mentioned but who had a large circle of useful, if shady, acquaintances.

The other Paris novels include Cast, In Order of Disappearance, Star Trap, Not Dead, Only Resting, What Bloody Man Is That?, A Reconstructed Corpse *and* Dead Room Farce. *The Mrs Pargeter books are* A Nice Class of Corpse, Mrs, Presumed Dead, Mrs Pargeter's Package, Mrs Pargeter's Pound of Flesh, Mrs Pargeter's Plot *and* Mrs Pargeter's Point of Honour. *The novels set in Fethering are* The Body on the Beach, Death on the Downs *and* The Torso in the Town.

| READ ON |

▶ To the Paris mysteries: Sebastian Shaw, *The Company of Knaves*; Marian Babson, *Encore Murder*; Jane Dentinger, *Who Dropped Peter Pan?*.
▶ To the Fethering books: ▷ Ann Granger, *Murder Among Us*.

BROOKMYRE, Christopher (born 1968)
Scottish novelist

Brookmyre's early novels are exuberant and blackly comic thrillers featuring Jack Parlabane, a cynical, drink-swigging journalist who finds himself involved in murder investigations. Parlabane is not an unfamiliar type in crime fiction but he is saved from cliché by the detail of the Scottish setting in which he operates and by Brookmyre's disenchanted views of Scottish society and politics which inform all the plots. In *Country of the Blind*, for example, the murder of a newspaper tycoon, apparently in a burglary gone badly wrong, turns out to be much more than it seems and involves Parlabane in a spectacular web of corruption which stretches from the Scottish Secretary of State downwards.

Brookmyre has also written a number of non-Parlabane books, all equally inventive and packed with a similar mixture of broad, often almost slapstick, humour and violent action. These have settings as diverse as an oil rig turned tourist spot which becomes the target of terrorists and a pre-millennium California filled with the deranged and the dangerous.

The Parlabane books are Quite Ugly One Morning *and* Country of the Blind. *Brookmyre's non-Parlabane novels are* Not the End of the World, One Fine Day in the Middle of the Night, A Big Boy Did It and Ran Away *and* The Sacred Art of Stealing.

| READ ON |

● *One Fine Day in the Middle of the Night* (farce and thriller combine as incompetent terrorists take over an international resort on an oil rig)
▶ Colin Bateman, *Divorcing Jack*; Charles Higson, *Getting Rid of Mister Kitchen*; ▷ Nicholas Blincoe, *Jello Salad*; ▷ Carl Hiaasen, *Double Whammy*.

BUNKER, Edward (born 1933)
US novelist

Virtually unique among crime writers in that he was himself a hardened criminal, Eddie Bunker's life reads like a plot drawn straight from the pages of a hundred hard-boiled novels. At seventeen, he was the youngest inmate at San Quentin prison and he started writing during his four-and-a-half-year jail sentence. After seventeen years and numerous attempts, his *No Beast So Fierce* was accepted for publication in 1973, while its author was awaiting trial for bank robbery and drugs charges. It was critically acclaimed – and filmed as *Straight Time* starring Dustin Hoffman – and Bunker's life changed for the better. More novels followed: *The Animal Factory, Little Boy Blue* and *Dog Eat Dog*, and he received an Oscar nomination for his work on the script of the 1985 film *Runaway Train*. In 1992 he achieved global recognition when he appeared as Mr Blue in Quentin Tarantino's film *Reservoir Dogs*. After this, his books were reissued and he received more film work, including the screenplay for his adaptation of *The Animal Factory*. His autobiography, *Mr Blue – Memoirs of a Renegade*, was published in 2000 and this searing, often brutal, account of his amazing life is perhaps his best work.

READ ON

▶ Donald Goines, *Black Gangster* (a novel by another writer who knew the crime scene from the criminal's point of view); ▷ George Pelecanos, *Hell to Pay*; Clarence Cooper Jr, *The Farm*.

BURKE, James Lee (born 1936)
US novelist

Burke began writing in the 1960s and published several novels but it was not until 1987 and the publication of *The Neon Rain* that he truly hit his stride. This was the first in what has become a series of books featuring Dave Robicheaux, an alcoholic Cajun detective who lives on the river in a beautifully depicted Louisiana. Atmospheric descriptions of the exotic settings contrast effectively with the evil and violence that Robicheaux encounters in his work. Alongside this are the confrontations with his own demons, either those lurking in the bottle(s) or from his dark past. So far he has appeared in twelve novels, ranging from the visceral early work like *Heaven's Prisoners* and *Black Cherry Blues* to the more mythical (and more lyrically titled) books such as *A Stained White Radiance* and *In the Electric Mist with Confederate Dead*. The most recent Robicheaux novel is *Jolie Blon's Bounce*.

As well as these, Burke has recently written three fine novels (*Cimarron Rose, Heartwood* and *Bitterroot*) featuring Billy Bob Holland, a former Texas ranger turned attorney. Set in the hills near Austin, Texas, these are lighter than the Robicheaux books but just as gripping.

READ ON

● *A Morning for Flamingos* (Robicheaux trails a killer into the dark heart of New Orleans in one of the best in the series).
▶ ▷ Robert Crais, *Voodoo River*; ▷ James Ellroy, *The Black Dahlia*;
▷ Dennis Lehane, *Prayers for Rain*; Martin Hegwood, *Big Easy Backroad*.

BURLEY, W(illiam) J(ohn) (born 1914)
British novelist

Burley spent many years as a science teacher and his first novel, *A Taste of Power*, featured a zoologist and amateur sleuth called Henry Pym. Pym appeared in one more novel but Burley's main series character – the one who has gained wide fame because of TV adaptations of the stories – is Wycliffe. Superintendent Wycliffe is a ruminative, pipe-smoking detective, an English Maigret who, instead of working in a city, solves cases in the towns and placid countryside of Cornwall. He likes to soak himself in the atmosphere of a place, watching and waiting as each case evolves – and this is satisfyingly balanced, again as in ▷ Simenon's Maigret books, by the tension and hysteria (often sexual) which underlie the crimes.

The Wycliffe books include To Kill a Cat, Death in a Salubrious Place, Wycliffe and the Schoolgirls, Wycliffe in Paul's Court, Wycliffe and the Quiet Virgin, Wycliffe and the Tangled Web, Wycliffe and the Dead Flautist, Wycliffe and the House of Fear *and* Wycliffe and the Guild of Nine.

> **READ ON**

▶ ▷ Peter Lovesey, *Upon a Dark Night*; R. D. Wingfield, *A Touch of Frost*; Janie Bolitho, *Snapped in Cornwall* (one of another, very different series set in Cornwall).

BURNETT, W(illiam) R(iley) **(1899–1982)**
US novelist and screenwriter

Burnett wrote films in Hollywood during the 1930s and 1940s and published over fifty books, chiefly westerns and crime thrillers. A pioneer of the gangster novel and a model for many of the pulp writers of the time, Burnett wrote two of the best-known crime novels of the first half of the twentieth century. *Little Caesar* (1929), later magnificently filmed with Edward G. Robinson in the lead role, is the story of Rico, a small-time Chicago gangster who bullies, betrays and kills his way to the top during Prohibition, only to fall. *The Asphalt Jungle* (1949), filmed by John Huston, is one of the first, and best, 'caper' novels, following in detail the progress of a spectacular crime.

> **READ ON**

● *High Sierra* (about an escaped murderer, also filmed, with Humphrey Bogart in the starring role).
▶ ▷ James M. Cain, *The Postman Always Rings Twice*; Raoul Whitfield, *The Virgin Kills.*

BUTLER, Gwendoline (born 1922)
British novelist

Under her own name, Gwendoline Butler has written a series of novels about Inspector (later Commander) Coffin of 'London's Second City' and his wife, a well-known actress – plainly told but meaty and atmospheric stories in which investigating a murder usually leads Coffin to unravel some far more tangled mystery. All the Coffin books have the word 'Coffin' in the title, although (confusingly) *A Coffin for Pandora* is a non-series book, a wonderful historical mystery set in 1880s Oxford. As Jennie Melville, Butler has written a series of novels starring policewoman Charmian Daniels.

A DARK COFFIN (1995)

Joe and Josie Macintosh are found dead in a theatre box, apparently as the result of a suicide pact. But little is ever what it seems in a Coffin novel and the Commander is soon facing some disturbing questions. Who exactly were the Macintoshes? And what was their connection with Inspector Harry Trent, the policeman who claims to be intent on tracking down his dangerous (and identical) twin brother? Plausibility is not always at a premium as Coffin unearths a bizarre story, with its roots far in the past.

The other Coffin novels include Coffin in Oxford, Coffin in Malta, Coffin in Fashion, Coffin in the Black Museum, Coffin on Murder Street, A Double Coffin, Coffin's Ghost *and* A Coffin for Christmas. *Jennie Melville's Charmian Daniels books include* Windsor Red, Witching Murder, Footsteps in the Blood, The Morbid Kitchen, The Woman Who Was Not There *and* Stone Dead.

| READ ON >

▶ to the Coffin books: ▷ P. D. James, *A Taste for Death*; ▷ Peter Robinson, *A Dedicated Man*; Patricia Hall, *Deep Freeze*.
▶ to the books written as Jennie Melville: Jo Bannister, *A Taste for Burning*.

C

CAIN, James M(allahan) (1892–1977)
US novelist

Cain's first novel, *The Postman Always Rings Twice* (1934), written when he was a struggling screenwriter, was a huge success and sold more than a million copies. A bitter story of two no-hopers in Depression Hollywood who become entangled in escalating, violent crime, it more than justifies one critic's description of Cain as 'the poet of the tabloid murder'. The book is exactly in the style of those black-and-white, rain-soaked crime melodramas Hollywood was turning out in the 1930s, and has itself been filmed several times. Its success has meant that it overshadows the rest of Cain's output, which is equally bleak and equally exciting. His best books are *Serenade*, *The Butterfly*, *Jealous Woman* and *The Magician's Wife*. A collection of three novellas, originally published as *Three of a Kind*, includes the masterly psychological thriller *Double Indemnity*, memorably filmed by Billy Wilder with Fred MacMurray, Barbara Stanwyck and Edward G. Robinson in the lead roles.

> READ ON

▶ Horace McCoy, *No Pockets in a Shroud*; ▷ Dashiell Hammett, *The Dain Curse*; ▷ Jim Thompson, *Pop. 1280*; William L. Gresham, *Nightmare Alley* (half-forgotten 1940s *noir* classic about the rise of a con-man).

CAMPBELL, Robert (1927–2000)
US novelist

Campbell is a versatile crime writer and his two main series are very different in style and tone. The Flannery books are set in Chicago and the central character is a volunteer worker for the Democrats. Politics plays a big part in the crimes Flannery investigates in what are well-plotted mysteries seasoned with punchy dialogue and amiable humour. The books set in La-La Land, i.e. Hollywood, are much darker. The protagonist, Whistler, is a failed actor turned private eye and he ventures regularly into a nightmare world that is the dark reflection of the Hollywood dream.

ALICE IN LA-LA LAND (1988)
Nell Twelvetrees hires Whistler as a bodyguard to protect her from her husband Roger, a well-known TV personality whom she believes is out to kill her. Blonde and beautiful, Nell is an enigma who draws Whistler into deep waters and Roger is very definitely more than he seems. Campbell reveals again the depravity beneath the glamour in LA and introduces a memorable killer.

The Flannery books include The Junkyard Dog, The 600-Pound Gorilla, Nibbled to Death by Ducks, Sauce for the Goose, The Lion's Share *and* Pigeon Pie.

The other Whistler books are In La-La Land We Trust, Sweet La-La Land *and* The Wizard of La-La Land.

READ ON ▷

▶ **to the Flannery books: Max Allan Collins,** *Chicago Confidential.*
▶ **to the Whistler books:** ▷ **Lawrence Block,** *Eight Million Ways to Die*; ▷ **James Ellroy,** *LA Confidential.*

CARR, John Dickson (1906–1977)
US novelist

Carr was one of the most inventive and imaginative writers of the classic detective story. He produced two dozen books starring Doctor Gideon Fell, an eccentric scholar with the brains of a Mycroft Holmes and a Falstaffian gusto for food, beer and pipe tobacco. Fell's hobby is solving such 'impossible' crimes as locked-room mysteries. The stories are tightly plotted, the mysteries ingenious, and Fell's character, if a bit fogeyish for today's tastes, is fascinating.

Under the pseudonym of Carter Dickson, Carr wrote a series of books featuring another eccentric – the large, shambling figure of Sir Henry Merrivale. Like Fell, Merrivale loves food, drink and impossible mysteries. But he is far grosser than Fell, far more self-indulgent and self-delighted. The reason Carr chose to use a pseudonym seems to be that he regarded his Fell books as serious, his Merrivale books as farce. He also wrote historical detective fiction, set in eighteenth- or nineteenth-century England.

The Doctor Fell books include The Blind Barber, The Case of the Constant Suicides, Hag's Nook, Till Death Us Do Part *and* The House at Satan's Elbow. *The Merrivale novels include* The White Priory Murders, The Judas Window, The Ten Teacups, My Late Wives *and* The Cavalier's Cup. *Among his historical novels are* The Bride of Newgate, The Devil in Velvet *and* Scandal at High Chimneys *(in which the detective is no less a personage than* ▷ *Wilkie Collins).*

READ ON ▷

▶ ▷ **Edmund Crispin,** *The Moving Toyshop*; **Anthony Boucher,** *The Case of the Solid Key*; ▷ **Michael Innes,** *Lament for a Maker.* **See also Read on a Theme: Locked-room Mysteries.**

CASPARY, Vera (1904–1987)
US novelist and screenwriter

Caspary's psychological mysteries grip by the second paragraph and never let go. She buttonholes the reader emotionally, writing swift, clipped prose with particularly punchy dialogue (a legacy of years of film work). Her chief skill lies in letting us inside the minds of her characters, particularly daydreamers and those whose personality is dominated by a single feeling (love, fear, jealousy) to an all but pathological extent.

THE MAN WHO LOVED HIS WIFE (1966)

Fletcher J. Strode, an ebullient, vital man, is devoted to his wife Elaine. When his larynx is removed because of cancer he is unable to cope. Feelings of inadequacy are compounded by paranoid jealousy of every man to whom his wife speaks. His diary tells how he first plans suicide, then begins to fantasize, first that Elaine wants him to kill himself, then that she intends to kill him herself. When he dies, the diary remains as evidence. The book stands out for superb character-drawing, not only of Strode himself, but of such minor characters as an ambitious, vain policeman, Strode's daughter and her weak-willed husband.

Caspary's other books include Laura *(made into a classic* film noir*)*, Stranger Than Truth, Thelma, Bedelia, A Chosen Sparrow, Final Portrait *and* Ruth.

> **READ ON**

▶ Leigh Brackett, *The Tiger Among Us*; Hilda Lawrence, *Death of a Doll*.

CHANDLER, Raymond (1888–1959)
US novelist

Born in the US, Chandler was brought to England as a boy and educated at Dulwich School (also the *alma mater* of P. G. Wodehouse). After a false start in England as a poet and literary journalist and war service in France, Chandler returned to the US. He became a successful executive in the oil industry until a fondness for the bottle resulted in unemployment. Broke and out of work, Chandler began writing stories for pulp magazines like *Black Mask*, treating violence, prostitution and betrayal in the cynical, hard-boiled style popular in films of the time. His ambition was to replace the kind of detective novels then most fashionable (stories of bizarre crimes solved by wildly eccentric detectives) with books about realistic crimes investigated in a plausible way by a detective who would be ordinary, with recognizable human hopes, fears and reactions.

Drawing on the example of writers he admired, like ▷ Hammett, and on his own secretly romantic temperament he created the character of Philip Marlowe. Marlowe is an honest, conscientious man who sweats, cowers and lusts just like anyone else. He is also a surprisingly chivalric figure – an urban knight errant walking the mean streets of Los Angeles, guided through the corruption, greed and dishonesty by his own code of behaviour. Marlowe narrates the stories himself, in the wisecracking, deadpan style that has become the target of a thousand parodies in the decades since Chandler first perfected it. The comic metaphors and similes ('A blonde to make a bishop kick a hole in a stained glass window') remain funny but they are matchable by a skilled parodist. Only Chandler could invest the language of crime fiction with the kind of poetic melancholy he often does. Only Chandler would describe old men sitting in a seedy LA bar, 'their faces like lost battlefields'. Emphasizing atmosphere and character even more than plot – 'the ideal mystery is one you would read if the end was missing', he once remarked – Chandler's novels were among the first to alert more snobbish critics to the potential of genre fiction. They remain great works of American literature, as readable and enjoyable as when they were first published.

FAREWELL, MY LOVELY (1940)

Marlowe is drifting with nothing particular to do when he is picked up (literally, by the scruff of the neck) by a muscle-bound ex-convict called Moose Malloy, memorably described as 'about as inconspicuous as a tarantula on a slice of angel food'. From this simple event, as ripples spread on a pond, the story grows to take in a priceless necklace, kidnapping, blackmail and murder. At its heart, like a man in the still centre of a whirlwind, Marlowe slouches from clue to clue, pushing open every door and investigating each alleyway even though he knows, from long experience, that he's likely to find painful or nasty surprises at every turn.

READ ON ▷

- ● *The Long Goodbye* (Marlowe helps a friend and finds himself in a deal of trouble in an archetypal Chandler exercise in hard-boiled romanticism).
- ▶ ▷ Dashiell Hammett, *The Maltese Falcon*; Robert B. Parker and Raymond Chandler, *Poodle Springs* (largely ▷ Parker's work on an unfinished novel Chandler began the year before his death); Howard Browne, *The Taste of Ashes*; ▷ Arthur Lyons, False Pretenses; ▷ Ross Macdonald, *The Drowning Pool*.

CHARTERIS, Leslie (1907–1993)
British/US novelist

Leslie Charteris (real name Leslie Charles Bowyer Yin) was born in Singapore and adopted his pseudonym early in his long, prolific and profitable career as a writer. Although he did write other books he is best known for the creation of Simon Templar, The Saint. Templar is a twentieth-century Robin Hood, an adventurer who rights wrongs, puts down the pompous, exposes frauds, rescues damsels in distress – and relieves crooks of their ill-gotten, excess cash. Charteris's early books, set largely in England, show The Saint in criminal circles, constantly one step ahead of plodding Inspector Teal of Scotland Yard. In later books, The Saint is based in the USA (Charteris became a US citizen in 1942) and has metamorphosed into an international troubleshooter, a kind of unlicensed, freelance James Bond. In both incarnations Templar is a character who now possesses much period charm.

Charteris's 1930s books include The Last Hero, The Saint in New York *and* The Saint Overboard. *His later books include* Send for the Saint *and* The Saint and the Templar Treasure. *Charteris also published two dozen books of short stories and novelettes, all with the word 'Saint' in the title, and many omnibuses.*

READ ON ▷

▶ ▷ John Creasey, *The Toff Steps Out*; E. W. Hornung, *Raffles: The Amateur Cracksman*.

CHASE, James Hadley (1906–1985)
British novelist

James Hadley Chase was the most frequently used pseudonym of René Brabazon Raymond. He was the author of dozens and dozens of gangster thrillers, although he remained best known for his first venture into the genre, *No Orchids for Miss Blandish* (1939). Violent (for its time) and hard-boiled, the book came to the disdainful notice of George Orwell, who gave it a blisteringly bad press in a 1944 essay, but it has been one of the best-selling crime books of all time. Even Orwell admitted that, although he thought it morally depraved, it was 'a brilliant piece of writing'. *No Orchids for Miss Blandish*, the story of an heiress kidnapped by gangsters, is set in the USA, as are many of Chase's other books. Chase only ever spent time in the US on short visits but absorbed the language and ambience of American crime stories and movies of the Thirties sufficiently that he was able to produce his own (idiosyncratic) versions from his writing desk in England.

Chase's other novels include The Dead Stay Dumb, Eve, You're Lonely When You're Dead, This Way for a Shroud, Tiger by the Tail, The Guilty Are Afraid *and the improbably titled* Goldfish Have No Hiding Place.

> **READ ON**

▶ ▷ Mickey Spillane, *Kiss Me, Deadly*; ▷ Peter Cheyney, *Can Ladies Kill?*.

CHESTERTON, G(ilbert) K(eith) (1874–1936)
British novelist, poet, essayist and critic

Chesterton published over 200 books and his writings ranged from nonsense verse to studies of Dickens and Shaw, from religious and political polemic to novels of fantasy and whimsy such as *The Napoleon of Notting Hill* and *The Man Who Was Thursday*. To lovers of mystery fiction he is known for his short stories featuring the meek, untidy Catholic priest Father Brown. Brown uses a sympathy honed in the confessional to think himself into the minds of criminals and so to solve the crimes. In the best of the stories Chesterton's gift for paradox is revealed in the ingenuity of the puzzles and their solutions and Father Brown, alert to the frailties of himself and others, is an endearing character.

The Father Brown stories appeared in the following collections: The Innocence of Father Brown *(which includes most of the best stories),* The Wisdom of Father Brown, The Incredulity of Father Brown, The Secret of Father Brown *and* The Scandal of Father Brown.

> **READ ON**

● *The Man Who Knew Too Much* (short stories about an English gentleman solving murders among the great and good).
▶ R. Austin Freeman, *Dr Thorndyke's Casebook*; Jacques Futrelle, *The Thinking Machine*; Baroness Orczy, *The Old Man in the Corner*; Ronald Knox, *The Viaduct Murder.*

CHEYNEY, Peter (1896–1951)
British novelist and short story writer

Cheyney was a British writer of American-style gangster novels who, in his heyday in the 1940s, sold millions of books worldwide. Considered racy at the time of publication, his novels now seem like period pieces but, as such, remain undemandingly readable. The Lemmy Caution books are about a hard-boiled, two-fisted New York G man. For some unaccountable reason they achieved almost cult status in France (not always a sign of quality in Anglophone crime writers) and a series of films appeared there in the 1950s and 1960s. The Slim Callaghan books are about a wisecracking, dry-witted private eye working in London's club- and gangland.

The Lemmy Caution novels include This Man is Dangerous, Don't Get Me Wrong, Never a Dull Moment, You Can Always Duck *and* I'll Say She Does. *Cheyney's many other books include a number featuring Slim Callaghan (e.g.* The Urgent Hangman, They Never Say When *and* Uneasy Terms*), spy thrillers (e.g.* Dark Duet *and* The Stars are Dark) *and collections of short stories (e.g.* Knave Takes Queen, Account Rendered *and* Dance Without Music*).*

READ ON

▶ ▷ **Mickey Spillane,** *Vengeance is Mine!*; **Michael Avallone,** *Kill Her – You'll Like It.*

CHILD, Lee (born 1954)
British novelist

In a few years Lee Child has carved out a career as a best-selling writer on the strength of his books featuring the footloose ex-militia man Jack Reacher. Reacher is the archetypal macho hero – taciturn, prone to violence and fond of weaponry and gadgetry. The books are not subtle and they are not the work of a great prose stylist but they are relentlessly fast-paced and exciting. In *Killing Floor* (1997), the first in the series, Reacher, who wanders nomadically around the States, pitches up in a small town in Georgia intent only on a bit of idle research into a blues musician who interests him. He is immediately arrested for murder. He has a sound alibi and is soon released but decides to stay in the town and, for reasons not entirely explained, root out the corruption at its heart. Child's books are extremely violent but, since the world he creates is, despite its surface realism, a fantasy one, this is not as disturbing as it might otherwise be.

Lee Child's other Jack Reacher novels are Die Trying, Tripwire, The Visitor, Echo Burning *and* Without Fail.

READ ON

▶ ▷ **Michael Connelly,** *The Concrete Blonde*; ▷ **James Patterson,** *Violets are Blue*; **John Sandford,** *Mind Prey.*

CHRISTIE, Agatha (1890–1976)
British novelist

Christie's eighty-four novels are models of the English 'Golden Age' of detective fiction. Each book chronicles a crime and its solution, with total efficiency. She never wastes a word and uses dialogue to speed her prose. Excitement mounts as we read, until none of us pauses long enough to examine each brilliantly placed (and even more ingeniously concealed) clue as carefully as we should. She often sets herself technical problems. In one novel, the narrator is the murderer; in another, all the suspects did the crime; in another there are no survivors.

Her series detectives include Superintendent Battle, Tommy and Tuppence Beresford (who appear first in *The Secret Adversary* (1922) as 'bright young things' and finally in *Postern of Fate* (1973) as 'bright old things'), and two of the best loved and most parodied detectives in the genre: Hercule Poirot and Miss Marple. Each of these has a besetting sin, essential to the sleuthing: Poirot's confidence in his 'little grey cells' and Miss Marple's nosiness. Poirot is at full stretch in *Murder on the Orient Express* (1934), a mystery for which he provides two entirely plausible solutions. Miss Marple uses her knowledge of people gained from gossip in the village of St Mary Mead to solve her crimes, and one of the best is *A Murder is Announced* (1950). Like a conjuror, Christie shows two vital clues with one hand, so to speak, while waving to distract our attention with the other.

Christie's Poirot books include Murder in Mesopotamia, Appointment with Death, Mrs McGinty's Dead, Cat Among the Pigeons, Five Little Pigs, Dead Man's Folly *and* The Clocks. *Her Marple books include* The Body in the Library, 4.50 From Paddington, They Do It With Mirrors, A Pocket Full of Rye, At Bertram's Hotel *and* Sleeping Murder. *Her non-series novels include* Ordeal by Innocence, Death Comes As the End *and* By the Pricking of My Thumbs. *Her 30 short-story collections include* The Labours of Hercules *and* Thirteen Clues for Miss Marple. *She also wrote plays (*The Mousetrap *has been showing in the West End for longer than many of us have been alive) and, using the pseudonym Mary Westmacott, romances.*

READ ON >

▶ **to the Poirot books:** Anthony Berkeley (▷ Francis Iles), *Death in the House.*
▶ **to the Miss Marple books:** ▷ Patricia Wentworth, *Miss Silver Intervenes.*
▶ **to Christie's books in general:** ▷ Ngaio Marsh, *Death in a White Tie*; Anthony Gilbert, *The Body on the Beam*; Georgette Heyer, *Envious Casca.*

READ ON A THEME: **CHRISTMAS**

▷ **Agatha Christie,** *Hercule Poirot's Christmas*
  K. C. Constantine, *Upon Some Midnights Clear*
▷ **Martha Grimes,** *The Man With a Load of Mischief*
▷ **Cyril Hare,** *An English Murder*
  Georgette Heyer, *Envious Casca*
▷ **Charlotte MacLeod,** *God Rest Ye Merry*
▷ **Ngaio Marsh,** *Tied Up in Tinsel*
▷ **Georges Simenon,** *Maigret's Christmas*

CLARK, Mary Higgins (born 1929)
US novelist

Known as the 'Queen of Suspense', Mary Higgins Clark, in truth, writes books that very often astutely combine both suspense fiction and romance fiction. In some of her fiction (e.g. *On the Street Where You Live*, in which a killer might just be the reincarnation of a nineteenth-century murderer) she even throws in a few elements from the supernatural/horror genre. Since her debut with *Where Are the Children?* in 1975, a story in which a woman's past and her possible involvement in the death of her children re-surfaces in her new life, she has written a sequence of books that have regularly reached the top of the bestseller lists. The plot of her first novel embodied one of the themes to which Mary Higgins Clark has returned again and again in her fiction – the threats and dangers that society presents to the vulnerable, especially women and children. Mary Higgins Clark is not strong on characterization – her people tend to talk more like people in soap operas than people in real life – but, in her complex plots and fast-paced melodramas-cum-mysteries, she does provide reliable entertainment.

PRETEND YOU DON'T SEE HER (1997)
Lacey Farrell, a Manhattan realtor, witnesses a murder and is sent by police, for her own safety, to live in Minneapolis. What the police at first don't know is that the victim spoke to Lacey before she died and entrusted her with a journal that might hold the clues to another suspicious death. The murderer, however, does seem to know this and Lacey is soon in as much danger in Minneapolis as she would have been in New York.

Mary Higgins Clark's other novels include Where Are the Children?, A Stranger is Watching, The Cradle Will Fall, While My Pretty One Sleeps, Let Me Call You Sweetheart, All Through the Night, Before I Say Goodbye, On the Street Where You Live *and* Daddy's Little Girl. He Sees You While You're Sleeping *and* Deck the Halls *were written in collaboration with her daughter, Carol Higgins Clark.*

| READ ON $>$

▶ **Carol Higgins Clark,** *Fleeced*; **Barbara Michaels,** *Be Buried in the Rain*; ▷ **James Patterson,** *2nd Chance*; **Judith Kelman,** *If I Should Die.*

CLYNES, Michael, see Paul DOHERTY

COBEN, Harlan (born 1962)
US novelist

Coben is the author of nine crime novels, of which seven feature his hero, Myron Bolitar. Bolitar is a former basketball player from New Jersey who was forced to retire from a promising career due to injury. Now he runs an agency representing sports stars and is a private eye in his spare time. All the books in the series feature some of the crispest and funniest dialogue in crime fiction and Myron's skill at delivering that perfect one-liner matches his ability on the court. Equally memorable is his ally, Windsor Horne Lockwood III, known as Win, which is what he always does. Handy to have around in that he's extremely rich and utterly flawless, the aristocratic Win is a kind of post-modern combination of Raffles, The Saint and Doc Savage. Is there anything he can't do? Yes, lose. Myron himself is a complex and hugely entertaining character: smart and very funny; tough and

very friendly; someone always ready to do the right thing even though, funda-
mentally, perhaps he only wants to do just *one* thing – play professional
basketball again. The series kicked off with *Deal Breaker* in 1994 and runs
up to *Darkest Fear*, in which Myron discovers that he may have a son, a child
whose mother is married to his long-time rival. Coben's next two books, *Tell No
One* and *Gone for Good*, are both stand-alone novels which, like the award-
winning Myron books, have met with huge acclaim and success.

The other Myron Bolitar novels are Dropshot, Fade Away, Back Spin, One False
Move *and* The Final Detail.

READ ON ▷

▶ ▷ **Robert Ferrigno,** *Heartbreaker*; **Jeremiah Healy,** *Invasion of Privacy*; **Michael
Stone,** *Totally Dead.*

CODY, Liza (born 1944)
British novelist

Two of the most distinctive female detectives operating in modern London have
both been the invention of Liza Cody. Anna Lee is a former police officer working
as the only woman detective in a private security agency – she has to fight to
prove her own worth to her male colleagues as well as deal with the cases thrown
her way. In *Under Contract* Lee is hired as security for a rock star about to embark
on a major tour. Pitched into the weird world of rock music, Anna struggles to
make sense of what she sees as she slowly realizes that the threat to the star is
very real indeed. Eva Wylie, who first appears when she is hired by Anna Lee, is a
security guard and one-time professional wrestler, known as the London Assassin or Bucket Nut, but now barred from the ring. Eva is big, ugly, foul-mouthed
and well able to look after herself when the going gets rough – as it frequently
does. Both the Anna Lee and the Eva Wylie books are rich in colourful characters
and a sense of the realities of London life, and they make strong, enjoyable, no-
nonsense reading.

The Anna Lee books are Dupe, Bad Company, Stalker, Headcase, Under
Contract *and* Backhand. *The novels featuring Eva Wylie are* Bucket Nut, Monkey
Wrench *and* Musclebound.

READ ON ▷

▶ ▷ **Sarah Dunant,** *Birthmarks*; ▷ **Lauren Henderson,** *The Black Rubber Dress*; ▷
Val McDermid, *Crackdown.*

COE, Tucker, see Donald E. WESTLAKE

COLE, Martina
British novelist

Martina Cole writes big, brassy novels, usually with big, brassy women as their
central characters. Her women are survivors, well schooled in the brutalities of

life, but determined to fight their corner and protect their own. Her men are hard and often violent – often on the wrong side of the law but possessed of their own codes of honourable behaviour none the less. The books are usually set in the East End of London (be prepared for more cockney rhyming slang than you would Adam and Eve) or on the wilder shores of Essex. The novels win no points for sensitive psychological subtlety (they're not aiming to) but they do have great energy and narrative vitality. Her first novel, *Dangerous Lady*, was about a clever and beautiful young woman outwitting London mobsters and set the pattern for the string of bestsellers that Cole has enjoyed since.

LADYKILLER (1993)
A London hard man's beloved daughter falls victim to a sex killer and his frenzied search for revenge leads him into unlikely cooperation with the police in the shape of Detective Inspector Kate Burrows. Together they try to bring the killer to justice of some kind. The characters of Kate Burrows and Patrick Kelly resurfaced in *Broken* in 2001.

Martina Cole's other novels are Dangerous Lady, Goodnight Lady, The Jump, The Runaway, Two Women, Broken, Faceless *and* Maura's Game.

READ ON >

▶ **Lynda La Plante, *The Widows*; Lesley Pearse, *Till We Meet Again*; ▷ James Patterson, *1st to Die*.**

COLLINS, Wilkie (1824–1889)
British novelist

Collins was a friend of Dickens and he wrote the kind of expansive, unhurried prose characteristic of the nineteenth century. However, he was also the leading exponent of what came to be known as 'sensation fiction', which often took mystery and crime as its subject matter. His long novel *The Woman in White* (1860) is a melodrama of thwarted love and skulduggery over an inheritance, all linked by the mysterious apparition of the Woman in White herself. It also includes a memorable villain in the fat, suave and sinister Italian, Count Fosco. *The Moonstone* (1868) is a more straightforward (though not shorter) tale of intrigue, haunting and death, centred on a jewel stolen from an Eastern statue of Buddha. It is often claimed by historians of the genre as the forerunner of all modern detective novels; it also contains, in the shrewd and melancholy Sergeant Cuff, the first working policeman in English literature to use 'scientific' methods of investigation.

READ ON >

● ***The Law and the Lady* (later Collins crime story suggested by the contemporary trial of Madeline Smith for allegedly poisoning her lover).**
▶ **Charles Dickens, *Bleak House*; ▷ Freeman Wills Crofts, *Inspector French's Greatest Case*.**

READ ON A THEME: COMEDY CRIME

▷ Christopher Brookmyre, *One Fine Day in the Middle of the Night*
▷ Tim Dorsey, *Florida Roadkill*
▷ Janet Evanovich, *One for the Money*
  Liz Evans, *Who Killed Marilyn Monroe?*
▷ Peter Guttridge, *The Once and Future Con*
▷ Sparkle Hayter, *Nice Girls Finish Last*
▷ Carl Hiaasen, *Double Whammy*
▷ Jonathan Latimer, *Headed for a Hearse*
  Gregory McDonald, *Fletch*
▷ Lawrence Sanders, *McNally's Secret*
▷ Laurence Shames, *Sunburn*
▷ Donald E. Westlake, *What's the Worst That Could Happen?*

CONNELLY, Michael (born 1946)
US novelist

Author of ten hard-boiled novels, Connelly is one of the very best of the newer breed of crime writers. Seven of his books feature Hieronymus 'Harry' Bosch, a world-weary detective in the LAPD. A Vietnam veteran and former 'tunnel rat', Bosch has a personal history that's harsh, complex and fascinating. Working from the Hollywood division in a superbly realized Los Angeles, Bosch is a very good cop in that he solves crimes and puts the criminals away but not so good in that he invariably faces suspension by his antagonistic, pen-pushing superiors. Bosch is a maverick who works to his own rules and code of honour rather than that of the system. Although maverick cops with drink problems and dysfunctional love lives are standard fare, Bosch is different. Connelly has succeeded in making him a sympathetic and compelling character, partly through his dry humour and partly because the reader knows, whatever the odds, that Bosch will be right – that he is the moral centre of the fiction and the authority he is always prepared to defy is self-serving.

Connelly's first book, *The Black Echo*, was published in 1992 and won an Edgar Award. It was followed by four others and then the first non-Bosch book, *The Poet* (see below), which became a bestseller. Two other novels without Bosch are *Blood Work*, which featured Terry McCaleb, a former FBI agent retired through ill-health, and *Void Moon*, a more light-hearted book set largely in Las Vegas and featuring a female thief called Cassie Black, an unlikely but likeable heroine. In *A Darkness More Than Night*, Connelly boldly teams up Bosch with McCaleb, and Bosch returns alone in *City of Bones*, perhaps Connelly's darkest book to date.

THE POET (1996)
Jack McEvoy's twin brother, a cop, is found dead in his car – apparently a suicide. McEvoy, a crime reporter, is drawn into investigating other police suicides around the country and becomes central to the pursuit of a serial killer with a fondness for the verse of Edgar Allan Poe. As improbable in its plot as nearly every other recent American serial-killer thriller, *The Poet* is none the less completely riveting and Connelly keeps the surprise twists and turns going until the last few pages.

Michael Connelly's other novels are The Black Echo, The Black Ice, The Concrete Blonde, The Last Coyote, Trunk Music, Blood Work, Angel's Flight, Void Moon, A Darkness More than Night *and* City of Bones.

READ ON ▷

● *The Black Echo* (the first of his Harry Bosch novels).
▶ ▷ David Baldacci, *The Simple Truth*; ▷ Jeffery Deaver, *The Bone Collector*; Ridley Pearson, *Probable Cause*; Stuart Woods, *Dead in the Water*.

CONSTANTINE, K. C. (born 1934)
US novelist

The series of crime novels by K. C. Constantine featuring Mario Balzic, chief of police in Rocksburg, Pennsylvania, has been praised (quite rightly) as much for its portrait of small-town American life as for its qualities as mystery fiction. Constantine is one of those crime writers who uses the genre very skilfully to explore a wider range of themes than those interested solely in crafting a successful mystery. Rocksburg is a town in economic decline and Constantine is expert at showing the ways in which that decline affects its inhabitants, from Balzic himself to men who have lost their jobs and their self-respect. He also has a superb ear for the language people use and rivals ▷ George V. Higgins in the dialogue he gives to his characters. A typical Balzic novel is *The Man Who Liked to Look at Himself*, in which the investigation of a murder is the hook on which Constantine hangs his observations of character and society. Constantine's most recent novels, still set in Rocksburg, have featured not Balzic but a younger cop, 'Rugs' Carlucci. The atmosphere and the dialogue remain compelling.

Constantine's other novels include The Rocksburg Railroad Murders, The Man Who Liked Slow Tomatoes, Upon Some Midnights Clear, Sunshine Enemies, Cranks and Shadows, Family Values *and* Grievance.

READ ON ▷

▶ ▷ George V. Higgins, *The Rat on Fire*; Gabriel Cohen, *Red Hook*.

COOPER, Natasha (born 1951)
British novelist

Natasha Cooper's first half a dozen crime novels were light-hearted, tongue-in-cheek mysteries featuring Willow King, a prissy civil servant during the week who leads a double life as a romantic novelist. The books make no pretences to be anything other than well-plotted entertainments (although they do hint at the more serious concerns of Cooper's later books) and, as such, they succeed very well. A typical example is *Rotten Apples*, in which Willow King looks into the death of an art historian and finds herself drawn into a tangled web of tax fraud and murder. Natasha Cooper's more recent books, which star a barrister called Trish Maguire, have grown progressively darker and more realistic, concerning themselves with genuine social issues, often involving children, and entering territory where Willow King would not tread.

FAULT LINES (1999)

A woman who was to have been Trish Maguire's star witness in a case of abuse at a children's home is found brutally murdered. It looks as if the witness may have been the latest victim of a serial killer and rapist known to the police already but not yet caught. The murdered woman has left Trish Maguire a note which leads her to a man named Blair Collons, a creepy obsessive who has been sacked from his job in local government and is full of tales of corruption and conspiracy. As the barrister tries to discover the truth about her witness's terrible death and the truth, if any, behind Collons's stories, she is drawn into danger herself.

The other Trish Maguire novels are Creeping Ivy, Prey to All *and* Out of the Dark. *The* Willow King *books are* Bitter Herbs, Rotten Apples, Festering Lilies, Poison Flowers, Bloody Roses, Fruiting Bodies *and* Sour Grapes. *Natasha Cooper has also written two psychological thrillers,* Clutch of Phantoms *and* Those Whom the Gods Love, *under the name of Clare Layton.*

READ ON

▶ to the Willow King books: Veronica Stallwood, *Oxford Knot*.
▶ to the Trish Maguire books: Jo Bannister, *Echoes of Lies*; Patricia Hall, *Death in Dark Waters*: Kate Ellis, *The Bone Garden*; ▷ Frances Fyfield, *The Nature of the Beast*.

CORNWELL, Patricia (born 1956)

US novelist

Each of Cornwell's thrillers begins with the discovery of a gruesomely mutilated body, which is then sent to Kay Scarpetta, Chief Medical Examiner of Richmond, Virginia. Scarpetta's post-mortem is the beginning of a spiral of serial killing, political machinations (she is not popular with corrupt official colleagues), personal involvement and nail-biting suspense. A favourite secondary character is her niece Lucy, a brilliant adolescent whose computer wizardry is equalled only by her social awkwardness. Since 1991 and the publication of *Post-Mortem*, the first of the Scarpetta books, Cornwell's combination of clinical and forensic expertise with tight plotting has made her books unputdownable.

POINT OF ORIGIN (1998)

Grisly murder comes once again to Scarpetta's home town of Richmond and once again Scarpetta's past returns to dog her. A farmhouse in Virginia has been destroyed in a fire and the remains of a body found there reveal clear signs of brutal murder. Meanwhile Carrie Grethen, a killer who tangled with Scarpetta in *The Body Farm*, has escaped from a psychiatric hospital and is sending Kay cryptic messages threatening revenge.

The other Scarpetta novels (best read in sequence, though self-contained) are Post-Mortem, Body of Evidence, All That Remains, Cruel and Unusual, The Body Farm, From Potter's Field, Cause of Death, Unnatural Exposure, Black Notice *and* The Last Precinct. Hornet's Nest, Southern Cross *and* Isle of Dogs *are non-Scarpetta novels.*

READ ON ▷

▶ ▷ Jonathan Kellerman, *Over The Edge*; ▷ Carol O'Connell, *Mallory's Oracle*; ▷ Kathy Reichs, *Déjà Dead*; Lisa Scottoline, *Mistaken Identity*; Louise Hendricksen, *Grave Secrets*; Linda Fairstein, *Cold Hit*. See also Read on a Theme: Serial Killers.

READ ON A THEME: COURTROOM DRAMAS

William Bernhardt, *Perfect Justice*
Henry Cecil, *According to the Evidence*
Dexter Dias, *False Witness*
Philip Friedman, *Inadmissible Evidence*
▷ Erle Stanley Gardner, *The Case of the Hesitant Hostess* (or almost any other of the Perry Mason cases)
Steve Martini, *Compelling Evidence*
▷ Scott Turow, *Presumed Innocent*

See also: Legal Eagles

COXE, George Harmon (1901–1984)
US novelist

In his long writing career, which lasted from the heyday of pulp magazines like *Black Mask* to the 1970s, Coxe wrote hundreds of short stories and over 150 crime novels. His best-known series features Kent Murdock, a newspaper photographer whose profession gains him entry to all levels of society, but also tangles him in other people's conspiracies, divorces and murders. Typical Murdock books are *The Jade Venus, The Hidden Key, An Easy Way To Go* and *The Last Commandment*. A good example of his non-series books is *The Candid Impostor* (1967), in which a reporter agrees to impersonate a friend, go to Panama and collect $10,000 – at which point, all kinds of entertaining hell breaks loose.

READ ON ▷

▶ ▷ Jonathan Latimer, *Murder in the Madhouse*; ▷ Ross Thomas, *Briarpatch*; ▷ Stuart M. Kaminsky, *Bullet for a Star*.

CRAIS, Robert (born 1953)
US novelist

A native of Louisiana, Crais trained as an engineer before taking up writing. In 1976, he moved to Los Angeles and, after scripting numerous episodes of such TV shows as *Cagney & Lacey, Hill St Blues* and *Miami Vice*, published *The Monkey's Raincoat* (1987), the first of eight novels featuring wisecracking private eye Elvis Cole and his tough, taciturn sidekick Joe Pike. Cole and his enigmatic partner make a dynamite team and the books are packed with charm, humour and large helpings of nail-biting suspense. They also possess a zen-like ambience, evidenced by Pike's occasional Zen mutterings, Cole's rigorous tai chi sessions and his rather epigrammatic conversations with his cat (who talks about as much as Pike). That the two sleuths wash down their Vietnamese takeaways with Falstaff ale, coupled with the fact that most of the action seems to take place under the pervasive glare of LA's constant sunshine, gives the novels an Eastern exoticism that only adds to their considerable appeal. The duo's last outing, the magnificent *LA Requiem*, examined their past, particularly that of the mysterious but charismatic Pike, aloof and stolid behind his shades which, being such a permanent fixture, appear to be surgically attached. Crais has since written *Demolition Angel* and *Hostage*, two stand-alone novels.

The Elvis Cole novels are Stalking the Angel, Lullaby Town, Free Fall, Voodoo River, Sunset Express, Indigo Slam, LA Requiem *and* The Last Detective.

READ ON

▶ ▷ Harlan Coben, *One False Move*; ▷ Dennis Lehane, *Gone, Baby, Gone*; ▷ Dick Lochte, *Sleeping Dog*; J. L. Abramo, *Catching Water in a Net.*

CREASEY, John (1908–1973)
British novelist and playwright

Few writers have matched John Creasey's awesome productivity. In a working life of forty years he produced more than 500 full-length novels, as well as short stories, plays and edited collections. He used twenty-two pseudonyms and wrote well over 20 million words. Inevitably many of his books were potboilers. He wrote three series of books, however, which remain well worth reading. The Toff books (with 'Toff' in every title) are light-hearted stories that now have a period charm, about a gentleman adventurer who sleuths for the fun of it.

The Inspector West books (with 'West' in each title) feature a Scotland Yard detective and combine brilliant investigation with a persuasive picture of the detective's private and family life. The Gideon books (written as J. J. Marric and with 'Gideon' in every title) are London police procedurals, mostly set in the 1950s and 1960s, and showing Gideon and his Scotland Yard colleagues patiently working on several interlocking crimes at once.

READ ON

▶ to the Toff books: ▷ Leslie Charteris, *Enter the Saint.*
▶ to the Inspector West books: ▷ Dorothy Simpson, *Wake the Dead*; ▷ Sheila Radley, *Fate Worse Than Death.*
▶ to the Gideon books: Eric Bruton, *The Laughing Policeman*; ▷ Robert Barnard, *Death and the Princess.*

READ ON A THEME: CRIMES TO COME
(crime fiction set in the future)

Isaac Asimov, *The Caves of Steel*
Greg Bear, *Queen of Angels*
Alfred Bester, *The Demolished Man*
▷ Peter Dickinson, *King and Joker*
William Gibson, *Neuromancer*

Terence M. Green, *Barking Dogs*
▷ Philip Kerr, *A Philosophical Investigation*
J. D. Robb, *Naked in Death*

CRISPIN, Edmund (1921–1978)
British novelist

Edmund Crispin was the pseudonym of Bruce Montgomery, a contemporary and friend of Philip Larkin and Kingsley Amis at Oxford, who was known under his own name as a composer, notably of film music for British comedies of the 1940s. His books feature one of the great 'English eccentric' detectives: Gervase Fen. Fen is a professor of English literature at Oxford, a man who 'attracts curiosities' as a flower attracts bees, a delicious amalgam of Sherlock Holmes and Jacques Tati. Crispin's plots similarly blend the intriguing, the macabre and the farcical – he is particularly good at chase endings, simultaneously unravelling knots and tying up loose ends in a scramble as hilarious as the last reel of any film comedy. Typical of his books are two Oxford University romps, *The Case of the Gilded Fly* (1945) and *The Moving Toyshop* (1946).

Crispin's other novels are Holy Disorders, Swan Song, Love Lies Bleeding, Buried for Pleasure, Frequent Hearses, The Long Divorce *and* The Glimpses of the Moon. Beware of the Trains *and* Fen Country *are collections of short stories.*

READ ON ▷

● *Buried for Pleasure* (in which Fen goes to the remotest and sleepiest of English villages to stand for parliament and finds – as always – a crew of wildly murderous eccentrics, as if he had stumbled on the cast of a peculiarly black Ealing comedy).
▶ ▷ Michael Innes, *The Weight of the Evidence*; ▷ Cyril Hare, *When the Wind Blows*; ▷ Dorothy L. Sayers, *Gaudy Night*.

CROFTS, Freeman Wills (1879–1957)
British novelist

Crofts's novels are masterly accounts of meticulous, plodding policework, his detective (in most novels, Inspector French) unpicking tightly woven tissues of lies and alibis with painstaking, unhurried care. The books are also often redolent of a long-gone, pre-Beeching era of the railways. Many of the alibis – and hence the stories – hinge on train times; as ▷ John Dickson Carr was to the locked-room mystery, so Crofts was to the timetable. The thirty French novels begin with *Inspector French's Greatest Case* and include *Sir John Magill's Last Journey*, *The Mystery of the Sleeping Car Express*, *Death of a Train*, *Anything to Declare* and *The 12.30 from Croydon*, in which obsession with timetables not only leads to the solution of the crimes, but is what causes them in the first place.

READ ON ▷

▶ Christianna Brand, *Green for Danger*; R. Austin Freeman, *Mr Pottermack's Oversight*.

CROMBIE, Deborah (born 1952)
US novelist

Like some other US novelists, such as Elizabeth George, Deborah Crombie writes well-crafted, traditional crime fiction set in England. The dangers of writing about a country other than one's own are obvious – the potential for gaffes lurks on every page – but Crombie's series featuring Superintendent Duncan Kincaid and Sergeant Gemma James is convincing and compelling. A romantic relationship between the two protagonists develops through the series and this provides one of the focuses of the books, but they owe their success primarily to the strength of Crombie's plotting and the quality of her writing. Typical Kincaid and James mysteries are *Dreaming of the Bones* (1997), in which the death of Kincaid's ex-wife leads him into an investigation that also encompasses the apparent suicide, several years earlier, of a poet, and *A Finer End* (2001), set largely in Glastonbury where ancient secrets and New Age shenanigans attract their attention.

Deborah Crombie's other novels include A Share in Death, All Shall Be Well, Leave the Grave Green, Mourn Not Your Dead, Kissed a Sad Goodbye *and* Justice, There is None.

READ ON

▶ ▷ Elizabeth George, *A Great Deliverance*; Jill McGown, *Scene of Crime*; Clare Curzon, *Body of a Woman*.

CROSS, Amanda (born 1926)
US novelist

Amanda Cross is the pseudonym of Carolyn Heilbrun, a former professor of English at Columbia University. Her sleuth, Kate Fansler, is also a professor and her investigations often involve some kind of literary detection. A wry view of the place of women, both in literature and society, colours but never overwhelms the plots: *A Death in the Faculty*, for example, is very funny about Harvard men's attitudes to a woman professor, and about militant feminism. Cross's stories move swiftly and yet have time for the rich, leisurely dialogue about books, music, politics and everything under the sun which is one of the chief pleasures of her novels.

SWEET DEATH, KIND DEATH (1984)
Professor Patrice Umphelby, unpopular for her views on the status of women in academic life, unexpectedly kills herself. Kate Fansler investigates, drawing ideas from the suicide notes of Stevie Smith and Virginia Woolf.

Amanda Cross's other books include In the Last Analysis, The James Joyce Murder, Poetic Justice, The Theban Mysteries, A Question of Max, A Trap for Fools, An Imperfect Spy, The Puzzled Heart *and* Honest Doubt.

READ ON

▶ Edith Skom, *The Mark Twain Murders*; ▷ Joan Smith, *A Masculine* Ending; Anna Clarke, *The Deathless and the Dead*.

CRUMLEY, James (born 1939)
US novelist

Crumley has not been a prolific writer. He has published only six crime novels in more than a quarter of a century. However, all six have met with much critical acclaim. Crumley, largely uninterested in the crime novel as whodunit or as psychological thriller, uses the genre to explore his own interests and preoccupations. Crime is the vehicle used to investigate character, the mythology of the American West and traditional masculinity. War abroad is the defining experience for Crumley's two main characters – C. W. Sughrue fought in Vietnam and Milo Milodragovitch in Korea – and the books are about their attempts to live the life of the American individualist, for which they believe they fought, in a society that has changed. Violence and drugs feature strongly in the books but Crumley writes with a spare lyricism that transcends his resolutely macho subjects. As his limited production of novels suggests, he is a literary craftsman and all his sentences are carefully honed and polished. He's also very funny with a nice line in deadpan wisecracks.

BORDERSNAKES (1997)
Crumley's two protagonists, Milo Milodragovitch and C. W. Sughrue ('Sugh as in sugar, rue as in rue the goddamn day') join forces in a drink and drug-fuelled journey through Texas and Mexico in search of revenge on assorted bad men who've done them wrong. As always with Crumley, the elaborately labyrinthine plot is not the main reason for staying the course – the pleasure is in the language and in his fantasy vision of two ageing but indomitable individualists who refuse to be broken by the system and the rich and powerful men who run it.

James Crumley's other novels are The Last Good Kiss, The Mexican Tree Duck, The Wrong Case, Dancing Bear *and* The Final Country.

> READ ON ▷

- ● *The Last Good Kiss* (the novel that introduced C. W. Sughrue).
- ▶ ▷ James Ellroy, *Brown's Requiem*; ▷ George Pelecanos, *Nick's Trip*; Zachary Klein, *Still Among the Living*; Jonathan Valin, *The Lime Pit*.

READ ON A THEME: CYBER CRIME
(computers, new technology and virtual reality)

Sally Chapman, *Love Bytes*
Phillip Finch, *F2F*
Duane Franklet, *Bad Memory*
William Gibson, *Neuromancer*
▷ Philip Kerr, *Gridiron*
Cole Perriman, *Terminal Games*
Christopher Priest, *The Extremes*

DAVIS, Lindsey (born 1949)
British novelist

In a series of novels featuring Marcus Didius Falco, 'the Philip Marlowe of Ancient Rome', as more than one reviewer has described him, Lindsey Davis brings the world of the Roman empire back to life. The stories are briskly told, filled with unobtrusive scholarship, and Falco is an inspired creation. Narrating his own adventures, he is witty and cynical, streetwise yet still enough of a romantic to pursue his unlikely, on-off relationship with the feisty senator's daughter Helena Justina. In 14 Falco novels Davis has sent her hero to very nearly all the furthest-flung corners of the empire and involved him with most of its dodgiest and most villainous citizens.

THE SILVER PIGS (1989)
The first in the series remains one of the best. Falco is sent to what is probably the most godforsaken of all outposts of empire – Britain – in order to investigate fraud in the silver mines which are the colony's only major asset. He shivers and shakes in the inhospitable climate, makes the acquaintance of Helena Justina for the first time and only narrowly escapes meeting his end far away from civilization.

The other Falco novels are (in sequence, although each is self-contained) Shadows in Bronze, Venus in Copper, The Iron Hand of Mars, Poseidon's Gold, Last Act in Palmyra, Time to Depart, A Dying Light in Corduba, Three Hands in the Fountain, Two for the Lions, One Virgin Too Many, Ode to a Banker, A Body in the Bath House *and* The Jupiter Myth. *She has also written* The Course of Honour, *a novel not starring Falco but set in the same period – the reign of the Emperor Vespasian.*

READ ON >

- ● *Last Act in Palmyra* (Falco's adventures with a travelling theatre troupe in Syria).
- ▶ ▷ Steven Saylor, *Roman Blood* (the first novel featuring the other candidate for Ancient Rome's Philip Marlowe, Gordianus the Finder); John Maddox Roberts, *SPQR: The Catiline Conspiracy*; Rosemary Rowe, *The Germanicus Mosaic* (first in a series set in second-century Roman Britain); Marilyn Todd, *I, Claudia*; David Wishart, *Old Bones*.
See also Read on a Theme: Rome.

DEAVER, Jeffery (born 1950)
US novelist

Rather like ▷ Lawrence Block, Deaver is such a prolific author and one with so many facets to his writing career that, sometimes, it's hard to keep up. Writing under the name of William Jefferies, he penned three novels featuring John Pellam, a film director who hit the bottle and, when it hit back, wound up in San Quentin. Now a Hollywood location scout, Pellam has appeared in three mysteries originally written in the 1990s: *Shallow Graves, Bloody River Blues* and *Hell's Kitchen*. Another film-based series, starring sassy punk Rune, an aspiring director who works in a video store in New York, has three novels in the can so far – *Manhattan is My Beat, Death of a Blue Movie Star* and *Hard News*.

Although loaded with the requisite thrills and suspense, these are more light-hearted than Deaver's usual work and Rune is an engaging heroine.

By far Deaver's most successful creation is Lincoln Rhyme, a quadriplegic forensic expert and former NYPD detective. A kind of hi-tech Mycroft Holmes, this sedentary sleuth is assisted by his partner, the more mobile Amelia Sachs, and together they have appeared in four thrillers. The latest, *The Stone Monkey*, is set in New York's Chinatown.

Deaver has also written a number of other novels including *The Devil's Teardrop* (featuring a guest appearance by Rhyme), *Praying for Sleep* and *The Blue Nowhere*, as well as *Mistress of Justice*, another novel with a female character, Taylor Lockwood, a paralegal by day, jazz pianist by night and amateur sleuth in between.

THE BONE COLLECTOR (1997)

Lincoln Rhyme brings his masterful mind and a dazzling array of technological gadgets to bear on the case of a serial killer who is re-creating murders from the past and providing police with the clues to stop the next one – if only they can work out what they mean. Deaver combines the graphic, visceral detail that seems *de rigueur* in today's thrillers with an implausible but none the less gripping plot.

READ ON ▷

▶ ▷ **Lee Child**, *Tripwire*; ▷ **Michael Connelly**, *Blood Work*; ▷ **James Patterson**, *Along Came a Spider*; **John Sandford**, *Eyes of Prey*.

DEXTER, Colin (born 1930)
British novelist

Since the days of Holmes and Watson there has been no surer ingredient of long-term success in detective fiction than an alliance between two apparently mismatched characters who are, in fact, devoted to one another. As the readers of his books – and the millions who have watched the TV films – know, Colin Dexter created just such an alliance in the partnership of Chief Inspector Morse and Detective Sergeant Lewis of the Oxford police. Morse is grumpy, intellectual, fond of booze, opera and crosswords, and a bachelor. Lewis is stolid, reliable, diligent but slightly unimaginative. Together they form a classic genius/sidekick duo. The third constant in the Morse books is Oxford. The city of dreaming spires provides the ideal setting for the complicated crimes Morse and Lewis investigate. However, plot, particularly in the early books, is not sacrificed to character and place. Dexter is a one-time national crossword champion and his narrative twists and turns have the ingenuity of the most cryptic of crossword clues.

The full-length Morse novels are: Last Bus to Woodstock, Last Seen Wearing, The Silent World of Nicholas Quinn, Service of All the Dead, The Dead of Jericho, The Riddle of the Third Mile, The Secret of Annexe 3, The Wench is Dead, The Jewel That Was Ours, The Way Through the Woods, The Daughters of Cain, Death is Now My Neighbour *and* The Remorseful Day. Morse's Greatest Mystery *is a collection of short stories, some about Morse, some not.*

READ ON >

- *The Way Through the Woods* (one of Morse's most satisfying cases, in which a chance newspaper headline sets him on the trail of a Swedish girl missing for a year).
- ▷ Reginald Hill, *An Advancement of Learning*; ▷ John Harvey, *Easy Meat*; Patricia Hall, *Skeleton at the Feast*; Veronica Stallwood, *Oxford Exit*; R. D. Wingfield, *A Touch of Frost* (one of a series that shares with Dexter's books TV success and a grumpy central character).

DIBDIN, Michael (born 1947)
British novelist

Dibdin's early novels, including a wicked reworking of Sherlock Holmes (*The Last Sherlock Holmes Story*) and one in which the Victorian poet Robert Browning plays amateur detective in Florence, are enjoyable mixtures of authentic crime fiction and pastiche. His finest creation, however, and one of the most appealing protagonists in contemporary crime writing, is Aurelio Zen, investigator for the Criminalpol section of the Italian Ministry of the Interior. Zen, unlike the one-dimensional ciphers of so much detective fiction, is a rounded and convincing character. Struggling to maintain what moral integrity he can amid the labyrinthine bureaucracy and corruption of Italian society, he tries to unearth as much of the truth about the cases he is assigned as circumstances allow. Dibdin himself lived and worked in Italy for a number of years and the richness and unobtrusive detail of the Italian settings – Venice, Rome, the impoverished south – add to the pleasures of reading the novels. In addition to the Zen novels, Dibdin continues to write other books in which he cleverly manipulates the conventions of crime fiction to produce challenging and witty narratives.

CABAL (1992)
Cabal opens with startling suddenness as a man plummets to his death from the gallery in St Peter's, Rome, while a priest is celebrating mass. The man is a gambler, playboy and prominent Catholic aristo, and the initial assumption is that he committed suicide. Zen is brought in by the Vatican police force to rubber stamp this verdict, but soon concludes that the case is not that simple. The dead man was involved in dubious financial skulduggery and, as murder begins to seem the likeliest option, potential witnesses join the ranks of the dead. Caught between the Vatican and his own superiors, Zen suspects far-reaching conspiracies and secret organizations ruthlessly intent on covering up their misdeeds.

The other Zen novels (each one self-contained) are Ratking, Vendetta, Dead Lagoon, Cosi Fan Tutti, A Long Finish, Blood Rain *and* And Then You Die. *Dibdin's other books include* The Last Sherlock Holmes Story, Dark Spectre, Dirty Tricks, The Tryst *and* Thanksgiving.

READ ON >

- *Dirty Tricks* (a non-Zen novel, the darkly humorous story of a teacher returning from Europe to Britain who finds himself involved in adultery and murder).
- to *The Last Sherlock Holmes Story*: Nicholas Meyer, *The Seven-Per-Cent Solution*; ▷ Loren D. Estleman, *Dr Jekyll and Mr Holmes*.

▶ to the Zen novels: ▷ Donna Leon, *The Death of Faith* (one of another crime series with Venetian police detective; ▷ Iain Pears, *Giotto's Hand*; ▷ Ian Rankin, *The Hanging Garden*; ▷ Reginald Hill, *Bones and Silence*; ▷ Magdalen Nabb, *The Marshal and the Murderer*.

DICKINSON, Peter (born 1927)
British novelist

In the 1960s and 1970s Dickinson wrote several novels featuring Superintendent Pibble of Scotland, a man as characterless as blotting paper. Pibble's lack of notability is vital, enabling him to move unobtrusively through the very bizarre communities in which Dickinson places the crimes: a group of New Guinea aboriginals living in the attic of a North London house (*Skin Deep*, 1968); a crazy religious sect waiting for the apocalypse on a remote Scottish island (*The Seals*, 1970); a community of brain-damaged, psychically sensitive children (*Sleep and His Brother*, 1971). In later books, Dickinson abandoned Pibble but kept the bizarreness. In *King and Joker* (1976), for example, someone commits murder in a Buckingham Palace inhabited by an egalitarian, trendy-left royal family.

Dickinson's books since the 1980s are less crime novels than novels including crime. Our interest is in the people and their relationships, and in Dickinson's virtuoso writing technique – he is particularly fond of moving backwards and forwards between historical periods, showing how people's behaviour in the present is affected by betrayals, love affairs and murders in the past.

Dickinson's other crime novels include The Lizard in the Cup, Walking Dead, One Foot in the Grave, Death of a Unicorn, Skeleton-in-Waiting, The Yellow Room Mystery *and* Some Deaths Before Dying.

READ ON ▷

● *Perfect Gallows* (a murder and its solution and the effects over a lifetime on the person who discovered the body are all unravelled in this rich and rewarding novel).
▷ H. R. F. Keating, *Death and the Visiting Firemen*; ▷ Andrew Taylor, *Waiting for the End of the World*; ▷ Elizabeth Ferrars, *Ninth Life*.

DICKSON, Carter, see John Dickson CARR

DOBYNS, Stephen (born 1941)
US novelist and poet

Dobyns's Charlie Bradshaw novels, which have been appearing since the mid-1970s, spoof every cliché of the private eye genre. Bradshaw, a wisecracking retired policeman, runs a down-at-heel detective agency in Saratoga Springs. His former boss dislikes him for his mouthiness. His contacts with the racing world mean that he constantly runs up against arrogant rich bastards and bitches with plenty to hide. Whenever murder happens – and that means frequently – either Bradshaw or his sidekick Vic Plotz seems to get the blame. As Charlie tries to track down the real villains, the books prove to be amiable, charming and often very funny. More recently Dobyns has written several psychological thrillers which inhabit a much darker world than the Saratoga Springs of the Bradshaw books.

SARATOGA HEADHUNTER (1985)

McClatchy, a crooked jockey about to give prosecution evidence against his former cronies, appears at Bradshaw's cottage late one night asking for protection. When he is found decapitated the next day, Bradshaw is the chief suspect. He has to clear his name by finding the real murderer, but every potential source of information quickly ends up dead.

The other Charlie Bradshaw books are Saratoga Longshot, Saratoga Snapper, Saratoga Swimmer, Saratoga Bestiary, Saratoga Hexameter, Saratoga Haunting, Saratoga Backtalk, Saratoga Fleshpot *and* Saratoga Strongbox. *His other novels include* The Wrestler's Cruel Study, The Church of Dead Girls *and* The Boy in the Water.

> READ ON

- **The Church of Dead Girls (a series of killings tears apart a small American community).**
- ▷ **Dick Francis, Forfeit (more horse-racing crime, although Francis's style could hardly be more different from Dobyns's).**

DOHERTY, Paul (born 1946)
British novelist

Doherty is one of the most prolific of contemporary writers of historical crime fiction. As well as the medieval and ancient Egyptian novels he has published under his own name, he has produced books under so many pseudonyms that he may well have lost track of them all himself. He publishes books at the rate of five or six a year and yet continues to maintain a remarkably high standard. The historical background, particularly in the medieval stories, is convincing in its detail but the emphasis remains on the mysteries which are, for the most part, genuinely intriguing. Under his own name Doherty's two medieval series feature Hugh Corbett, investigator and spy-master to Edward I, and the pilgrims from Chaucer's *Canterbury Tales* who are given extra tales of murder to tell. His Egyptian series, set in Thebes in the fifteenth century BC, features the judge Amerotke as he looks into cases of murder and treachery.

As Paul Harding, Doherty has produced the Brother Athelstan series about a Dominican friar living in medieval Southwark and working as secretarius to Sir John Cranston, Coroner of London. As Michael Clynes, he writes mysteries set in the reign of Henry VIII and featuring Roger Shallot, a roguish investigator employed by Cardinal Wolsey. Under the name of Ann Dukthas, Doherty has produced an ingenious series involving Nicholas Segalla, a man who travels through time to look into well-known historical mysteries such as the fate of the Dauphin, later Louis XVII, during and after the French Revolution.

The Hugh Corbett novels include Satan in St Mary's, The Prince of Darkness, The Assassin in the Greenwood, The Devil's Hunt *and* Corpse Candle. *The Brother Athelstan mysteries include* The Nightingale Gallery, The House of the Red

Slayer, The Assassin's Riddle, The Devil's Domain *and* The Field of Blood. *The Egyptian novels are* The Mask of Ra, The Horus Killings, The Anubis Slayings *and* The Slayers of Seth. *The Ann Dukthas novels are* A Time for the Death of a King, The Prince Lost to Time, The Time of Murder at Mayerling *and* In the Time of the Poisoned Queen.

READ ON >

▶ to the medieval novels: ▷ Michael Jecks, *The Leper's Return*; ▷ Kate Sedley, *The Eve of St Hyacinth*; A. E. Marston, *The Wolves of Savernake*.
▶ to the Egyptian novels: Anton Gill, *City of the Horizon*; Lauren Haney, *The Right Hand of Amon*; Lynda S. Robinson, *Drinker of Blood*.
See also Read on a Theme: Medieval Mystery, Egypt.

DORSEY, Tim (born 1961)
US novelist

Since penning *Miami Roadkill* in 1999, Dorsey has followed with three more crime novels at a rate of one a year: *Hammerhead Ranch Motel*, *Orange Crush* and *Triggerfish Twist*. Each one is set in a Florida so garish and grotesque, it's as if Dorsey had created a new genre: dayglo noir. Serge Storms, the psychotic protagonist of all of the books, is probably what puts them ahead of a very crowded field. An inspired creation, Storms has something of the zeal and love for the splendours of Florida that one would encounter in a Carl Hiaasen character, but, refreshingly, is an utter lunatic with the morals of a shark and the attention span of a minnow. A walking encyclopedia on all things pertaining to the Orange State, Storms is never happier than when he is enlightening whomever he's with about a piece of local history, no matter what he's doing at the time – driving a stolen car at high speed, having sex, or just killing someone. Aided, abetted and often impeded by his drug-guzzling cohorts, Coleman and the deliriously desirable Sharon, Storms races through Tallahassee, Miami and the Keys, leaving behind a trail of destruction and hysteria that's, well, hysterical.

READ ON >

▶ ▷ Carl Hiaasen, *Stormy Weather*; ▷ Laurence Shames, *Sunburn*; Tom Corcoran, *Bone Island Mambo*.

DOYLE, Sir Arthur Conan (1859–1930)
British novelist

Doyle came from a family of artists and writers but his original intention was to pursue a career in medicine. He qualified as a doctor and set up a practice in Southsea, Portsmouth, only turning to fiction when patients proved few and far between. Within a few years he had created Sherlock Holmes and Dr Watson, destined to become the most famous characters in crime fiction. The pair first appeared in 1887 in *A Study in Scarlet* and made their real mark in a series of short stories published in *The Strand* magazine in the 1890s. Doyle, who was proudest of his historical fiction (which now seems very ponderous and dry), was famously resentful of the attention given to Holmes and tried to kill him off by sending him over the Reichenbach Falls in the clutches of Professor Moriarty.

The public was having none of this and demanded his return. Doyle reluctantly complied, first in the novel *The Hound of the Baskervilles* and then in further short stories and novels.

What is the enduring appeal of Holmes, the supremely rational detective able to make sweeping deductions from the smallest piece of evidence, and of Watson, his stolid and dependable sidekick? Maybe the idea of an omniscient detective, able to solve the most baffling of mysteries, is a perennially reassuring one. However, plenty of other writers have created omniscient, supermen detectives and none has even come remotely close to rivalling Holmes. Doyle's stories themselves often contain weak plots and repetitive dialogue but Holmes and Watson transcend petty limitations. They have escaped the boundaries of the fiction in which they appear in a way that few characters, other than some of Shakespeare's and some of Dickens's, have done. Whatever the reasons for this, it is safe to assume that they will remain semi-mythical figures for as long as crime fiction continues to be read.

THE HOUND OF THE BASKERVILLES (1902)
In what is probably the most famous of all detective novels, Holmes and Watson exchange the fog-enshrouded streets of London for the fog-enshrouded moors of Devon. Detective meets devilish dog in Doyle's potent story of the ancient curse on the Baskerville family that may still be at work in the present. ('Mr Holmes, they were the footprints of a gigantic hound!') The short stories are, perhaps, where Holmes and Watson are seen at their most archetypal, but the chilling melodrama of *The Hound of the Baskervilles* is still guaranteed, a century after its first publication, to enthral all readers with any imagination at all.

The other Holmes novels are A Study in Scarlet, The Sign of Four *and* The Valley of Fear. *The fifty-six short stories are gathered in the following collections:* The Adventures of Sherlock Holmes, The Memoirs of Sherlock Holmes, The Return of Sherlock Holmes, His Last Bow *and* The Casebook of Sherlock Holmes.

READ ON ▷

▶ ▷ G. K. Chesterton, *The Innocence of Father Brown*; Arthur Morrison, *Martin Hewitt, Investigator*; Jacques Futrelle, *The Thinking Machine*; August Derleth, *The Adventures of Solar Pons* (half-parody, half-homage, these stories feature a Holmes-like detective operating from rooms in Praed Street).
See also Read on a Theme: Holmes Beyond Doyle, Rivals of Sherlock Holmes.

DUFFY, Stella (born 1963)
British novelist

Too often British private eyes seem to operate in some indeterminate era that could be almost any time from the 1960s to the present day. One of the great strengths of Stella Duffy's original and likeable dyke detective Saz Martin is that she is so immediately and recognizably contemporary. The novels in which she appears are not only cleverly constructed and filled with wit and one-liners but they take place in convincing turn-of-our-century settings.

WAVEWALKER (1996)
Maxwell North is famous as a therapist and guru. People queue up to pay tribute to the powers of his 'healing' process. Yet dark secrets lurk behind North's public

persona. Saz Martin, hired by a mystery employer known to her only as the Wavewalker, is drawn into an investigation of North that reaches back into 1970s San Francisco and propels her into danger in today's London.

The other Saz Martin books are Calendar Girl, Beneath the Blonde *and* Fresh Flesh.

READ ON >

▶ ▷ Lauren Henderson, *Too Many Blondes*; J. M. Redmann, *Death by the Riverside*; Kate Calloway, *First Impressions*.
See also Read on a Theme: Gay and Lesbian Detectives.

DUKTHAS, Ann, see Paul DOHERTY

DUNANT, Sarah (born 1950)
British novelist

Sarah Dunant's heroine Hannah Wolfe has been described by one reviewer as 'one of the best private eyes, either sex, either side of the Atlantic'. This intelligent and spirited private investigator appeared in three novels in the early 1990s, each a well-paced mystery combined with plenty of wry social commentary and barbed observations of life, love and relationships. In recent novels Dunant has abandoned her heroine and the private eye genre in favour of the psychological thriller. In *Mapping the Edge* (1999), for example, she weaves together parallel narratives about the disappearance of a single mother with great skill, in a book which is more about the challenges and risks of modern non-nuclear families than it is about a mystery and its resolution.

FATLANDS (1993)
Hannah Wolfe takes a job keeping an eye on the rebellious teenage daughter of a well-known scientist. What seems a brief involving no more than shepherding her charge on shopping trips to Knightsbridge becomes a journey into the world of animal rights extremists and yet more sinister organizations.

The other Hannah Wolfe novels are Birthmarks *and* Under My Skin. *Dunant's other novels are* Snow Storms in a Hot Climate, Transgressions *and* Mapping the Edge.

READ ON >

▶ to the Hannah Wolfe books: ▷ Liza Cody, *Bad Company*; ▷ Sara Paretsky, *Hard Time*.
▶ to the psychological thrillers: ▷ Nicci French, *The Red Room*; ▷ Frances Fyfield, *The Nature of the Beast*.

E

EARLY, Jack, see Sandra SCOPPETTONE

READ ON A THEME: EGYPT
(ancient and relatively modern)

▷ Agatha Christie, *Death on the Nile*
▷ Paul Doherty, *The Mask of Ra*
   Aaron Elkins, *Dead Men's Hearts*
   Anton Gill, *City of the Horizon*
▷ Michael Pearce, *The Mamur Zapt and the Return of the Carpet*
▷ Elizabeth Peters, *Crocodile on the Sandbank*
   Lynda S. Robinson, *Murder in the Place of Anubis*

READ ON A THEME: ELIZABETHAN MYSTERIES

   Fiona Buckley, *To Shield the Queen*
   P. R. Chisholm, *A Plague of Angels*
   Judith Cook, *Death of a Lady's Maid*
   Philip Gooden, *Sleep of Death*
   Karen Harper, *The Poyson Garden*
▷ Faye Kellerman, *The Quality of Mercy*
   Edward Marston, *The Mad Courtesan*
   Leonard Tourney, *The Bartholomew Fair Murders*

ELLROY, James (born 1948)
US novelist

Few crime writers have been more obviously driven to the genre by their own personal demons than James Ellroy. As his luridly readable autobiography *My Dark Places* makes clear, his was not an all-American, apple-pie upbringing. His mother was murdered when he was ten years old and his adolescence and early manhood were overshadowed by drink, drugs and sexual obsessions. (Breaking into women's apartments in order to sniff their underwear is but one of the confessions he makes in the book.) More than most writers, his writing has clearly been a lifeline to some kind of sanity and self-respect.

His first few novels were straightforward hard-boiled cop thrillers but *The Black Dahlia* was something else. Taking a famous unsolved murder of the 1940s – one with clear resonances with his own mother's killing – Ellroy created a dark and compelling narrative in which real-life individuals interacted with bruised and obsessed characters of his own creation. It was the beginning of his best and most intense work, the books collectively known as the LA Quartet. These comprise an extraordinary retelling of California's secret history seen through the eyes of its corrupt and cynical police officers. Marshalling dozens of characters and a tangled web of competing plots and sub-plots, Ellroy creates his own alternative history of the decades in which American dreams began to turn to nightmares. Recent novels have been even more ambitious but there are signs that Ellroy is teetering perilously close to the edge of self-parody. His prose, which was always idiosyncratic, has become in, say, *The Cold Six Thousand*, a strange sort of telegraphese in which sentences rarely exceed half a dozen words and adjectives and adverbs are so ruthlessly excised that the reader falls upon any that still exist like a starving man coming upon an unexpected feast. Over 600 pages, this abbreviated style is very hard to take. Nothing, however, can make one forget the power of the LA Quartet, which remains one of the great achievements of modern hard-boiled writing.

The books in the LA Quartet are The Black Dahlia, The Big Nowhere, LA Confidential *and* White Jazz. *Ellroy's other novels are* Brown's Requiem, Clandestine, Blood on the Moon, Because the Night, Suicide Hill, American Tabloid *and* The Cold Six Thousand. My Dark Places *is an autobiography that chronicles his own years of seedy delinquency and his attempts to learn the truth about his mother's murder.*

READ ON ▷

- *American Tabloid* **(Ellroy's ambitious and daring attempt to use the crime genre to re-examine American history in the run-up to the JFK assassination).**
- ▶ ▷ **Michael Connelly,** *The Last Coyote*; ▷ **James Crumley,** *Bordersnakes*; ▷ **James Lee Burke,** *Cadillac Jukebox.*
See also Read on a Theme: Tinseltown Murders.

ENGEL, Howard (born 1931)
Canadian writer

Engel's private eye, Benny Cooperman, is a Jewish Canadian from Grantham, Ontario. He is shrewd, funny and soft-hearted – he must be the only sleuth ever forced to tell all by a hood threatening to remove the leaves one by one from his mother's rubber plant. The ace in his hand is that he was born and bred in Grantham, and really knows the area – both the American and Canadian sides of the border. He is no loner, and has a wry but friendly relationship with the police. But with his clients and the people he meets he can be just as much a twenty-minute egg as any other private eye.

A CITY CALLED JULY (1986)
Cooperman is hired by Jewish community leaders to investigate the disappearance of a local solicitor and his client's cash. The search sends him snooping round government contracts, mobsters and the close-knit Geller family. Engel's plot is beautifully complex and clues are handsomely shared with the reader (though concealed in local colour); the conclusion is brilliant.

The other Benny Cooperman books include The Suicide Murders, Murder on Location, A Victim Must Be Found, Dead and Buried, There Was an Old Woman *and* Getting Away With Murder. *Engel has also written a delicious historical mystery novel set in 1920s Paris,* Murder in Montparnasse.

READ ON ▷

▶ ▷ **Robert B. Parker,** *The Godwulf Manuscript*; ▷ **Loren D. Estleman,** *The Midnight Man.*

ESTLEMAN, Loren D. (born 1952)
US novelist

Estleman's city is Detroit – 'the place where the American Dream stalled and sat rusting in the rain', as he once described it. It's the city where his private eye, Amos Walker, works. Walker is an investigator of the old school – short of money, long on tolerance for life's losers. He is not quite as laconic as Spade or Marlowe but he's working on it. ('What happened to your face?' 'I walked into a floor.') Detroit has its quota of mean streets and Walker gets to go down most of them. Estleman's style is an up-to-date version of the greats, and he is as good as his models at writing about eccentric or larger-than-life characters without making them seem mere freaks.

The Amos Walker novels are Motor City Blue, Angel Eyes, The Midnight Man, The Glass Highway, Sugartown, Every Brilliant Eye, Lady Yesterday, Silent Thunder, Sweet Women Lie, Never Street, The Witchfinder, The Hours of the Virgin *and* A Smile on the Face of the Tiger. *Estleman has also written non-Walker books set at different periods in Detroit's history* (Whiskey River, Edsel, Jitterbug *and others) and three books about Peter Macklin, a professional hit-man (*Kill Zone, Roses are Dead *and* Any Man's Death*).*

READ ON ▷

▶ ▷ **Lawrence Block,** *Eight Million Ways to Die*; **Richard Whittingham,** *Their Kind of Town.*

EVANOVICH, Janet (born 1943)
US novelist

In the decade or so since her first appearance in print, Janet Evanovich's feisty motormouth of a heroine, Stephanie Plum, has established herself as one of the most vivid and appealing female characters in contemporary crime fiction. An unlikely bounty hunter – she works for her cousin's bail bond business – Stephanie is pitched into increasingly weird situations as she goes about the simple business of trying to earn a reasonably honest buck. Most seem to involve some member of her large and eccentric extended family or the sexy cop Joe Morelli, or both. Set in Trenton, New Jersey, the Stephanie Plum novels are unashamed entertainments. There's very little gritty realism but lots of wisecracking, comic set-pieces and escalating farce.

ONE FOR THE MONEY (1994)

Stephanie has just lost her job as a lingerie buyer in a Newark store and is forced to ask her cousin Vinnie, a bail bondsman, for a job. She's soon got her first assignment – to bring in Joe Morelli, a suspended cop who's accused of murder. She and Morelli know one another very well – he was her first lover – but that doesn't make it any easier to put the cuffs on him. Nor do the distractions of finding that she is being stalked by a psycho heavyweight boxer and of having her borrowed car bombed. Her first foray into bounty-hunting is soon spiralling into chaos and a sequence of very bad-hair days.

The other Stephanie Plum novels are Two For the Dough, Three to Get Deadly, Four to Score, High Five, Hot Six, Seven Up *and* Hard Eight.

| READ ON |

▶ ▷ Laura Lippman, *Baltimore Blues*; Kathy Hogan Trocheck, *Homemade Sin*; Katy Munger, *Legwork*.

F

FAIR, A. A., see Erle Stanley **GARDNER**

READ ON A THEME: **FEMALE DETECTIVES**

▷ Linda Barnes, *Cold Case* (Carlotta Carlyle)
  Janet Dawson, *Where the Bodies are Buried* (Jeri Howard)
▷ Sarah Dunant, *Birthmarks* (Hannah Wolfe)
▷ Antonia Fraser, *Quiet as a Nun* (Jemima Shore)
▷ Sue Grafton, *A is for Alibi* (Kinsey Millhone)
▷ P. D. James, *An Unsuitable Job for a Woman* (Cordelia Gray)
▷ Karen Kijewski, *Katwalk* (Kat Colorado)
▷ Val McDermid, *Common Murder* (Lindsay Gordon)
▷ Marcia Muller, *Listen to the Silence* (Sharon McCone)
▷ Sara Paretsky, *Toxic Shock* (V. I. Warshawski)
  Gillian Slovo, *Close Call* (Kate Baier)

FERRARS, Elizabeth (1907–1995)
Scottish novelist

Elizabeth Ferrars is the pseudonym of Morna Brown. She wrote more than seventy crime and psychological thrillers which take the lives of ordinary, pleasant-seeming people and curdle them. Her style is light and easy, in marked contrast to the bizarre or horrific events she describes. She writes well about women, and is fond of analysing close-knit communities, such as small towns (in *Alive and Dead*) or the academic world (in *Hanged Man's House*, in which doubt is thrown on the apparent suicide of the director of a plant research station when a mummified body is found in his house). Often Ferrars sets her stories among a group of people who share some special interest: gourmet cookery, for example (in *Ninth Life*) or travel (in *The Small World of Murder*, set on a world cruise).

Elizabeth Ferrars's other books include Give a Corpse a Bad Name, Alibi for a Witch, The Wandering Widows, No Peace for the Wicked, A Stranger and Afraid, Blood Flies Upward, Witness Before the Fact, Experiment With Death, Death of a Minor Character, Thy Brother Death *and* Answer There Came None.

READ ON ▷

▶ Marian Babson, *Death in Fashion*; Joan Aiken, *Last Movement*; ▷ Margaret Yorke, *The Point of Murder*.

FERRIGNO, Robert (born 1947)
US novelist

Since his debut with *Horse Latitudes*, Ferrigno has produced five superb novels, all set in the half paradise/half purgatory of southern California. Two of these, *The Cheshire Moon* and *Dead Man's Dance*, feature a journalist named Quinn, a typical Ferrigno protagonist in that he's a smart, endearing maverick ready to fight for what is, or should be, his. *Dead Silent* appeared in 1996 and cocked an ear to the inharmonious world of the LA music scene. One-hit wonder Nick Carbonne is enjoying life as a semi-successful producer and husband to lawyer Sharon when former band member Perry re-emerges from their murky past. Before Nick can say 'One-two-three-four!' Perry and Sharon are dead and unless he wants to end up permanently out of time, Nick has to start producing a few hits of his own. *Heartbreaker* (1999) opens in Ferrigno's home turf of Florida but swiftly moves to California, where undercover cop Val Duran has to tackle sociopath drug dealer Junior and the beautiful daughter of a wealthy and very dysfunctional family. *Flinch* features another journalist, the resourceful Jimmy Gage, who returns from Europe in time to track down a serial killer while engaging in a long-standing and obsessive sibling rivalry with his brother Jonathan, a successful plastic surgeon. Trouble is, Jonathan is now married to Jimmy's gorgeous ex-girlfriend Olivia and is also looking very likely as the murderer. Like all Ferrigno's books, this has a dynamite plot, an irresistible setting and dialogue to die for.

> READ ON

▶ ▷ Harlan Coben, *Fade Away*; ▷ Dennis Lehane, *Darkness, Take My Hand*; ▷ Elmore Leonard, *Get Shorty*.

READ ON A THEME: FLORIDA CRIMES

Tom Corcoran, *The Mango Opera*
▷ Tim Dorsey, *Florida Roadkill*
▷ James W. Hall, *Buzz Cut*
▷ Carl Hiaasen, *Tourist Season*
▷ John D. Macdonald, *A Deadly Shade of Gold*
▷ Laurence Shames, *Welcome to Paradise*
Randy Wayne White, *Sanibel Flats*
▷ Charles Willeford, *Miami Blues*

READ ON A THEME: FOOD AND DRINK

Claudia Bishop, *Murder Well-Done*
Michael Bond, *Monsieur Pamplemousse*
Anthony Bourdain, *Bone in the Throat*
Diane Mott Davidson, *Sticks and Scones*
Nan and Ivan Lyons, *Someone is Killing the Great Chefs of Europe*
Tamar Myers, *Too Many Cooks Spoil the Broth*
Katherine Hall Page, *The Body in the Cast*
Phyllis Richman, *Murder on the Gravy Train*
▷ Rex Stout, *Too Many Cooks*

FRANCIS, Dick (born 1920)
British novelist

Authenticity is a priceless commodity in crime fiction and thriller writing. Pick up any Dick Francis novel and it is immediately apparent that he knows the world of racing inside out and is familiar with the characters who people it. It is this authenticity (and his ability to fashion a tightly constructed plot) that has kept him a bestseller for nearly forty years. Francis was champion jockey in 1953/4 and was riding the Queen Mother's horse Devon Loch in the 1956 Grand National when it fell so mysteriously with victory in sight. In a later fall Francis was badly injured and forced to give up riding. He turned to journalism and in 1962 published his first novel, *Dead Cert*. Many others have followed, all of them providing that first-hand knowledge of the racing game which fans so much enjoy.

Dick Francis's almost forty other novels include For Kicks, Blood Sport, Bonecrack, High Stakes, Reflex, Bolt, The Edge, Comeback, Wild Horses, Come to Grief, To the Hilt, 10lb Penalty, Second Wind *and* Shattered.

> **READ ON**

- *Trial Run* (Francis moves outside the world of racing in a story of attempts to sabotage the Moscow Olympics).
- ▶ John Francome, *Dead Weight*; Michael Maguire, *Slaughter Horse*.

FRASER, Antonia (born 1932)
British novelist and historian

Best known for her historical biographies of figures like Cromwell and Mary, Queen of Scots, Antonia Fraser has also written a series of light and enjoyable crime novels featuring TV reporter and part-time sleuth Jemima Shore. Jemima Shore is impossibly chic and glamorous, dresses in the finest designer wear and spends her time in a variety of locations (a convent, a Scottish laird's castle, Oxford during the end-of-year balls). Wherever she goes, murder is committed and everyone hurries to tell her their innermost thoughts and motives. The stories move effortlessly along until the final chapters, when Fraser puts her brain into gear, sorts out the situation and writes a suspenseful, satisfying ending. Typical is *The Wild Island* (1978), which involves Shore in dark family passions and a baroque nationalist movement in a remote Highland glen, and culminates in a spectacular stalk – not for deer but for human prey.

The other Jemima Shore books are Quiet as a Nun, A Splash of Red, Cool Repentance, Oxford Blood, Your Royal Hostage, The Cavalier Case *and* Political Death.

> **READ ON**

- ▶ Hazel Holt, *Mrs Malory and the Fatal Legacy*.

FREELING, Nicolas (born 1927)
British novelist

Before Freeling began writing, he worked for fifteen years as a hotel chef all over Europe, and a strong feeling for place fills his novels. Most are police procedurals, starring the Dutch Inspector Van der Valk or the French Inspector Castang. Freeling's atmospheric style, full of asides and comments, lets us see his characters' reactions as they investigate, and he writes well about their home lives. He has also written a number of tense thrillers, for example *A City Solitary* (1985), in which an act of petty vandalism triggers an 'ordinary, decent man' to take furious, murderous revenge.

KING OF THE RAINY COUNTRY (1965)
Jean-Claude Marschal, head of a vast secretive financial empire, disappears, and Van der Valk is assigned to find him. The trail leads Van der Valk into two kinds of unfamiliar territory: Europe's jet-set ski resorts and the seductive snares of a passionately jealous woman.

Freeling's Van der Valk novels include Love in Amsterdam, Because of the Cats, Gun Before Butter, Double Barrel, Over the High Side, One Damn Thing After Another *and* Sand Castles. *His Castang books include* A Dressing of Diamond, What are the Bugles Blowing For?, Castang's City, Those in Peril, The Pretty How Town *and* The Seacoast of Bohemia.

> READ ON

- **The Pretty How Town** (Henri Castang finds himself up to his neck in intrigue amid the bureaucracy and politicking of the European Union headquarters).
- ▶ To the Van der Valk novels: ▷ Georges Simenon, *Maigret's Pipe*; ▷ Michael Dibdin, *Ratking*; Jan Willem de Wetering, *The Corpse on the Dike*.

FREMLIN, Celia (born 1914)
British novelist

Fremlin describes the everyday lives of ordinary people – schoolgirls, shop-keepers, mothers with young children – and burns them with the acid of psychological disturbance or the supernatural. Because the surroundings are so humdrum, the menace seems all the greater, and suspense is heightened because she builds it up so gradually, page by page and chapter by chapter, to a perfectly logical, terrifying end.

THE HOURS BEFORE DAWN (1959)
Why has a schoolteacher chosen to take lodgings in Louise's house, with its harassed mother, squalling children and self-satisfied, carping husband? What is her secret – and will Louise survive the domestic pressure long enough to find out?

Celia Fremlin's other novels include Uncle Paul, Seven Lean Years, Appointment with Yesterday, The Long Shadow, The Spider Orchid, The Parasite Person *and* Listening in the Dusk.

READ ON >

- *With No Crying* (about a schoolgirl who pretends pregnancy, until she must find a baby somewhere).
▶ ▷ Margaret Yorke, *The Smooth Face of Evil.*

FRENCH, Nicci
British novelist

Nicci French is the name used by the husband-and-wife writing team of Nicci Gerrard (born 1958) and Sean French (born 1959). Since 1997 they have produced a sequence of tautly written and intelligent psychological thrillers which explore the power of the past over the present and the dangerous intensities of erotic obsession. In *The Memory Game* (1997) the discovery of the remains of a murdered girl and the ambivalent memories uncovered by psychotherapy work together to unsettle the life of the central character and, in a twisting plot, secrets buried (in several senses) for a quarter of a century re-emerge. *Killing Me Softly* (1999) tells the disturbing story of a woman well in control of her life who loses nearly everything through her obsession with a charismatic, sexually attractive but (as she discovers) violent man. The most compelling of Nicci French's novels so far is *The Safe House* (1998). Samantha Laschen is a psychiatrist specializing in post-traumatic disorders and has just moved from London to open her own clinic. The police ask her to take in a teenage girl who has survived a brutal attack in which she saw both her parents killed. By agreeing, Samantha unleashes a sequence of events that turn her life upside down and put her and all those she loves into danger. *The Safe House* shows Nicci French's particular combination of psychological acuity and skilful plotting at its best.

Nicci French's other novels are Beneath the Skin *and* The Red Room.

READ ON >

▶ Barbara Vine (▷ Ruth Rendell), *A Fatal Inversion*; ▷ Minette Walters, *Acid Row*;
▷ Val McDermid, *A Place of Execution.*

FRIEDMAN, Kinky (born 1944)
US novelist

Kinky Friedman's first career was as front-man for a Jewish country and western band who performed such unlikely numbers as 'They Don't Make Jews Like Jesus Any More'. With a pedigree like that, it was a safe bet that, when he turned his hand to crime fiction, he would come up with something original. The protagonist of his novels bears a startling resemblance to the writer. He is called Kinky or the Kinkster, he's worked as a musician etc. He lives in New York where he has a fondness for tequila, cigars, wild women, cats and the solving of mysteries. Little is taken seriously in Friedman's novels and the wisecracks come hurtling towards the reader off every page (rather relentlessly so in the more recent, less effective books) but there are genuinely well-constructed plots in the best books and crimes there to be solved.

A CASE OF LONE STAR (1987)

One of the earliest and most enjoyable of the Kinkster's adventures centres on a Manhattan bar, the Lone Star Café, where country musicians play when in New York. The Barkin Brothers play the Lone Star but one of them is found in his dressing room battered to death with his own guitar. After some reluctance Kinky launches himself into the investigation and finds himself in pursuit of a killer with a fan's appreciation of the songs of Hank Williams.

Kinky Friedman's other novels include Elvis, Jesus and Coca Cola, Armadillos and Old Lace, God Bless John Wayne, Blast from the Past, The Mile High Club *and* Steppin' on a Rainbow. *Some of the books, which are relatively short, have been collected in compilation volumes which include* The Kinky Friedman Crime Club *and* More Kinky Friedman.

 READ ON

▶ Gregory McDonald, *Fletch*; ▷ Carl Hiaasen, *Tourist Season*; ▷ Sandra Scoppettone, *I'll Be Leaving You Always* (for the Greenwich Village setting).

FYFIELD, Frances (born 1948)
British novelist

In a series of stylish and intelligent novels, Frances Fyfield has established herself as a writer to rival ▷ Minette Walters and ▷ Ruth Rendell in the creation of psychological suspense and menace. She provides all the traditional delights of crime fiction but adds to them her own subtle insights into human motivation and character. Several of her books feature Crown Prosecutor Helen West and her partner Detective Chief Superintendent Geoffrey Bailey. Both the neat plotting and the changing, often difficult relationship between West and Bailey sustain our interest. In *Deep Fire*, for example, West and Bailey, used to London and separate homes, have moved together to the country. This provides its own tensions and then the two are drawn into a murder case where the one likely suspect is the partner of West's only friend in the area.

THE NATURE OF THE BEAST (2001)

A train crashes on a journey through Kent. People are killed and one of them is thought to be Amy Petty, the wife of a man engaged in a libel action against a national newspaper. In fact, Amy has taken the opportunity of the chaos following the accident to walk away from her life. Is it her life with her overbearing, brutal husband that she wants to escape or are there other secrets in her past from which she is running? Fyfield's narrative, which includes some memorably nasty characters, slowly and skilfully reveals familial and marital dysfunction behind respectable façades.

Frances Fyfield's other novels include Trial by Fire, Deep Sleep, Shadow Play, Perfectly Pure and Good, Blind Date *and* Undercurrents.

She has also written three novels as Frances Hegarty: The Playroom, Half Light *and* Let's Dance.

READ ON >

- *Deep Sleep* (Helen West refuses to accept that the death of a pharmacist's wife is what it seems).
- ▷ Minette Walters, *The Ice House*; Barbara Vine (▷ Ruth Rendell), *A Dark-Adapted Eye*; ▷ Joan Smith, *What Men Say*.

G

GARDNER, Erle Stanley (1889–1970)
US novelist

Gardner began publishing stories in pulp magazines of the 1920s and 1930s such as the legendary *Black Mask*. By the end of his career he had written some 1000 short stories (westerns, crime, science fiction), dozens of television scripts and over 150 novels. As A. A. Fair he wrote twenty-nine comic private-eye novels about the little-and-large team of Donald Lam and Bertha Cool. (Titles include *The Bigger They Come*, *Double or Quits*, *Fools Die on Friday* and *Beware the Curves*.) Under his own name he wrote eighty-two novels and many short stories starring Perry Mason, a superman Los Angeles lawyer who knows how every type of character will behave in any circumstance, and exactly which question in court will instantly bring the reply he needs to win the case. Each book climaxes in a courtroom scene where Mason's brilliance completely outshines the bumbling district attorney Hamilton Burger. The books, all of which aré entitled *The Case of . . .*, are formulaic (and old-fashioned) hokum but they remain immensely readable. Good examples of the series are *The Case of the Howling Dog*, *The Case of the Curious Bride*, *The Case of the Hesitant Hostess*, *The Case of the Footloose Doll*, *The Case of the Terrified Typist*, *The Case of the Glamorous Ghost* and *The Case of the Daring Decoy*.

READ ON $\triangleright$

▶ To the Perry Mason books: Thomas Chastain, *The Case of the Burning Bequest* (Perry Mason rides again in a novel using Gardner's characters); Hillary Waugh, *Parrish for the Defence*; ▷ Rex Stout, *Triple Jeopardy*.

GASH, Jonathan (born 1933)
British novelist

Lovejoy is probably best known from the TV series starring Ian McShane but the character of the shady and lecherous antiques dealer was first to be found in a series of novels written by Jonathan Grant under the pen name of Jonathan Gash. Lovejoy is chronically short of funds and prepared to do most things to try to remedy this situation. His private life is a mess and, to make it even messier, he's always after another woman. But, whatever his difficulties, he always has his love and knowledge of antiques to fall back on. The books usually follow an agreeably familiar pattern. Lovejoy is in search of a rare and valuable antique. So too are others, even more unscrupulous than he is. Lovejoy is only distracted from the pursuit of the antique by his pursuit of women. Murder and mayhem follow

Lovejoy around but the tone of the books is essentially light-hearted and the central character himself is that comparatively rare bird in crime fiction, a lovable rogue who is genuinely appealing. Jonathan Gash has more recently begun a darker and more serious series of books set in Manchester and featuring Dr Clare Burtonall and her lover, a male escort called Bonn.

THE RICH AND THE PROFANE (1998)
Through a beautiful young woman with an interest in learning how to steal antique jewellery, Lovejoy is introduced to members of her family, including the prior of Albansham Priory. The priory is said to be a treasure trove of rare antiques. Lovejoy and an associate break into the priory to investigate. All goes badly and, unsurprisingly, wrong. The prior disappears. So too does Lovejoy's accomplice and it looks as if he's been murdered. Lovejoy is off on another wild-goose chase which will lead him to the Channel Islands and another series of attempted scams, mishaps and dangerous encounters.

The other Lovejoy novels include The Grail Tree, The Vatican Rip, The Sleepers of Erin, The Gondola Scam, The Very Last Gambado, The Lies of Fair Ladies, The Grace in Older Women *and* A Rag, A Bone and a Hank of Hair. *The Burtonall and Bonn series consists of* Different Women Dancing, Prey Dancing, Die Dancing *and* Bone Dancing.

> READ ON ▷

▶ ▷ Kyril Bonfiglioli, *The Mortdecai Trilogy;* ▷ Peter Guttridge, *The Once and Future Con;* ▷ Donald E. Westlake, *The Hot Rock.*

READ ON A THEME: **GAY AND LESBIAN DETECTIVES**

   George Baxt, *A Queer Kind of Death* (Pharaoh Love)
   Sarah Dreher, *Shaman's Moon* (Stoner McTavish)
▷ Stella Duffy, *Calendar Girl* (Saz Martin)
   Katherine V. Forrest, *Sleeping Bones* (Kate Delafield)
▷ Joseph Hansen, *Fadeout* (Dave Brandstetter)
▷ Dan Kavanagh, *Duffy*
▷ Laurie King, *A Grave Talent* (Kate Martinelli)
▷ Val McDermid, *Report for Murder* (Lindsay Gordon)
   Michael Nava, *The Burning Plain* (Henry Rios)
▷ Sandra Scoppettone, *Everything You Have is Mine* (Lauren Laurano)
   Richard Stevenson, *Strachey's Folly* (Don Strachey)

GEORGE, Elizabeth (born 1949)
US novelist

Like ▷ Deborah Crombie and ▷ Martha Grimes, Elizabeth George is an American writer who sets her fiction in England. Her long and rewarding novels, meticulously researched and plotted, combine elements of traditional English crime fiction of the past with those of the most up-to-date and contemporary police procedural. One of her leading characters, Inspector Thomas Lynley, who is also the 8th Earl of Asherton, harks back to the upper crust detectives of ▷ Sayers and ▷ Allingham. The other, Detective Sergeant Barbara Havers, is from a much less exalted background and, at first, resents Lynley and all he represents. Particularly in the first novel, *A Great Deliverance*, there is much tension between the two which adds its own undercurrents to the narrative. Other characters recur in the books and one of the pleasures of reading Elizabeth George's books lies not only in watching the changing relationship between Lynley and Havers but in coming to appreciate the personal histories of a wide cast of characters. All the novels are long and satisfying reads in a traditional sense and, once you decide to ignore the inherent improbability of a police officer who is also a member of the House of Lords, the police procedural elements work as well.

PAYMENT IN BLOOD (1989)

In the second of the Lynley/Havers books, the ill-matched couple are investigating the murder of a woman playwright in a remote Scottish manor house. Lynley is at his most discreet in his enquiries. Not only were prominent people present in the house at the time of the murder, but one of them is Lady Helen Clyde with whom he has shared a complicated friendship. (Later in the series the two are to marry.) The blunt Havers is disgusted by what she sees as special treatment of the socially successful and risks much by undertaking a less subtle search for the truth. Eventually Elizabeth George's craftily constructed narrative leads us to the secrets behind the killing.

The other Lynley novels are Well-Schooled in Murder, A Suitable Vengeance, For the Sake of Elena, Missing Joseph, Playing for the Ashes, In the Presence of the Enemy, Deception on his Mind, In Pursuit of the Proper Sinner *and* A Traitor to Memory. I, Richard *is a collection of five stories.*

READ ON ▷

▶ ▷ Deborah Crombie, *A Finer End*; ▷ P. D. James, *Death in Holy Orders*; ▷ Ann Granger, *Cold in the Earth*; ▷ Martha Grimes, *The Man With a Load of Mischief*.

GIFFORD, Barry (born 1947)
US novelist

Probably best known for his novels *Wild at Heart* and *The Wild Life of Sailor and Lula* and his scripts for film director David Lynch, Gifford is a uniquely gifted writer, one who could best be described as haunting the fringes of crime fiction. He resembles a figure, in fact, like many of his characters – a man on the outside, looking in. Reminiscent of the work of such great hard-boiled novelists as ▷ Jim Thompson, ▷ David Goodis, ▷ James M. Cain, and ▷ Charles Willeford, Gifford's writing also has a Beat-like quality to it. In many ways, he combines the styles of the Depression-era writers like Cain and Horace McCoy, and 1950s hipsters such as Jack Kerouac and his freewheeling followers. Though Gifford's characters may be on the road, they would be on the road to nowhere, probably in a stolen car, with somebody else's girl and a gun.

Alongside his screenplays and such novels as *The Sinola Story* and *Wyoming*, Gifford has written a number of interesting non-fiction books. Of these, *Out of the Past* is a brilliant examination of the *film noir* genre, from classic A-list pictures to obscure B-movies. *The Phantom Father* is a poignant memoir of his own father, a fascinating if shadowy type who ran an all-night liquor store in Chicago, was connected to the rackets and died when his son was eleven. He has also contributed fiction to photographer David Perry's evocative images in *Bordertown* and *Hot Rod*. *Night People* and the memorably titled *My Last Martini* are collections of short, and very sharp, stories.

READ ON ▷

▶ ▷ Jim Thompson, *The Grifters*; ▷ Charles Willeford, *Pick-Up*; Chuck Pahlaniuk, *Invisible Monsters*.

GILBERT, Michael (born 1912)
British novelist

Michael Gilbert has written all kinds of crime novels from police procedurals to thrillers. He is perhaps best known for his books featuring Inspector Hazelrigg of Scotland Yard. Titles include *Close Quarters*, *Smallbone Deceased* and *Fear to Travel*. However, he has also written slightly old-fashioned but enjoyable adventure stories such as *The Long Journey Home* (1985), about an English engineer whose attempts to expose corruption in a multi-national company lead him into trouble with the Mafia, and *Trouble* (1987), in which the unmasking of an IRA bombing campaign in London triggers all kinds of tension, racial and professional, among those who have to deal with it.

READ ON ▷

▶ ▷ Cyril Hare, *Tenant for Death*; Colin Watson, *Coffin, Scarcely Used*; Christianna Brand, *Green for Danger*; Roy Lewis, *A Form of Death*.

READ ON A THEME: **GOLDEN AGE DETECTIVES**

▷ Margery Allingham, *Death of a Ghost* (Albert Campion)
▷ John Dickson Carr, *Hag's Nook* (Gideon Fell)
▷ G. K. Chesterton, *The Innocence of Father Brown*
▷ Agatha Christie, *Murder on the Orient Express* (Hercule Poirot);
　　The Murder at the Vicarage (Miss Marple)
▷ Arthur Conan Doyle, *The Memoirs of Sherlock Holmes*
▷ Ngaio Marsh, *Artists in Crime* (Roderick Alleyn)
▷ Dorothy L. Sayers, *Murder Must Advertise* (Lord Peter Wimsey)
▷ Rex Stout, *Fer-de-Lance* (Nero Wolfe)
▷ S. S. Van Dine, *The Bishop Murder Case* (Philo Vance)
▷ Josephine Tey, *The Man in the Queue* (Inspector Grant)

GOODIS, David (1917–1967)
US novelist and screenwriter

Goodis found success with his early hard-boiled novels – *Dark Passage* was made into a Bogart and Bacall movie and the novelist was tempted to Tinseltown

– but his own demons drove him further and further into obscurity. He left Hollywood to return to his native Pennsylvania and became a virtual recluse, dying while still in his forties.

Only since his death has he been recognized as, in the words of one critic, 'a poet of the gutter'. Goodis's central characters are nearly all losers or, a reflection of his own stalled career, once-successful men brought down by love or obsession. In *Down There* (filmed by Truffaut as *Shoot the Piano Player*), for example, the anti-hero is a former concert pianist whose wife committed suicide. He has dropped out of his old life and works in the seedier dives of Philadelphia as a piano player. A waitress he meets seems to offer some hope of redemption but Goodis doesn't 'do' redemption and the relationship with the waitress is as fated as his marriage. As this précis suggests, Goodis is nothing if not darkly and broodingly sentimental but his writing, *noir* to its very core, is undeniably powerful.

THE MOON IN THE GUTTER (1953)
Obsessed by the suicide of his sister, William Kerrigan also dreams of escape from his working-class life and from the drink and violence of his family circumstances. When he meets a cool blonde from the other side of the tracks, he sees his chance. 'From now on everything's gonna be different, gonna be better.' But, in Goodis's *noir* world there is no escape from one's destiny and Kerrigan's destiny is to 'ride through life on a fourth-class ticket'.

David Goodis's other novels include Dark Passage, Black Friday, The Blonde on the Street Corner, Street of No Return, Down There (*also published as* Shoot the Piano Player) *and* Fire in the Flesh.

READ ON ▷

▶ ▷ Jim Thompson, *The Nothing Man*; ▷ Cornell Woolrich, *The Bride Wore Black*; Horace McCoy, *No Pockets in a Shroud*.

GOSLING, Paula (born 1939)
US novelist

Paula Gosling's early novels were atmospheric crime thrillers, fast-paced and suspenseful. In *A Running Duck* (1978) an assassin stalks the one woman in the country who has seen and can recognize him. In *Monkey Puzzle* (1985) the blackmailing professor of a university English department is murdered, and in that dark, closed community things rapidly go from bad to very much worse. Her most recent novels have mostly been set in a small community, Blackwater Bay, in the Great Lakes region, and feature Sheriff Matt Gabriel. Lighter and quirkier than the earlier books, the Blackwater Bay books were described by one reviewer 'as if Garrison Keillor was meeting Miss Marple for the first time'. They certainly have the same kind of small-town charm as Keillor's tales but there is grit in the oyster. They retain some of the bite of Gosling's earlier books and work well as involving mysteries.

THE BODY IN BLACKWATER BAY (1992)
According to Daria Grey, her ex-husband is stalking her and threatening to harm her. According to her neighbours on the small island in Blackwater Bay, her ex-

husband hasn't been seen in the area. Until he turns up dead on Daria's front lawn. Kate Trevorne, old friend of Daria, and Jack Stryker investigate.

Paula Gosling's other novels include The Wychford Murder, Backlash, A Few Dying Words, The Dead of Winter, Death and Shadows, Underneath Every Stone *and* Ricochet.

READ ON ▷

▶ **to the early novels: ▷ Ruth Rendell, *The Lake of Darkness*.**
▶ **to the Blackwater Bay books: Virginia Lanier, *Death in Bloodhound Red*; Deborah Adams, *All the Dirty Cowards*.**

GRAFTON, Sue (born 1940)
US novelist

Sue Grafton's 'alphabet' books have made up one of the most consistently entertaining crime fiction series of the last twenty years and Kinsey Millhone, her California private investigator, is just about the best of today's crop of feisty, self-confident and independent-minded female detectives. Beginning with *A is for Alibi* in 1982, Grafton has already made her way through two thirds of the twenty-six letters. The books can be read as stand-alone novels but, since one of the pleasures of the series is to watch Kinsey's character grow and develop over the books, it is perhaps best to start at the beginning of the alphabet and go from there. All the books are very readable but some of the cleverest in the series are *E is for Evidence* (Kinsey becomes her own client to investigate why she's being framed for an insurance fraud), *I is for Innocent* (Kinsey is employed to look for new evidence in the case of a man tried and acquitted for the murder of his wife) and *O is for Outlaw* (in which skeletons from her past life and her long-ago marriage to a hard-living vice cop return to rattle their bones).

The full Alphabet series so far consists of A is for Alibi, B is for Burglar, C is for Corpse, D is for Deadbeat, E is for Evidence, F is for Fraud, G is for Gumshoe, H is for Homicide, I is for Innocent, J is for Judgment, K is for Killer, L is for Lawless, M is for Malice, N is for Noose, O is for Outlaw, P is for Peril *and* Q is for Quarry.

READ ON ▷

▶ ▷ **Janet Evanovich, *One for the Money*; ▷ Laura Lippman, *Butchers Hill*; Katy Munger, *Legwork*.**
See also Read on a Theme: Female Detectives.

GRAHAM, Caroline (born 1931)
British writer

Most of Graham's novels are set in small communities where everyone knows everyone else's business – or thinks they do. The communities appear to be closely knit and peaceful, but the investigation of a crime by Graham's central character, the avuncular and sympathetic Inspector Barnaby, reveals hidden secrets and petty jealousies. The tensions and rivalries are gradually revealed as Barnaby and his less genteel colleague, Sergeant Troy, patiently probe beneath the apparently tranquil surface. Murder and crime are shown to spring from ordinary human failings rather than grand passions as Graham moves her plots skilfully towards far from predictable conclusions. She is working in the great tradition of classic English crime established in the 1920s and 1930s and she shows that it is still alive and well.

THE KILLINGS AT BADGER'S DRIFT (1987)

Badger's Drift is the sort of idyllic English village that now only exists in Caroline Graham's brand of crime fiction. Emily Simpson is an elderly spinster who is shocked to witness a naked couple making love in the woods. Soon afterwards she is dead, apparently from natural causes. Inspector Barnaby is, at first, reluctant to investigate but when he does so, he soon realizes that all is not as it seems. A second killing demonstrates how right he is to have suspicions about life (and death) in the apparently sleepy village.

The other Inspector Barnaby novels are Death of a Hollow Man, Death in Disguise, Written in Blood, Faithful Unto Death *and* A Place of Safety.

| READ ON ▷

● *Murder at Madingley Grange* (a non-Barnaby novel set during a 'murder weekend' at a country house).
▶ Christine Green, *Death in the Country*; Jill McGown, *Murder at the Old Vicarage*; Susannah Stacey, *Dead Serious*.

GRANGER, Ann (born 1939)
British writer

Ann Granger writes crime fiction that is up to date and recognizably set in the modern world, yet possesses all the virtues of the English detective story in its 'Golden Age' of the 1930s and 40s. She works in two main series. The Mitchell and Markby books feature civil servant Meredith Mitchell, who works in London, and Superintendent Alan Markby, who is in charge of law and order in an area of the Cotswolds where Meredith has a weekend cottage. As one might expect, Markby's beat sees more than its fair share of crime and murder – much more than is really consistent with credibility – but these modern takes on the English village detective story are wittily told and deftly plotted. And the on–off, occasionally acerbic relationship between the two main characters is always entertaining. More recently Granger has started a series of books featuring Fran Varady, an unconventional young would-be actress who finds herself drawn into murder investigations, often among the homeless and unemployed.

The Mitchell and Markby novels include Cold in the Earth, Where Old Bones Lie, Flowers for His Funeral, A Touch of Mortality, A Word After Dying, Call the Dead Again, Beneath These Stones *and* A Restless Evil. *The Fran Varady novels are* Asking for Trouble, Keeping Bad Company, Running Scared *and* Risking It All.

| READ ON ▷

▶ ▷ Deborah Crombie, *Dreaming of the Bones*; ▷ Peter Robinson, *A Dedicated Man*; Jill McGown, *Scene of Crime*.

READ ON A THEME: GREECE ANCIENT AND MODERN

> Anna Apostolou (▷ Paul Doherty), *A Murder in Macedon*
> T. J. Binyon, *Greek Gifts*
> Sarah Caudwell, *The Shortest Way to Hades*
> Daniel Chavarria, *The Eye of Cybele*
> Desmond Cory, *The Mask of Zeus*
> Margaret Doody, *Aristotle Detective*
> Reg Gadney, *Stealing Greece*
> ▷ Emma Lathen, *When in Greece*
> ▷ Margaret Yorke, *Grave Matters*

GRIMES, Martha (born 1931)
US novelist

Martha Grimes was inspired to write her first mystery when she was browsing in a book of British pub names and came across a pub called The Man with a Load of Mischief. The unusual name immediately suggested the beginnings of a story and the novel of that name, a tale of multiple murder in an English village, was published in 1981. All her novels since take their titles from genuine British pub names and all the stories involve a pub as the setting for at least some of the action. All the books also feature the handsome and urbane Inspector Jury of Scotland Yard and his languid, aristocratic friend Melrose Plant. Grimes owes a lot to classic-era writers like ▷ Allingham, ▷ Marsh and (especially) ▷ Dorothy L. Sayers, whose Lord Peter Wimsey is, in different ways, the original for both Jury and Plant. However, she has her own, very individual gift for eccentric characterization and a prose style that is witty and engaging. Her books may be firmly in the tradition of the English classic mystery but as a modern American writer she has brought her own perspective to it.

JERUSALEM INN (1984)
It is Christmas and it seems Jury is obliged to spend the festive season with disagreeable relatives. However, when a woman he meets and to whom he is attracted, is found murdered the following day, he joins the investigation into her death. Soon another body is found at a country house where Melrose Plant and his Aunt Agatha have joined a group of upper-class idlers and dilettantes to celebrate Christmas. Grimes's variant on the house-party setting so familiar from so many 1930s English mysteries is cleverly done and leaves room for plenty of surprises as Jury learns how the remote country pub, Jerusalem Inn, provides the links between the two murders.

Other Richard Jury novels include The Anodyne Necklace, Help the Poor Struggler, I Am the Only Running Footman, The Old Contemptibles, The Horse You Came In On, The Blue Last *and* The Grave Maurice.

READ ON ▷

▶ ▷ Elizabeth George, *A Great Deliverance*; ▷ Deborah Crombie, *Mourn Not Your Dead*; ▷ Caroline Graham, *The Killings at Badger's Drift*.

GRISHAM, John (born 1955)
US novelist

Before turning to fiction, Grisham practised law and he has become the most successful writer of the legal thriller genre in which lawyers play central roles and the intricacies of the law often provide the fuel for the plot. His first novel, *A Time to Kill* (1989), with its story of a lawyer defending a black father who has killed his daughter's rapists, had many of what would be later recognized as the classic ingredients of a Grisham plot. But it was with his second book, *The Firm* (1990), that Grisham really hit his stride and propelled himself into the bestseller ranks. The central character is a brilliant and ambitious young lawyer who joins a prominent law firm and gradually discovers that it is a front for the Mafia, working solely for the benefit of organized crime. The novel follows his attempts to break free of the dangerous web in which the firm has entangled him. Grisham cranks up the tension with great skill and the legal details are neatly dovetailed into a plot that twists and turns with satisfying suspense.

For many of his fans *The Firm* remains Grisham's best book but he has followed it with a number of other thrillers that are almost equally engrossing. In *The Client* (1992) a senator has been the victim of a Mafia hitman and a small boy is the only person who knows the identity of the killer. He becomes the innocent centre of a legal battle. In *The Brethren* (1999) three judges, imprisoned for assorted crimes, concoct a blackmail plot which goes disastrously astray when they pick the wrong man to blackmail.

A Painted House (2001) shows a desire to get away from the courtroom and is a nostalgic story of a boy growing up in the rural mid-West in the 1950s. His change of pace and style will have surprised many of his readers, although it is safe to assume that this does not mean we have seen the last of Grisham's expertly crafted legal thrillers.

Grisham's other novels are The Partner, The Pelican Brief, The Runaway Jury, The Testament, The Rainmaker, The Street Lawyer, The Chamber *and* The Summons.

| READ ON ▷ |

- **The Runaway Jury (gripping story of the manipulation of a jury in a high-profile case is not one of Grisham's best-known novels but is one of his best-constructed).**
- ▶ ▷ **Scott Turow, *Presumed Innocent*; ▷ James Patterson, *Along Came a Spider*; Michael Crichton, *Rising Sun*; Steve Martini, *The Attorney*.**

GUTTRIDGE, Peter (born 1951)
British novelist

Peter Guttridge has written a series of unashamedly farcical crime novels featuring Nick Madrid, a journalist and yoga devotee, who stumbles into unlikely nightmares of murder and mystery wherever he goes. In the first of the series, *No Laughing Matter* (1997), Nick is locked in a particularly difficult yoga position when a naked woman plummets past his fourteenth-floor hotel room window. His attempts to find out why she died lead him through the world of international stand-up comedy, where few of the comics are as funny or agreeable offstage as they are on. *The Once and Future Con* (1999) finds Nick and his regular companion Bridget Frost, the 'Bitch of the Broadsheets', in that haven of New Age nonsense, Glastonbury, where King Arthur's grave site may have been discovered. The heritage industry is in full cry at the prospect but Nick is more concerned by the possibility that a serial killer is loose amid the West Country millennial madness. The books are all more Tom Sharpe than ▷ Ruth Rendell but, as well as the enjoyable flow of jokes and comic set-pieces, Guttridge makes sure that he also supplies an engaging mystery.

The other Nick Madrid novels are A Ghost of a Chance, Two to Tango *and* Foiled Again.

READ ON ▷

▶ ▷ **Jonathan Gash,** *Every Last Cent*; ▷ **Mike Ripley,** *Bootlegged Angel*; **Nancy Livingston,** *Death in a Distant Land.*

H

HALL, James W. (born 1947)
US novelist and poet

Florida seems to have inspired more than its fair share of crime novelists – ▷ John D. Macdonald, ▷ Carl Hiaasen and ▷ Laurence Shames spring to mind. One practitioner of this semi-genre, less celebrated though just as good, is James Hall, author of eleven excellent thrillers all set in the *noir*-soaked sunshine state. The first, *Under Cover of Daylight*, appeared in 1987 and introduces readers to Thorn, an amiable, if moody, anti-hero who falls just short of being a sociopath and who is certainly too individual to have a first name. This reluctant sleuth has been pretty busy, however, and has so far appeared in most of Hall's novels, including *Tropical Freeze*, *Mean High Tide*, *Gone Wild*, *Buzz Cut* and *Red Sky at Night*, where he is injured and temporarily paralysed. In the appropriately named *Bones of Coral*, Hall covers the affliction of multiple sclerosis and its link with the US military, who were secretly testing chemical warfare in Key West during the 1950s. He also introduces a truly memorable villain in Dougie Barnes, a fascinatingly demonic and moderately retarded character whom the author has described as having 'a weakness for silly rhymes and little girls'. *Body Language* is a caper story that gives Thorn a breathing space and features instead a beautiful crime-scene photographer, Alexandra Rafferty.

> READ ON

▶ ▷ Carl Hiaasen, *Tourist Season*; ▷ Laurence Shames, *Welcome to Paradise*; ▷ Tim Dorsey, *Florida Roadkill*.

HAMMETT, Dashiell (1894–1961)
US novelist and short story writer

A former Pinkerton detective, Hammett wrote stories and serials for pulp magazines, and later became a Hollywood scriptwriter. He perfected the private eye story, in which kidnappings, thefts and murders are investigated by laconic, wisecracking individuals who are always just on the side of the angels and just one step ahead of the police. Hammett, like ▷ Chandler later, far transcended the limitations of the pulp tradition in which he worked. Chandler wrote of him that he 'gave murder back to the kind of people that commit it for reasons, not just to provide a corpse, and with the means at hand, not with hand-wrought dueling pistols, curare and tropical fish'. He is not a 'realistic' writer in a documentary sense but his spare prose, his own knowledge of crime from his days with the Pinkerton agency and his unsentimental view of human nature combine to make his novels appear to reflect reality in a way that no crime fiction before him had done. His best-known detectives are Sam Spade (made famous by Humphrey Bogart), the urbane Nick Charles (made famous in William Powell's Thin Man films) and 'The Continental Op'.

Hammett's novels are The Dain Curse, Red Harvest, The Glass Key, The Maltese Falcon *and* The Thin Man; *his story collections include* The Continental Op *and* The Big Knockover and Other Stories.

$\boxed{\text{READ ON}}$ ▷

▶ ▷ **Raymond Chandler,** *The Lady in the Lake*; ▷ **James M. Cain,** *Double Indemnity*; ▷ **Ross Macdonald,** *The Drowning Pool*; ▷ **Jim Thompson,** *The Killer Inside Me*; **Paul Cain,** *Fast One*; **Raoul Whitfield,** *Green Ice*.

HANSEN, Joseph (born 1923)
US novelist

Joseph Hansen is best known for his Dave Brandstetter novels. Brandstetter, an insurance claims investigator in LA, is in the classic private eye tradition established by writers like ▷ Chandler. Like most of the private eyes in that tradition he is tough, masculine and not averse to the odd fist-fight. Very much unlike most of them he is gay and quite contentedly so. In the years since the first Brandstetter novel was published, many more gay detectives have come out of the closet but Hansen's hero, who ages and changes in the course of the series, remains one of the best and the novels in which he appears remain some of the best-written and convincingly plotted crime books of the last thirty years.

FADEOUT (1970)
Folk singer Fox Olson's car has been found wrecked. There is no sign of Olson. His family believe he is dead. Brandstetter doesn't and notes with interest the close relationship between Olson's wife and his manager and the sudden re-appearance after twenty years of an old friend. Something is not quite right and Brandstetter is determined to find out what that is.

The other Brandstetter novels are Gravedigger, Skinflick, The Man Everybody Was Afraid Of, Death Claims, A Country of Old Men, The Boy Who Was Buried This Morning, Early Graves, The Little Dog Laughed, Nightwork. *His other fiction includes* Backtrack *and* Steps Going Down.

$\boxed{\text{READ ON}}$ ▷

▶ **George Baxt,** *A Queer Kind of Love*; **Richard Stevenson,** *Ice Blues*; **Michael Nava,** *The Little Death*.
See also Read on a Theme: Gay and Lesbian Detectives.

HARDING, Paul, see Paul DOHERTY

HARE, Cyril (1900–1958)
British novelist

Alfred Gordon Clark, a county court judge, wrote nine classic detective stories under the pseudonym of Cyril Hare. His books are the work of a cool, drily witty legal mind, and many star the barrister Francis Pettigrew, an unassuming man whose career has never fulfilled its youthful promise. Although Hare's plots are scrupulously fair, and his glimpses of the English legal system are fascinating, it is the details of character and location which give his books their zest. *Tragedy at Law* (1942), Hare's own favourite, is a wonderful character study of Pettigrew himself – charming, gentlemanly, rueful about his lost potential. The setting of *With a Bare Bodkin* (1946) is the offices of a London ministry during the Second World War. *An English Murder* is the story of a murder in a snowbound mansion which is investigated not by Pettigrew but by the eccentric Czech refugee Dr Bottwink.

Hare's other Pettigrew books are When the Wind Blows, That Yew Tree's Shade *and* He Should Have Died Hereafter. *Another detective, Inspector Mallett of Scotland Yard, appears alone in three books (*Tenant for Death, Death is No Sportsman *and* Suicide Excepted*), and also plays walk-on roles in several of the Pettigrew novels.*

READ ON

▶ ▷ Michael Gilbert, *Sky High*; ▷ Michael Innes, *Hamlet, Revenge!*; Christianna Brand, *Green for Danger*; Henry Cecil, *No Bail for the Judge*; Edward Grierson, *Reputation for a Song*.

HARVEY, Jack, see Ian RANKIN

HARVEY, John (born 1938)
British novelist

In his Charlie Resnick novels, John Harvey has produced some of the most convincing British police procedurals of the last two decades. Set in Nottingham, the books centre on the scruffy, overweight, jazz-loving Resnick but the supporting cast of characters (who, like Resnick himself, change and develop as the series progresses) is equally important. Harvey is a downbeat, unflashy writer but the books – there are ten in all – have built up into a surprisingly powerful portrait of British society, adrift in the 1980s and 90s, as filtered through the experiences of one provincial policeman and his colleagues.

STILL WATER (1997)
In a typically multi-stranded novel, Harvey has Resnick dealing with the murder of a young girl whose body has been found in a Nottingham canal, the theft of some paintings which takes him into dodgier corners of the London art world, the ongoing troubles of a policeman who was the victim of a male rape and the troubled marriage of some friends of his partner Hannah Campbell. Harvey manages to sustain our interest in all the elements of his plot as they both diverge and dovetail in the course of the book.

The other Resnick novels are Lonely Hearts, Rough Treatment, Cutting Edge, Off Minor, Wasted Years, Cold Light, Living Proof, Easy Meat *and* Last Rites. *His non-Resnick books include* Junkyard Angel, Neon Madman, Dancer Draws a Wild Card *and* In a True Light.

READ ON ▷

▶ ▷ Reginald Hill, *Bones and Silence*; ▷ Ian Rankin, *Knots and Crosses*; ▷ Peter Robinson, *Gallows View*; Stephen Booth, *Black Dog*.

HAYTER, Sparkle (born 1958)
Canadian novelist

Sparkle Hayter's Robin Hudson series will never win any prizes as tightly constructed murder mysteries but they are some of the wildest and funniest novels in contemporary crime fiction. Like her creator, Robin Hudson ('Jerry Lewis's nutty professor in the body of Rita Hayworth', as she describes herself) works in the media and finds herself dragged unwillingly into the most bizarre and dangerous of situations. In *Nice Girls Finish Last* the murder of her gynaecologist (the only man to have seen her naked in months) leads her into the weird world of sado-masochism and the Marquis de Sade Society, reluctantly accompanied by her Aunt Mo. A series of chance encounters in *The Last Manly Man* pitches her into an improbable plot involving murder, a mysterious chemical called Adam 1 and testosterone-fuelled primates, both human and chimpanzee. Satire, surrealism and sheer high sprits come together in Sparkle Hayter's fiction. As one wit has said, she is 'the funniest thing to come out of Canada since the moose'.

WHAT'S A GIRL GOTTA DO? (1994)
Robin Hudson's private life is a mess. Her husband has just left her for a younger woman. Her professional life as a TV news reporter has gone downhill since she committed the *faux pas* of belching into her microphone at a White House press conference. She's being blackmailed. What more can go wrong?

Sparkle Hayter's other Robin Hudson novels are Nice Girls Finish Last, Revenge of the Cootie Girls, The Last Manly Man *and* The Chelsea Girl Murders.

READ ON ▷

▶ ▷ Janet Evanovich, *One for the Money*; Katy Munger, *Out of Time*; Scarlett Thomas, *Seaside*.

HEGARTY, Frances, see Frances FYFIELD

HENDERSON, Lauren (born 1966)
British novelist

The last few years have seen the publication of a refreshingly contemporary series of English crime novels by Lauren Henderson, all featuring her female detective-cum-sculptress Sam Jones. The books are all prime examples of what one anthology (co-edited by Henderson) calls 'tart noir'. Sexy, savvy and frequently foul-mouthed, Sam is unashamedly fond of drink, drugs and men. She also has an accident-prone habit of falling into murder investigations. The Sam Jones books are all very readable – funny, convincing in their London milieux (the art world, theatre, the clubbing scene) and written with energy and panache.

THE BLACK RUBBER DRESS (1997)
Sam's latest sculpture is to have its preview in the atrium of a City bank. Donning a figure-hugging black rubber dress, she sets out to wow potential patrons. Things don't work out as expected. One of the guests is murdered and, as more bodies follow, Sam is drawn into an unfamiliar world of old and new money, Sloanes and merchant bankers, in her search for the truth.

The other Sam Jones novels are Dead White Female, Too Many Blondes, Freeze My Margarita, The Strawberry Tattoo, Chained! *and* Pretty Boy.

> READ ON

▶ ▷ Sparkle Hayter, *The Chelsea Girl Murders*; Scarlett Thomas, *Dead Clever*; Liz Evans, *Don't Mess with Mrs In-Between.*

HIAASEN, Carl (born 1953)
US novelist

Carl Hiaasen knows the world of which he writes with such black relish in his comedy thrillers. Born and raised in Florida, the setting for his books, he has worked as a journalist investigating the kinds of corruption and chicanery that provide the fuel on which his plots run. Hiaasen's novels have the suspense and mystery of the best crime fiction but it is safe to assume that what readers remember of them are the manic, comic energy, the grotesque villains (and, often, even more grotesque heroes) and the writer's ability to focus on one seemingly trivial incident, spinning out its consequences to logical but bizarre lengths. Only in a Hiaasen novel is a hit-man a seven-foot-tall Amish. Only in a Hiaasen novel does a deranged bad guy spend the second half of the book with a dead dog's rotting head firmly embedded by the teeth in his forearm. And only a Hiaasen plot can begin with the theft of blue-tongued mango voles from the Kingdom of Thrills in Key Largo and escalate into an insane confrontation between environmentalists and a mobster-developer which results in the total destruction of the Kingdom. As P. J. O'Rourke once pointed out (correctly), 'Reading Hiaasen will do more to damage the Florida tourist trade than anything except an actual visit to Florida.'

TOURIST SEASON (1986)
A band of anti-tourist terrorists is on the loose in Florida, led by a rogue newspaperman appalled by the destruction of the state's natural beauty and resources. The head of Miami's Chamber of Commerce has been found dead with a toy rubber alligator lodged in his throat. More murders follow. Another reporter turned private eye is given the job of tracking down the terrorists, a job which soon turns into one of Hiaasen's characteristic excursions along the wilder highways and byways of the Sunshine State. And beneath the mayhem, violence and dark farce, the author's serious environmental concerns are apparent.

Hiaasen's other novels are Double Whammy, Skin Tight, Native Tongue, Strip Tease, Stormy Weather, Lucky You *and* Sick Puppy. *He has also written three novels with William Montalbano* (Powder Burns, Trap Line *and* A Death in China), *less anarchic than his solo fiction.*

| READ ON ⟩ |

- *Sick Puppy* (environmentalists and land developers, both equally deranged, clash in a typically insane and off-the-wall Hiaasen plot).
- ▷ Laurence Shames, *Sunburn*; Dave Barry, *Big Trouble*; ▷ Charles Willeford, *The Shark-Infested Custard*; ▷ Doug J. Swanson, *Dreamboat*; ▷ Tim Dorsey, *Orange Crush*; Charles Higson, *King of the Ants* (for an English version of Hiaasen's mix of grotesquerie, violence and comedy).

HIGGINS, George V(incent) (1939–1999)
US novelist

Working as a lawyer (which included several years as assistant DA for Massachusetts) gave Higgins an insight not just into crime, but into the minds of criminals and those politicians and businessmen who do exactly as they please without ever actually turning crooked. His books use the crime-novel formula, and are exciting reading, with superbly convincing dialogue and deadpan wit. But they also dissect and discuss the state of the late twentieth-century USA, with its problems of drugs, poverty, racism and moral bankruptcy. These are crime stories not just to pass the time but to make you think.

Higgins's novels include the trilogy The Friends of Eddie Coyle, The Digger's Game *and* Defending Billy Ryan, *and the self-standing books* Cogan's Trade, Outlaws, Impostors, Trust, Wonderful Years, Wonderful Years, A Change of Gravity *and the last book completed before his death,* At End of Day. The Sins of the Fathers *is a collection of short stories.*

| READ ON ⟩ |

- ▷ Elmore Leonard, *City Primeval*; ▷ K. C. Constantine, *Cranks and Shadows*; Richard Price, *Clockers*.

READ ON A THEME: HIGHER EDUCATION
- ▷ Amanda Cross, *A Death in the Faculty*
  Judith Cutler, *Dying by Degrees*
  Ruth Dudley Edwards, *Matricide at St Martha's*
- ▷ Paula Gosling, *Monkey Puzzle*
- ▷ Reginald Hill, *An Advancement of Learning*
- ▷ P. D. James, *Shroud for a Nightingale*
- ▷ Janet Neel, *Death among the Dons*
- ▷ Josephine Tey, *Miss Pym Disposes*

See also: Oxbridge

HIGHSMITH, Patricia (1921–1995)
US novelist

Except for *The People Who Knock on the Door* (1982, about the disintegration of an 'ordinary' American family whose father becomes a born-again Christian), Highsmith's books are chiefly psychological thrillers. They show the planning and commission of horribly convincing, 'everyday' crimes, and the way murder erodes the murderer's moral identity. Few writers screw tension so tight in such functional, unemotional prose. Highsmith's most chilling insight is how close the criminally insane can be to people just like ourselves. Ripley has several times been the subject of films, played by Dennis Hopper, Alain Delon, Matt Damon and, in 2002, by John Malkovich.

RIPLEY'S GAME (1974)
Ripley, who appears in several Highsmith books, is a charming American psychopath who lives in France. In this book, out of boredom, he sets up circumstances to snare an entirely innocent man into committing murder. But the murder-victim is a Mafia boss, and soon assassins begin to hunt down both Ripley and his dupe. The plot is exciting, but Highsmith's main concern is the comparison between Ripley's icy amorality and the conscience-racked flailings of the man he corrupts.

The other Ripley books are The Talented Mr Ripley, Ripley Under Ground, The Boy Who Followed Ripley *and* Ripley Under Water. *Highsmith's other novels include* Strangers on a Train, The Two Faces of January, The Story Teller/A Suspension of Mercy, The Tremor of Forgery, Edith's Diary, Found in the Street, Small g: a Summer Idyll *and* The Price of Salt/Carol. The Snailwatcher/Eleven, The Animal-Lover's Book of Beastly Murder, The Black House, Mermaids on the Golf Course *and* Tales of Natural and Unnatural Catastrophes *contain short stories.*

> READ ON

- *The Glass Cell* (a typical non-Ripley book in which a man has had his character brutalized and his moral integrity destroyed by six years in prison. Tormented by the possibility of his wife's unfaithfulness, he sets out to discover the truth).
- ▶ Julian Symons, *The Man Who Killed Himself*; Barbara Vine (▷ Ruth Rendell), *A Fatal Inversion*; ▷ P. D. James, *The Skull Beneath the Skin*; ▷ Minette Walters, *The Echo*.

HILL, Reginald (born 1936)
British novelist

In his first novel, *A Clubbable Woman* (1970), Hill introduced the two characters who have been central to his books ever since – the aggressive, slobbish but shrewd Superintendent Dalziel and the eager, sensitive Inspector Pascoe. Each successive book has expanded our knowledge of the pair and shown Hill's increasingly confident use of humour, deft characterization and ingenious plotting to tell traditional crime stories in a contemporary setting. To many, Reginald Hill is now the best crime writer in Britain.

ON BEULAH HEIGHT (1998)

During a hot summer a village re-emerges from the reservoir which had covered it fifteen years earlier. At the time the villagers were evacuated three girls were missing and so too was the man suspected of abducting them. Now he seems to have returned, another girl is missing and Dalziel is obliged to face once again the most demanding and puzzling of cases from his past. Hill produces a crime story of satisfying complexity and depth which also manages, unpretentiously, to say something about the power of the past to haunt the present.

Hill's other Dalziel and Pascoe books are An Advancement of Learning, Ruling Passion, An April Shroud, A Pinch of Snuff, A Killing Kindness, Deadheads, Exit Lines, Child's Play, Under World, Bones and Silence, Recalled to Life, Pictures of Perfection, The Wood Beyond, Arms and the Women, Dialogues of the Dead *and* Death's Jest Book. *He has also written several novels about a Luton-based private investigator, Joe Sixsmith, and has also published fiction under the pseudonyms Dick Morland, Patrick Ruell and Charles Underhill.*

READ ON

▶ ▷ Val McDermid, *A Place of Execution*; ▷ Colin Dexter, *Death is Now My Neighbour*; ▷ Ian Rankin, *The Falls*; ▷ Peter Robinson, *In a Dry Season*.

HILLERMAN, Tony (born 1925)
US novelist

The novels of Tony Hillerman have been among the most original crime stories of the last thirty years, wholly convincing in their re-creation of a Navajo culture in which values are very different from those of the American society which surrounds it, and in which even words like 'crime' and 'punishment' have different meanings. Hillerman's early novels featured either Joe Leaphorn, a man caught between respect for the old ways and modern scepticism, or Jim Chee, younger than Leaphorn but more willing to return to the shamanism and ceremony of the Navajo past. In *Skinwalkers* Hillerman brought his two characters together in the same novel and they have continued to work as a team since.

THE FALLEN MAN (1997)

A skeleton is found high on a sacred mountain in an Indian reservation. Who is he and how did he die? Leaphorn does not believe that a Navajo would choose to climb on sacred ground let alone kill on it but, in a world where mining rights and land claims can mean big money, who can be certain? Not the least of Hillerman's many virtues as a writer is his sense of place. He is expert at conjuring up the buttes and mesas of the American South West and, in *The Fallen Man*, the bleak beauty of the desert and mountain landscapes is central to the plot.

Hillerman's other mystery novels are The Blessing Way, Dance Hall of the Dead, Listening Woman *(all Leaphorn alone)*, People of Darkness, The Dark Wind, The Ghostway *(all Chee alone)*, Skinwalkers, A Thief of Time, Talking God, Coyote Waits, Sacred Clowns, The First Eagle *and* The Wailing Wind *(Leaphorn and Chee together)*.

READ ON >

▶ Dana Stabenow, *A Cold Day for Murder* (set in Alaska with an Aleut central character); Nevada Barr, *Track of the Cat*; Margaret Coel, *The Dream Stalker*; James D. Doss, *The Shaman's Bones*.

HIMES, Chester (1909–1984)
US novelist

Himes knew what it was to be an outsider. He began writing while serving a jail sentence for armed robbery and, for much of his later life, he was an exile from his native land, living and working in Europe. His Harlem novels, featuring the police detectives Coffin Ed Johnson and Grave digger Jones, began when a French publisher suggested he contribute to a *roman policier* series. The nine novels in the sequence tell of knifings, rapes and drug-pushing in the slums and streets of Harlem. But letting Johnson and Jones solve the crimes is one of the last things on Himes's mind. He is describing an urban nightmare, a surrealist ghetto filled with grotesque, unlikely characters. His real subjects are black identity in a white world, and the way evil seethes like lava beneath the surface of city life, just needing the smallest vent-hole to erupt. Himes wrote in a sharp, one-liner-packed style all his own. On the surface his books read like pacy, funny, violent crime stories – underneath they cut like knives.

A RAGE IN HARLEM (1957)
The first of the Harlem Cycle immediately set the style for those that followed. Jackson is a naïve, law-abiding citizen who is suckered by his beautiful girlfriend Imabelle into losing his life savings to con artists. Drawn even further into the wild side of Harlem, he steals money from his boss and then blows that as well. From there a spiralling journey downwards is guaranteed. Coffin Ed Johnson and Grave Digger Jones, Himes's unforgettable duo of detectives, appear only as secondary characters in this edgy and witty story of one man's downfall but they already seemed marked for greater things to come.

Chester Himes's other novels include The Crazy Kill, The Real Cool Killers, All Shot Up, The Big Gold Dream *and* Cotton Comes to Harlem.

READ ON >

▶ Grace F. Edwards, *No Time to Die* (one of a series set in 1990s Harlem); ▷ Walter Mosley, *A Red Death*; ▷ James Sallis, *The Long-Legged Fly*.

HOAG, Tami (born 1959)
US novelist

Tami Hoag began her career with early bestsellers such as *Still Waters* (1992), a fat, page-turning story of a glamorous journalist arriving in a small Minnesota town and becoming the suspect in a vicious murder. These are as much romances as crime novels – the steamy attraction between the blue-eyed hunk of a sheriff and the reporter gets a lot of attention in *Still Waters*. Her more recent books have been more clearly the work of a crime writer. They are not subtle novels. They are big and brash, and plot and character are both painted in bright primary colours for those who like to know exactly what they are getting from a novel. But, give yourself over to them and they are satisfying and suspenseful reads.

ASHES TO ASHES (1999)

A serial killer, nicknamed the Cremator because he burns his victims alive, is on the loose in Minneapolis. A girl has witnessed the latest killing but she is saying nothing. A former FBI agent and a top psychological profiler work uneasily together to find out what the girl knows and to predict the next move of a killer who always seems to be one step ahead of them.

Tami Hoag's other novels include Cry Wolf, Dark Paradise, Night Sins, Guilty as Sin, A Thin Dark Line, Dust to Dust *and* Dark Horse.

> READ ON

▶ ▷ **James Patterson, *1st to Die*; Sandra Brown, *The Witness*; John Sandford, *Rules of Prey*.**

HOLDEN, Craig
US novelist

Holden's first novel, *The River Sorrow* (1995), drew on his experiences working as a lab technician at a medical centre. This powerful book tells the story of Adrian Lancaster, a doctor with a dark past that includes heroin addiction and obsessive love for a *femme fatale*. Both of these return to haunt him. Holden has a knack of using classic *noir* devices to kick-start his story and then takes off from there, his foot to the floor. In *The Last Sanctuary*, a Gulf War veteran is searching for his younger brother when he accepts a ride from a couple and gets involved with a Waco-like cult. Before long, he's wanted for robbery and murder, criss-crossing the country and pursued by the FBI, cult members and the Canadian Mounties. The past also comes back to haunt two cops in *Four Corners of Night*, when a radio call about a missing teenage girl triggers off still-simmering memories for one of them, whose own daughter vanished seven years ago, never to re-surface. Holden's fourth novel, *The Jazz Bird*, differs from its predecessors in that it is based on a real event: the 1920s murder trial of notorious bootlegger George Remus, who shot his wife.

> READ ON

▶ **to Holden's first three books:** ▷ **Lee Child, *Running Blind*; Steve Hamilton, *The Hunting Wind*.**
▶ **to *The Jazz Bird*:** ▷ **Loren D. Estleman, *Whiskey River*.**

READ ON A THEME: HOLMES BEYOND DOYLE

▷ **Michael Dibdin, *The Last Sherlock Holmes Story***
    Adrian Conan Doyle and ▷ **John Dickson Carr, *The Exploits of Sherlock Holmes***
▷ **Loren D. Estleman, *Dr Jekyll and Mr Holmes***
    Quinn Fawcett, *The Scottish Ploy* (one of a series of adventures of Mycroft Holmes, Sherlock's smarter elder brother)

Mark Frost, *The List of 7* (Arthur Conan Doyle as investigator)

Michael Hardwick, *Prisoner of the Devil* (Holmes involves himself in the Dreyfus case)

William Hjorstberg, *Nevermore*

▷ Laurie King, *The Beekeeper's Apprentice* (on the eve of the First World War a young girl meets a retired Sherlock Holmes and learns the art of detection)

Michael Kurland, *The Infernal Device* (Moriarty moves centre stage)

Nicholas Meyer, *The Seven-Per-Cent Solution*

Barrie Roberts, *Sherlock Holmes and the Railway Maniac*

M. J. Trow, *Lestrade and the Deadly Game* (one of a series in which the blundering Scotland Yard detective of the Doyle stories shows he's not such a blunderer after all)

See also: Rivals of Sherlock Holmes

I

ILES, Francis (1893–1971)
British novelist

Francis Iles was a pseudonym of Anthony Berkeley Cox, who also wrote as Anthony Berkeley. Under the name Iles, he published a handful of short stories and three highly regarded novels that pioneered the psychological crime story. They show the deterioration of minds under intolerable stress or delusion and the inexorable progress of crimes whose perpetrators and motives we know from the start of the book. Iles blends creepiness with sharp social criticism of the 1930s upwardly mobile: snobbery is the corrosive force which destroys his people's lives.

MALICE AFORETHOUGHT (1931)
Bickleigh, a small town doctor, has married 'above him' and his wife never lets him forget the fact. His unhappiness leads him first to flirting with pretty women, then to a love affair, then to murder. He thinks that he is committing the perfect crime, and he is wrong.

The other two Iles novels are Before the Fact *and* As For the Woman. *As Anthony Berkeley, Cox wrote books which simultaneously celebrate and spoof the standard English detective novel of the 1920s and 1930s. Many of them feature Roger Sheringham, an amateur, upper-class sleuth who is conceited, nosy, patronizing and highly likely to jump to completely wrong conclusions. The novels include* The Wychford Poisoning Case, The Poisoned Chocolates Case, The Silk Stockings Murders, Murder in the Basement *and* Panic Party.

> **READ ON**

- ▶ to *Malice Aforethought*: C. S. Forester, *Payment Deferred*; ▷ Ruth Rendell, *The Face of Trespass* (a book by the great modern exponent of the psychological crime story which Iles pioneered).
- ▶ to the Roger Sheringham books: ▷ E. C. Bentley, *Trent's Last Case*; Kingsley Amis, *The Riverside Villas Murder* (a more recent novel that both sends up the conventional old-fashioned detective story and celebrates its merits).

INNES, Michael (1906–1994)
British novelist and critic

Michael Innes was the pseudonym of the Oxford don J. I. M. Stewart. His fifty detective novels (starring Appleby or Honeybath) are set in the unhurried world of Oxford colleges and English country houses, aglow with fine port and old-master paintings. They are replete with endless, erudite quotations which everyone – from detective to potboy, from rural yokel to damsel in distress – seems immediately able to recognize. Privilege and farce go hand in hand, in an unhurried, dazzling charade. At its worst Innes's style can seem irritatingly affected and dated. At his best (in *The Daffodil Affair* or *Private View*) few classic detective writers so effortlessly combine mystification, urbanity and grotesquerie.

Innes's crime novels include Death at the President's Lodging, Lament for a Maker, Appleby on Ararat, The Weight of the Evidence, A Night of Errors *and* Stop Press. *Under his own name he wrote non-detective novels including a quintet of books about Oxford life, beginning with* The Gaudy *in 1974.*

READ ON ▷

▶ ▷ Edmund Crispin, *The Moving Toyshop*; Glyn Daniel, *The Cambridge Murders*. See also Read on a Theme: Oxbridge.

IRISH, William, see Cornell WOOLRICH

READ ON A THEME: ITALY

▷ Michael Dibdin, *Ratking*
  Gregory Dowling, *See Naples and Kill*
▷ Sarah Dunant, *Mapping the Edge*
▷ Michael Gilbert, *The Etruscan Net*
  Timothy Holme, *A Funeral of Gondolas*
▷ Donna Leon, *A Venetian Reckoning*
  Carlo Lucarelli, *Almost Blue*
▷ Magdalen Nabb, *The Marshal and the Murderer*
▷ Elizabeth Peters, *The Seventh Sinner*

IZZI, Eugene (1953–1997)
US novelist

Izzi was a fascinating figure who could well have been a character out of any of the numerous novels that he wrote before his untimely and mysterious death, aged forty-three. Raised in Hegewisch on the south-east side of Chicago, he was the son of a drunken father who was in and out of jail. After dropping out of high school and joining the army, he started writing, but following his discharge, he worked in the local steel mills. Married with a family, he too started drinking heavily, was frequently arrested and, during this traumatic period, apparently contemplated suicide. After writing six unpublished novels, Izzi finally got a break when *The Take* came out in 1987. With books such as *Booster*, *The Eighth Victim*, *King of the Hustlers*, *Prime Roll* and *Tony's Justice*, he hit his stride, accruing acclaim and increasing sales, his life seemingly turned around. There are no detectives in these extremely tough books, no heroes. Each features a character enmeshed in the rackets, someone always looking for that last big score before leaving and heading for the good life. Following a dispute over his publisher, Izzi didn't publish under his own name for three years. In December 1997 his body was found hanging outside the apartment where he did his writing and a verdict of suicide was recorded. His final novel, *The Criminalist*, perhaps his hardest and most compelling, was published posthumously and, ironically, garnered some of the best reviews Izzi had ever received.

READ ON >

▶ ▷ Michael Connelly, *The Black Ice*; ▷ George Pelecanos, *The Sweet Forever*; Thomas Perry, *Sleeping Dogs*.

J

JAMES, Bill (born 1929)
British novelist

Bill James has written some of the finest British police procedurals of the last twenty years. Focusing on the morally ambivalent world where cops and crooks meet and mingle, all intent on their own interests, his novels brilliantly combine tense plotting, blackly comic dialogue and believable characters. Set mostly in Wales and the south-west, the books feature Detective Chief Superintendent Colin Harpur and his unscrupulous, self-serving superior, Assistant Chief Constable Desmond Iles. Harpur, often battling against drug gangs and corruption, is necessarily no angel himself but it is his flawed character that provides one of the many strengths of these intelligent, distinctively written books.

The Harpur and Iles novels include You'd Better Believe It, The Lolita Man, Gospel, The Detective is Dead, Lovely Mover, Eton Crop, Panicking Ralph, Pay Days *and* Double Jeopardy.

READ ON ▷

▶ ▷ John Harvey, *Rough Treatment*; ▷ Ian Rankin, *Black and Blue*; Ken Beven, *The Killing of the Tinkers*.

JAMES, P(hyllis) D(orothy) (born 1920)
British novelist

Although James is often described as the 'Queen of Crime', ▷ Agatha Christie's heir, she is more like a cross between ▷ Sayers and ▷ Highsmith. The crimes in her books are brutal, are committed by deranged, psychopathic people, and are described in chilling, unblinking prose, as objective as a forensic report. Her principal detective, Adam Dalgliesh, is a poet and aesthete, combining brilliant detective instincts with a liberal conscience and a dandyish distaste for what he does. Although the books at first seem long and leisurely, James racks tension inexorably tighter until her dénouement: not a cosy Christieish explanation round the library fire, but a scene of pathological, cathartic violence.

A TASTE FOR DEATH (1986)
A lonely spinster, taking flowers to decorate her local church, finds the throat-cut corpses of a tramp, Harry Mack, and a prominent Tory MP, Sir Paul Berowne. Berowne has been the subject of recent slanderous accusations, and Dalgliesh's investigation must begin by deciding whether he was murdered or committed suicide after killing Mack. The story gradually sucks in various members of

Berowne's large and mutually hostile family, his servants and his mistress. As well as showing us this, and describing the police work in exact, unhurried detail, the book also concerns itself with the lives and preoccupations of Dalgliesh's assistants, especially Inspector Kate Miskin, the newest member of the team.

James's other novels are Cover Her Face, A Mind to Murder, Death of an Expert Witness, Unnatural Causes, Shroud for a Nightingale, An Unsuitable Job for a Woman (*which introduces James's female private investigator, Cordelia Gray*), The Black Tower, Innocent Blood, The Skull Beneath the Skin, Original Sin, Devices and Desires, A Certain Justice *and* Death in Holy Orders. Children of Men *is set in England in 2021, when there are no children and there is therefore no future.* Time To Be in Earnest *is a memoir.*

READ ON ▷

▶ ▷ **Ngaio Marsh, *Surfeit of Lampreys*; ▷ Marjorie Allingham, *The Tiger in the Smoke*; ▷ Ruth Rendell, *A Sleeping Life*; ▷ Colin Dexter, *The Way Through the Woods*.**

JAPRISOT, Sebastien (born 1931)
French novelist

Jean-Baptiste Rossi has been publishing strange and tricksy crime fiction under the pseudonym of Sebastien Japrisot since the 1960s. His novels were post-modern before the term had been invented, playing sophisticated games with ideas of identity and with readers' expectations of the genre. His earlier novels appeared in the aftermath of the French Nouvelle Vague in the cinema and Japrisot's books always read a bit as if they should be the bases for films by Truffaut, Godard and other Nouvelle Vague directors. (In one or two instances they have been.) Typical titles are *The Lady in the Car with Glasses and a Gun* and *Trap for Cinderella*, which both set up plots in which the central character loses, or fears she is losing, a sense of personal identity. In the first a young and beautiful blonde borrows her boss's car and drives from Paris to the south of France. En route she encounters one bizarre incident after another. When she discovers the body of a man in the car boot, she begins to believe she is losing her mind. In *Trap for Cinderella* a fire destroys a beach house at a French resort. Of the two girls inside only one survives, burned beyond recognition and in a state of total amnesia. Which of the two girls who entered the beach house is she? And is she a killer or an intended victim? Japrisot's novels are an acquired taste but it is one worth taking time to acquire.

Japrisot's other novels include The 10.30 From Marseille, One Deadly Summer, Rider in the Rain *and* Women in Evidence.

READ ON ▷

● *A Very Long Engagement* (a thriller about a woman trying to discover the fate of her fiancé, missing in action in the First World War).
▶ ▷ **Daniel Pennac, *The Fairy Gunmother*; ▷ James Sallis, *The Long-Legged Fly*; Delacorta, *The Rap Factor*.**

JARDINE, Quintin (born 1945)
Scottish novelist

For the last ten years Quintin Jardine has been painting a dark portrait of the Edinburgh the tourists don't see, in his sequence of gripping, well-plotted novels featuring Deputy Chief Constable Bob Skinner. Sharing some of the same territory as ▷ Ian Rankin's Rebus books, the Skinner novels are, in some ways, more convincing as police procedurals and Skinner more believable as a genuine police officer than Rankin's hero. (The Rebus books, of course, have their own particular and undeniable strengths and virtues.) Jardine has had his tough and humane cop dealing with cases ranging from the investigation of a mid-air explosion (*Skinner's Ordeal*) to the thwarting of terrorists who are threatening the Edinburgh Festival (*Skinner's Festival*). All the Skinner books are well plotted and highly readable crime thrillers.

SKINNER'S RULES (1993)
The discovery of a badly mutilated body in a dark Edinburgh alley is followed by more brutal murders and the city seems to be harbouring an insane serial killer. But, when one of the later bodies turns out to be that of the fiancée of the first victim, Skinner finds it hard to believe that this is coincidence. As he pursues his investigation, he unearths a far-reaching and deadly conspiracy. In this first novel, Jardine showed the assured plotting and skill at evoking the dark side of Edinburgh that have been hallmarks of all the Skinner books that have followed.

The other Skinner novels are Skinner's Festival, Skinner's Trail, Skinner's Round, Skinner's Ordeal, Skinner's Mission, Skinner's Ghosts, Murmuring of Judges, Gallery Whispers, Thursday Legends, Autographs in the Rain *and* Head Shot. *Under the name of Matthew Reid, Jardine has also published several novels* (Blackstone's Pursuits, Screen Savers *and others)* about a London-based private investigator, Oz Blackstone.

READ ON ▷

▶ ▷ Ian Rankin, *Knots and Crosses*; Frederic Lindsay, *Darkness in My Hand*; Joyce Holmes, *Mr Big*; Peter Turnbull, *The Man With No Face*.

JECKS, Michael (born 1960)
British novelist

Medieval mysteries have proliferated in the last twenty years but few have been as well plotted and well researched as the series by Michael Jacks set in early fourteenth-century Devon and featuring Sir Baldwin Furnshill, Keeper of the King's Peace, and his friend Simon Puttock, the bailiff of Lydford Castle. Knights, squires, corrupt justices, jousting tournaments, boy bishops and all the more colourful paraphernalia of medieval life are to be found in the pages of Jecks's books but they are also all cleverly constructed mysteries which travel towards satisfying solutions. One of Jecks's cleverest touches is that he makes Sir Baldwin a former member of the Templars, whose order has been declared heretical and been destroyed, and several of the books refer back to his past life.

THE LAST TEMPLAR (1995)

In the first of the series Puttock, just appointed bailiff of Lydford Castle, is confronted by the apparently accidental death of a man in a fire. Lord of the manor Furnshill, recently returned from his European travels, is convinced that the man's death was not accidental and soon another killing in the area seems to prove him right. What connects the two deaths and what connection is there between events in Devon and the burning of Knights Templar in France a few years earlier?

Michael Jecks's other novels are The Merchant's Partner, A Moorland Hanging, The Crediton Killings, The Abbot's Gibbet, The Leper's Return, Squire Throwleigh's Heir, Belladonna at Belstone, The Traitor of St Giles, The Boy-Bishop's Glovemaker, The Tournament of Blood, The Sticklepath Strangler *and* The Devil's Acolyte.

READ ON ▷

▶ ▷ **Paul Doherty,** *The Assassin in the Greenwood*; **Edward Marston,** *The Elephants of Norwich*; **Alys Clare,** *The Tavern in the Morning*; **Susanna Gregory,** *An Unholy Alliance.*
See also Read on a Theme: Medieval Mystery.

JEFFERIES, Wilham, see Jeffery DEAVER

JOHNSTON, Paul (born 1957)
Scottish novelist

Johnston is the creator of an unusual and original crime series. His books are set in Edinburgh in the 2020s. Britain has broken up and a number of independent city-states have developed. Edinburgh, its economy bolstered by a year-long tourist festival, is one of them and is ruled by an austere Council of City Guardians, who have banned such individual luxuries as TV, cars and telephones. Private life is strictly regulated by the state and crime is rare. When murder does occur there are few able to deal with it. One of the few is Johnston's hero, Quint Dalrymple, a maverick private investigator who used to work for the Guardians. There are a few jarring notes in Johnston's imagined future scenarios – is it really likely that Dalrymple would be a devotee of blues and rock music from fifty years earlier, for example? – but, by and large, he works out his fantasy with impeccable logic. The books are enjoyable both as mysteries and as dark political satire.

BODY POLITIC (1997)

It is 2020 and there hasn't been a murder in independent Edinburgh for five years. Then one of the city's guardswomen is brutally killed and it looks as if a killer, long thought dead himself, has returned to disturb the state. Quint Dalrymple is chosen to investigate and soon finds himself up to his neck in the kind of corruption that the Council of City Guardians was supposed to have ended.

The other Dalrymple novels are The Bone Yard, Water of Death, The Blood Tree *and* The House of Dust. *Johnston has more recently started a new series featuring a Greek private investigator called Alex Mavros. The first title is* A Deeper Shade of Blue.

READ ON

▶ ▷ **Philip Kerr,** *A Philosophical Investigation*; **J. D. Robb,** *Naked in Death* **(New York in 2058).**

K

KAMINSKY, Stuart M. (born 1934)
US novelist

Kaminsky is best known for a series of books starring Toby Peters, a 1940s private eye sacked from his previous job as film studio security guard for cheeking Jack Warner. He still works in Hollywood and his speciality is investigating blackmail and murder involving film stars. The stars themselves take part in the investigations and the supporting casts include such luminaries as Babe Ruth, Joe Louis and Ernest Hemingway. For all their wisecracks, the books are serious crime novels, crammed with nuggets of gossip and movie history which will delight movie buffs without alienating readers who care nothing for Hollywood's great past. Typical Peters books are *High Midnight* (featuring Gary Cooper), *Bullet for a Star* (co-featuring Errol Flynn, Sydney Greenstreet and Peter Lorre) and *Murder on the Yellow Brick Road* (featuring, naturally, Judy Garland).

The prolific Kaminsky has produced at least two other series worth investigating. The Lieberman series, all of which have the central character's name in the title, feature an ageing Jewish police detective in Chicago. The books in the Porfiry Rostnikov series (typical titles are *Death of a Dissident*, *Blood and Roubles* and *Murder on the Trans-Siberian Express*) have a Moscow police inspector as their central character.

> **READ ON**

▶ to the Toby Peters series: George Baxt, *The Bette Davis Murder Case*; ▷ Andrew Bergman, *Hollywood and Levine*.
▶ to the Rostnikov books: Martin Cruz Smith, *Gorky Park*.

KAVANAGH, Dan (born 1946)
British novelist

Kavanagh is the pseudonym of novelist Julian Barnes who, during the 1980s, dashed off four witty and earthy crime novels featuring Duffy, an amiable, bisexual private eye. *Duffy* and *Fiddle City* appeared in 1980 and 1981 respectively, sandwiched in between Barnes's first two 'regular' novels. *Putting the Boot In* (1985) saw Duffy tackling the seedy world of third division football, while encountering the much graver problem of possible Aids infection. In *Going to the Dogs*, the last book to date, he investigates a suspicious death in a country mansion. As Barnes extends his career by branching out as a writer of short stories and essays and as a translator, further excursions for both Kavanagh and Duffy seem doubtful. Barnes claimed on his website that Kavanagh 'hasn't written anything for ages. He's jealous of my success', before ominously adding: 'Some nasty road accident in north London may be necessary to get rid of Kavanagh. Traditionally the author kills off his characters, but I don't see why an author shouldn't get killed off as well. Crushed by a beer barrel falling off a truck as he leaves a pub, or something. Poor old Dan.'

READ ON ▷

▶ John Milne, *Alive and Kicking*; P. B. Yuill, *Hazell and the Three Card Trick*;
▷ Mark Timlin, *A Street That Rhymed at 3 a.m.*

KAVANAGH, Paul, see Lawrence BLOCK

KEATING, H(enry) R(eymond) F(itzwalter) (born 1926)
British novelist

Keating has not only written some excellent crime novels, he has also, over the years, been a fine spokesman and promoter of the genre as a reviewer, editor and commentator. In the early 1960s he wrote a sequence of clever spoofs, each involving murder in a different, bizarre location: at a firefighters' conference (*Death and the Visiting Firemen*), at a residential course in Zen Buddhism (*Zen There Was Murder*), at a croquet championship (*A Rush on the Ultimate*). In 1964, with *The Perfect Murder*, he began a series starring Ganesh Ghote, a mild-mannered Bombay police inspector. The Ghote books are no-tricks mysteries that demonstrate a feeling for the sights, smells, sounds and eccentric characters of India. (This, despite the fact that when he wrote the first Ghote novels, he had never visited the country.) Ghote is a delightful hero: fussy, self-important, easily embarrassed, proud of his home, fond of his wife and, above all, wide-eyed with astonishment at the worlds into which his investigations plunge him. The series has proved remarkably consistent – each book is as fresh and enjoyable as the others.

The Inspector Ghote novels include The Perfect Murder, Inspector Ghote Hunts the Peacock, Inspector Ghote Trusts the Heart, Filmi, Filmi, Inspector Ghote, Under a Monsoon Cloud, The Body in the Billiard Room, The Iciest Sin *and* Breaking and Entering. *Keating's non-Ghote books include* Zen There Was Murder, The Dog It Was That Died, The Murder of the Maharajah *and* Murder by Death.

READ ON ▷

● *The Rich Detective* (a police detective wins money on the lottery which allows him to pursue a murderer whom only he believes to be guilty).
▶ to the Ghote novels: ▷ Ellis Peters, *Mourning Raga*; Paul Mann, *The Burning Ghats* (one of a darker series set in India).

KELLERMAN, Faye (born 1952)
US novelist

The central partnership in most of Faye Kellerman's novels is that between Pete Decker, a Los Angeles police detective, and Rina Lazarus, an Orthodox Jewish woman who is first his girlfriend and, later in the series, his wife. Kellerman uses these two characters and the relationship between them not only to portray the harsh realities of American police work – common enough in the work of dozens of writers – but also the rituals and beliefs of Judaism, a far less frequent element in crime fiction. In *Day of Atonement*, for example, Decker, newly married to Rina, finds he has to make efforts to understand a close-knit and close-mouthed Orthodox community when a troubled teenager goes missing from it. Unconventional in much of their subject matter but traditional in their use of tight plotting to draw the reader in, the Decker/Lazarus novels are all taut and exciting crime thrillers.

Faye Kellerman took a break from the series to produce a historical mystery, *The Quality of Mercy* (set in Elizabethan England), and *Moon Music*, about the search for a serial killer in Las Vegas. Her husband Jonathan is also a crime writer (see below).

PRAYERS FOR THE DEAD (1996)
A famous heart surgeon and Christian fundamentalist is brutally murdered. As Decker investigates the man's life and death, he finds that the surgeon's public persona and private self were at odds, that his family is divided and dysfunctional and, most worrying of all, that there is a strong link between at least one member of the family and his own wife.

Faye Kellerman's other Decker and Lazarus novels are The Ritual Bath, Sacred and Profane, Milk and Honey, Day of Atonement, False Prophet, Grievous Sin, Sanctuary, Justice, Serpent's Tooth, Jupiter's Bones, Stalker, The Forgotten *and* The Stone Kiss.

READ ON >

▶ ▷ Jonathan Kellerman, *The Clinic*; John Sandford, *Certain Prey*; ▷ Harry Kemelman, *Saturday the Rabbi Went Hungry* (one of a much gentler, less graphic series in which Judaism is an integral part of the plot); Joseph Telushkin, *The Unorthodox Murder of Rabbi Wahl*.

KELLERMAN, Jonathan (born 1949)
US novelist

Like his hero Alex Delaware, Kellerman is a professional psychologist, and his compulsive, chilling thrillers depend on unlocking the secrets in apparently demented minds. In *When the Bough Breaks* (1985), for example, Delaware is working with a disturbed seven-year-old girl who may have witnessed a brutal murder, and uncovers a story of pederasty, child prostitution and more murder. In *Over the Edge* (1987), a disturbed young man is the chief suspect in a case of multiple knife-murders, and Delaware must turn every stone in wealthy Los Angeles society to prove the boy's innocence. Kellerman's themes are grim and his books are long – sometimes overlong – but his writing is mesmeric. To begin each novel is to guarantee reading it through to the shattering, surprising ending.

The other Alex Delaware novels are Blood Test, Silent Partner, Time Bomb, Private Eyes, Devil's Waltz, Bad Love, Self-Defence, The Web, The Clinic, Survival of the Fittest, Monster, Doctor Death *and* Flesh and Blood.

READ ON >

- *Billy Straight* (a non-Delaware book in which a homeless boy witnesses a terrible crime).
- ▷ James Patterson, *Roses Are Red*; ▷ Jeffery Deaver, *The Stone Monkey*; Maxine O'Callaghan, *Only in the Ashes*.

KEMELMAN, Harry (1908–1996)
US novelist

David Small is a small-town Massachusetts rabbi, mild-mannered, easy-going and a touch too progressive for some members of his community. Wherever he goes, murders seem to happen, threatening the suburban tranquillity. Small solves them by worrying away at the problems in the way scholars puzzle at problems in the Talmud. The books are drily witty, the mysteries are beautifully worked out and Kemelman is unobtrusively insightful about ordinary American small-town life. Only in ▷ Chesterton's Father Brown stories have religion and murderous intrigue been so successfully mixed.

The Small books are Friday the Rabbi Slept Late, Saturday the Rabbi Went Hungry, Sunday the Rabbi Stayed Home, Monday the Rabbi Took Off, Tuesday the Rabbi Saw Red, Wednesday the Rabbi Got Wet, Thursday the Rabbi Walked Out, Someday the Rabbi Will Leave, One Fine Day the Rabbi Bought a Cross, The Day the Rabbi Resigned *and* That Day the Rabbi Left Town. The Nine Mile Walk *is a collection of stories of a quite different kind, about a Mycroft Holmesian figure who sits in his study solving cases by sheer brainpower.*

READ ON >

▶ ▷ Howard Engel, *Getting Away With Murder*; Joseph Telushkin, *The Final Analysis of Dr Stark*; Batya Gur, *Murder on a Kibbutz*.

KERR, Philip (born 1956)
British novelist

In his first three novels, published in the late 1980s, Philip Kerr created a memorably different private eye. Cleverly blending historical reality with the conventions of crime fiction, Kerr's Berlin Noir trilogy introduced readers to Bernie Gunther, a private investigator and former member of the German secret police who operates in Nazi Germany just before the outbreak of the Second World War. Since the publication of the third in the series, *A German Requiem*, in which Gunther becomes embroiled in the developing tensions post-war that were to shape the Cold War, Kerr has turned his back on the character. Instead he has moved on to the crafting of a series of very contemporary (sometimes futuristic) thrillers. All are expertly done and *A Philosophical Investigation*, the story of a search for a Wittgenstein-loving serial killer, set in the near future, is as good a thriller as you're ever likely to read. But crime fans may still mourn the passing of Bernie Gunther.

The Berlin Noir trilogy consists of March Violets, The Pale Criminal *and* A German Requiem. *Kerr's other thrillers include* Gridiron, Esau, The Shot *and* Dark Matter.

READ ON ▷

▶ to the Berlin Noir trilogy: Robert Harris, *Fatherland*; Alan Furst, *The World at Night*.

▶ to the other novels: Thomas Harris, *The Silence of the Lambs*; Michael Crichton, *The Terminal Man*.

KIJEWSKI, Karen (born 1943)
US novelist

Since the success of authors like ▷ Sara Paretsky and ▷ Sue Grafton in the 1980s, with their savvy and resourceful heroines, there has been no shortage of American crime novels involving feisty female private investigators. Some have been rather pale imitations of the originals. Others have been lively and engaging characters in their own right. High up among the latter category is Kat Colorado, series heroine of Karen Kijewski's novels. The first book, *Katwalk*, won several awards and those that have followed have maintained a high standard – they work well as mysteries and the character of Kat develops and changes as the series progresses.

ALLEY KAT BLUES (1995)
The mangled corpse of an apparent hit-and-run victim is haunting Kat Colorado's dreams. It was Kat who stopped her car and rescued the young woman's body from the middle of the road. It is Kat who has been hired by the victim's mother to prove that it was murder and not an accident. Meanwhile, Kat's cop boyfriend Hank is working on the case of a Las Vegas serial killer, the Strip Stalker, and possibly getting too interested in a young woman who believes her runaway sister may have been one of the killer's victims. *Alley Kat Blues* shows the mixture of devious plotting and feisty characterization that give the Kat Colorado books their bite.

The other Kat Colorado books are Katwalk, Katapult, Kat's Cradle, Copy Kat, Wild Kat, Honky Tonk Kat, Kat Scratch Fever *and* Stray Kat Waltz.

READ ON ▷

▶ ▷ Janet Evanovich, *Three to Get Deadly*; ▷ Sara Paretsky, *Toxic Shock*; Elizabeth M. Cosin, *Zen and the Art of Murder*; Maxine O'Callaghan, *Down for the Count*. See also Read on a Theme: Female Detectives.

KING, Laurie (born 1952)
US novelist

Laurie King has written three novels (*A Grave Talent*, *To Play the Fool* and *With Child*) featuring Kate Martinelli, a female homicide detective in San Francisco, and her partner Al Hawkin. In the first of the series, *A Grave Talent*, the newly promoted Martinelli is assigned to the world-weary Hawkin and, despite his initial misgivings, mutual respect develops as their investigation of the murders of three young girls leads them into the murky past of a famous artist. The novel met with great critical acclaim and won several awards. The other

Martinelli books are just as well done but they are not as striking as King's other series.

The Beekeeper's Apprentice is the story of a precocious young girl, Mary Russell, who meets and makes friends with a middle-aged man, living in retirement in the Sussex Downs and keeping bees. The man is Sherlock Holmes. He begins to teach Mary the art of detection but what starts as a sort of game between the two becomes very serious when an enemy from Holmes's past appears. There have been many – too many – Sherlock Holmes pastiches in the past but Laurie King's books are in a league of their own. Her Holmes is a character built upon the foundations of Doyle's original but genuinely given new life and individuality. *The Beekeeper's Apprentice*, and the books that have followed it, are highly engaging mysteries in their own right, well plotted and wittily written, and the knowledgeable allusions to Doyle, other literature and the history of the period add another layer to the reader's enjoyment.

The other Mary Russell books are A Monstrous Regiment of Women, A Letter of Mary, The Moor, O Jerusalem *and* Justice Hall.

> **READ ON**

▶ to the Martinelli novels: Katherine V. Forrest, *Amateur City*.
▶ to the Mary Russell novels: Quinn Fawcett; *The Scottish Ploy* (one of another series which makes use of Doyle's characters, in this case Mycroft Holmes, Sherlock's brother); ▷ Elizabeth Peters, *Crocodile on the Sandbank*; Gillian Linscott, *The Perfect Daughter*.

L

LANSDALE, Joe (born 1951)
US novelist

Any number of contemporary American crime writers attempt to marry farce with violent action in their narratives, but few do it with such pulp style as Joe Lansdale. Lansdale began as a horror writer but he is now best known for the series of novels featuring Hap Collins and Leonard Pine in over-the-top but enjoyable adventures. Hap, white and straight, and Leonard, black and gay, form an odd team for solving crime and some of the crimes they have to unravel are even odder, but Lansdale's zest for telling the tallest of tales carries the reader along with him.

THE TWO-BEAR MAMBO (1995)
Florida Grange, Leonard's lawyer and Hap's former lover, has disappeared. When they go in search of her they find themselves caught in a town full of redneck psychopaths who fail to see the good side of the cross-race male bonding of Hap and Leonard. Lansdale's hallmark mixture of high farce and almost cartoonishly over-the-top violence ensues.

The other Hap Collins and Leonard Pine novels are Mucho Mojo, Savage Season, Rumble Tumble *and* Captains Outrageous.

> **READ ON**

- *The Bottoms* (very different from the wild Collins and Pine novels – an elegiac combination of murder mystery and coming-of-age story set in 1930s East Texas).
- ▷ Doug J. Swanson, *Big Town*; ▷ Robert Crais, *The Monkey's Raincoat*; ▷ Tim Dorsey, *Hammerhead Ranch Motel*.

LATHEN, Emma
US novelist

Emma Lathen was the pseudonym of Mary Jane Latsis (1927–1997) and Martha Henissart (b. 1929), who also wrote together as R. B. Dominic. Their Lathen books combine big business, finance and murder. The mayhem in *Accounting for Murder* starts with the attempt to trace fraudulent computer accounts. *Double, Double, Oil and Trouble* deals with oil contracts, ransoms and Swiss bank accounts. In each book Lathen's investigator, John Putnam Thatcher of Wall Street's Sloan Guaranty Trust, comes hard up against the greed, naïvety and bad manners of the human race without ever being surprised by what he finds or condemning it. The banking and financial details are easy to understand, the characters are entertaining and the stories move effortlessly to exciting climaxes.

As R. B. Dominic the same authors wrote mysteries which are solved by US Congressman Ben Safford. These have the same structure, with Safford's family and colleagues appearing in each, but deal with wider issues: fraudulent doctors in *The Attending Physician*, for example, political corruption in *Epitaph for a Lobbyist* and security and aircraft research in *A Flaw in the System*.

Emma Lathen's other novels include Banking on Death, Death Shall Overcome, Murder Against the Grain, By Hook or By Crook, Green Grow the Dollars, Right on the Money *and* A Shark Out of Water.

READ ON ▷

▶ Arthur Maling, *The Koberg Link*; Janet Neil, *Death of a Partner*;
▷ Sara Paretsky, *Deadlock*; David Williams, *Murder for Treasure*.

LATIMER, Jonathan (1906–1983)
US novelist

Latimer was a Hollywood screenwriter in the 1940s and 1950s, and in the 1960s scripted the Perry Mason TV series. His 1930s comedy thrillers, starring the boozy private eye Bill Crane, combine comedy and suspense more successfully than almost any other novels in the genre. Of his non-Crane books, *Black is the Fashion for Dying* is a murder mystery set in Hollywood. Latimer also wrote a single novel, *The Search for My Great Uncle's Head*, using the pseudonym of Peter Coffin.

Latimer's Crane books include *Murder in the Madhouse*, *The Lady in the Morgue* and *Red Gardenias*. His other non-Crane novels are *Solomon's Vineyard*, *Sinners and Shrouds* and *Dark Memory*.

READ ON ▷

▶ ▷ Dashiell Hammett, *The Thin Man*; Howard Browne, *The Taste of Ashes*; Fredric Brown, *The Fabulous Clipjoint*.

LAYTON, Clare, see Natasha COOPER

READ ON A THEME: LEGAL EAGLES

   Catherine Arnold, *Due Process* (female attorney in Florida)
▷ John Grisham, *A Time to Kill*
▷ Cyril Hare, *Tragedy at Law*
   John Lescroart, *Nothing But the Truth*
   Paul Levine, *Fool Me Twice*
   Richard North Patterson, *Degree of Guilt*
   Lisa Scottoline, *The Vendetta Defense*
   Robert K. Tanenbaum, *No Lesser Plea*

See also: Courtroom Dramas

LEHANE, Dennis (born 1965)
US novelist

Born and bred in Dorchester, Massachusetts, Lehane is the author of six crime novels, all set in or around his native town and the Boston area. Five of these feature private investigators Patrick Kenzie and Angela Gennaro, along with their 'assistant', the barely civilized Bubba Rogowski. Set in largely blue-collar, rather than blue blood, parts of Boston, the books' razor-sharp wisecracks and dialogue don't disguise the fact that they inhabit exceptionally dark regions of the human soul. Several of them feature child abuse as a theme, and the domestic violence that runs through them seems so common as to be almost casual or expected. Friends since childhood and partners for years, Kenzie and Gennaro make a compelling and entertaining double act, running their investigation agency from the belfry of a Boston church. But as Patrick's father, a firefighter whom he ironically labels 'the hero', terrorized his family and Angie's husband is not averse to being brutal with her, both of them have an intimate knowledge of 'indoor fireworks'. Three of the novels have won crime fiction awards and all are superbly written.

MYSTIC RIVER (2001)
This is a stand-alone novel about three friends, Dave Boyle, Sean Devine and Jimmy Marcus, and of something that happened twenty-five years ago that killed that friendship. When Jimmy's daughter is murdered, the three men, on different sides of the law now, are united once more.

The Kenzie and Gennaro books are A Drink Before the War, Darkness, Take My Hand, Sacred, Gone, Baby, Gone *and* Prayers for Rain.

READ ON >

▶ ▷ Harlan Coben, *One False Move*; ▷ Robert Crais, *Sunset Express*; Chris Larsgaard, *The Heir Hunter*.

LEON, Donna (born 1942)
US novelist

Donna Leon's crime novels are set in Venice and the city's *calli* and *campi* provide the stage set on which the sympathetic figure of Commissario Guido Brunetti conducts his investigations. The charm of the novels has much to do with Venice itself. Leon is very precise in her descriptions and anyone who knows and loves Venice will recognize many of the places she writes about. But hers is not a sentimentalized version of the 'Pearl of the Adriatic', it's a city in which drugs, prostitution and corruption lurk in the shadows. Through it all moves the thoughtful and humane Brunetti, honestly determined to get at as much of the truth as he can.

FATAL REMEDIES (1999)
An act of vandalism destroys the windows of a travel agent in a Venice square. The vandal is Brunetti's wife Paola, protesting against sex tourism to the Far East. Brunetti, embarrassed by his wife's behaviour but sympathetic to her motives, is

faced with an even more dramatic conflict of interests when the owner of the agency is found murdered.

The other Commissario Brunetti books are Death at La Fenice, Death in a Strange Country, The Anonymous Venetian, A Venetian Reckoning, Acqua Alta, The Death of Faith, A Noble Radiance, Friends in High Places, A Sea of Troubles *and* Wilful Behaviour.

READ ON ▷

▶ ▷ **Michael Dibdin,** *Dead Lagoon*; ▷ **Magdalen Nabb,** *The Marshal and the Murderer*; **Timothy Holme,** *The Neapolitan Streak*.

LEONARD, Elmore (born 1925)
US novelist

Elmore Leonard began his career in the 1950s as a writer of westerns and it was not until the late 1960s that he turned his attention to the crime genre. His commercial success was immediate and several of his books were turned into films – mostly not very good ones, it has to be said – but it was not until the 1980s that he began to gather the critical acclaim that has attached itself to his work ever since. There is a case to be argued that he is the best living American crime writer. Like ▷ George V. Higgins and ▷ K. C. Constantine, Leonard is almost entirely uninterested in the puzzle element of crime writing. His great strength, like theirs, is his dialogue which is pacy, convincing and catches superbly the rhythms and cadences of everyday speech among the grifters, gangsters, mobsters and small-time hoodlums who people his novels. His books create an unforgettable and often very funny portrait of the low life and weirdos who make up his own vividly imagined criminal underworld in Detroit and, in later books, Florida. He has continued to attract the attention of film-makers, including (most famously) Quentin Tarantino, and this is no surprise. He writes dialogue which most scriptwriters would sell their souls to the Devil to match, and his books are always fast and furious in their action.

GET SHORTY (1990)
This book features one of Leonard's most engaging anti-heroes in Chili Palmer, an amiable, movie-obsessed mobster who travels to Hollywood in pursuit of an absconding debtor and finds himself right at home in Tinseltown. In fact, the big guns of the movie business seem a bit amateurish to him and he soon decides that his own particular combination of chutzpah, self-confidence and willingness to apply just the right amount of violence necessary to get results will take him far. He decides to become a producer.

Leonard's other novels include The Switch, City Primeval, Cat Chaser, Stick, La Brava, Glitz, Freaky Deaky, Maximum Bob, Rum Punch, Riding the Rap, Be Cool, Pagan Babies *and* Tishomingo Blues.

READ ON ▷

▶ ▷ **George V. Higgins,** *Outlaws* (for the dialogue); ▷ **Robert B. Parker,** *Night Passage*; ▷ **Loren D. Estleman,** *Motor City Blue*.

LIPPMAN, Laura (born 1959)
US novelist

Laura Lippman's entertaining and much-acclaimed crime novels feature her journalist turned private investigator Tess Monaghan. Tess is a fine creation and a likeable character – intelligent, honest, funny and persevering. The Baltimore in which most of the mysteries take place, and with which Tess has a love/hate relationship, is brought vividly to life (both its past and its present) and the plots are cunningly and tightly structured. *Baltimore Blues*, in which Tess first appears and turns her talents from reporting to snooping, has her involved in a murder which looks very much as if it may be the work of a close friend. *Charm City* follows her investigation of the death of Wink Wynkowski, a flamboyant promoter who was set to bring a professional basketball team to Baltimore – an investigation that involves more deaths and surprises before the truth is reached.

IN BIG TROUBLE (1999)
The mystery begins for Tess Monaghan when she receives an anonymous letter enclosing a photo of her ex-boyfriend. Attached is the ominous message, 'In Big Trouble'. The rest of the novel slowly unfolds the 'big trouble' to which the message refers. Concerned about her ex, Tess travels to Texas, where he is playing in a band. All seems well – he is insistent that he is OK but, before long, a body turns up and secrets from the past begin to emerge. *In Big Trouble* has Tess operating away from the familiar streets of her beloved Baltimore but showing the same gutsy determination to get at the truth that she always does.

The other Tess Monaghan books are Baltimore Blues, Charm City, Butchers Hill, The Sugar House, In a Strange City *and* The Last Place.

READ ON

▶ Jan Burke, *Sweet Dreams, Irene*; Edna Buchanan, *You Only Die Twice*; Julie Smith, *House of Blues*.

LOCHTE, Dick (born 1944)
US novelist

New Orleans-born journalist Lochte is a highly ebullient author who has written a number of screenplays, six novels (two of them with a co-author) and a volume of stories. His first book, *Sleeping Dog*, was published in 1985 and featured two engaging narrators: Leo Bloodworth, a middle-aged, bourbon-friendly private eye, and Serendipity Dahlquist, a precocious fourteen-year-old girl. *Laughing Dog* appeared in 1988 and starred the same unlikely duo, with Serendipity assisting Leo while driving him to distraction. Set in Los Angeles, both books are supremely entertaining, with much humour derived from the protagonists' contrasting viewpoints and narrative styles. A discreet but palpable sexual frisson between the budding young woman and the battered old sleuth adds to their appeal.

Lochte's next two books featured a minor character from their predecessors, New Orleans private eye Terry Manion. Assisted by his mentor, J. J. Legendre, Manion solves the crimes in *Blue Bayou* and *The Neon Smile*. Manion, Legendre and Bloodworth and Serendipity all appear in Lochte's story collection, *Lucky*

Dog & Other Tales of Murder, published in 2000. Lochte has also collaborated with Christopher Darden, a prosecutor in the O. J. Simpson trial on *The Trials of Nikki Hill* and *LA Justice*, both featuring black female prosecutor Hill.

READ ON ▷

▶ ▷ Robert Crais, *The Monkey's Raincoat*; Julie Smith, *New Orleans Mourning* (for New Orleans setting).

READ ON A THEME: LOCKED-ROOM MYSTERIES

  Anthony Boucher, *The Case of the Solid Key*
▷ John Dickson Carr, *The Witch of the Low Tide*
  Carter Dickson (▷ John Dickson Carr), *The Ten Teacups*
▷ Michael Gilbert, *Smallbone Deceased*
  Georgette Heyer, *Envious Casca*
▷ Edgar Allan Poe, *The Murders in the Rue Morgue* (short story that is the
    grandfather of all locked-room mysteries)
▷ Ellery Queen, *The Chinese Orange Mystery*
▷ Maj Sjöwall and Per Wahlöö, *The Locked Room*
  Israel Zangwill, *The Big Bow Mystery*

READ ON A THEME: LONDON

▷ Margery Allingham, *The Tiger in the Smoke*
▷ Gwendoline Butler, *Coffin in Fashion*
▷ Arthur Conan Doyle, *A Study in Scarlet*
  Anthony Frewin, *London Blues*
▷ Dan Kavanagh, *Duffy*
  Cameron McCabe, *The Face on the Cutting Room Floor*
  John Milne, *Shadow Play*
▷ Anne Perry, *Resurrection Row*
▷ Mark Timlin, *Paint It Black*

LOVESEY, Peter (born 1936)
British novelist

Since his debut novel in the 1970s Peter Lovesey has proved one of the most versatile and consistently readable of British crime writers. His first series featured two Victorian London policemen, Sergeant Cribb and Constable Thackeray. Well researched and well plotted, the Cribb and Thackeray books take the reader down some of the more intriguing byways of Victorian history: walking races (*Wobble to Death*), the music hall (*Abracadaver*), spiritualism (*A Case of Spirits*), prize-fighting (*The Detective Wore Silk Drawers*). Lovesey's other novels include several which involve Bertie, Prince of Wales (later Edward VII), in the solving of mysteries and a number of books set in the present day in which Peter Diamond, head of the murder squad in Bath, investigates unlawful deaths in the spa town.

The Sergeant Cribb novels are Wobble to Death, The Detective Wore Silk Drawers, Abracadaver, Mad Hatter's Holiday, Invitation to a Dynamite Party, A Case of Spirits, Swing, Swing Together *and* Waxwork. *The Peter Diamond series began with* The Last Detective *and includes* The Summons, Upon a Dark Night *and* The Vault.

READ ON ▷

- ● *The False Inspector Dew* (ingenious story of a murderer taking on a false identity and being asked to investigate murder).
- ▶ to the Cribb novels: ▷ Anne Perry, *Death in the Devil's Acre*; Francis Selwyn, *The Hangman's Child*; Ray Harrison, *Death of a Dancing Lady*.
- ▶ to the Peter Diamond novels: ▷ Reginald Hill, *Bones and Silence*; Morag Joss, *Fearful Symmetry* (another, very different crime story set in Bath).

LYONS, Arthur (born 1946)
US novelist

Arthur Lyons is firmly in the tradition of ▷ Hammett and ▷ Chandler, and his wisecracking detective Jacob Asch owes much to Philip Marlowe while being an original enough creation to make Lyons's novels well worth reading. The mean streets Asch walks are contemporary ones. The books are largely set in the seedier, sleazier realms of Hollywood and Asch has to negotiate his way through a rat's nest of B-movie starlets, junkies, pimps and corrupt officials in search of the truth.

The Jacob Asch novels are The Dead Are Discreet, All God's Children, The Killing Floor, Dead Ringer, Castles Burning, Hard Trade, At the Hands of Another, Three With a Bullet, Fast Fade, Other People's Money *and* False Pretenses.

READ ON ▷

- ▶ ▷ Raymond Chandler, *Farewell, My Lovely*; ▷ Howard Engel, *There Was an Old Woman*; Roger L. Simon, *The Big Fix*.

M

McBAIN, Ed (born 1926)
US novelist

Ed McBain is best known for the police procedural novels he has been publishing since the 1950s, set in the 87th Precinct of a city not too unlike New York. The books star various members of the precinct and, although Steve Carella is often the most prominent figure, they gain their strength from the ensemble of characters McBain has created. As the series proceeds, the characters grow and develop so that we come to know them like members of a family. Several of the books include an arch-villain, the Deaf Man, possessed of a grippingly macabre sense of humour. If the blend of humour and harshness, social comment and personal drama in the 87th Precinct novels seems familiar, then it's because many of the finest American TV cop series – *Hill Street Blues*, for example – ultimately derive from it. McBain has also written a second series featuring a Florida attorney/detective, Matthew Hope.

The 87th Precinct books include Cop Hater, Killer's Choice, Give the Boys a Great Big Hand, Eighty Million Eyes, Fuzz, Hail, Hail, the Gang's All Here, Let's Hear It for the Deaf Man, Blood Relatives, Eight Black Horses, The Big Bad City *and* The Last Dance. *The Matthew Hope novels (all of which refer to fairy tales or children's rhymes in their titles) include* Goldilocks, Rumpelstiltskin, Snow White and Red Rose, The House That Jack Built, Three Blind Mice, There Was a Little Girl *and* Gladly the Cross-Eyed Bear.

> READ ON >

▶ to the 87th Precinct novels: ▷ Joseph Wambaugh, *The Choirboys*; William Caunitz, *One Police Plaza*.
▶ to the Matthew Hope novels: Stephen Greenleaf, *Past Tense*.

McCRUMB, Sharyn
US novelist

Sharyn McCrumb is known for two series of crime books. The best known and most original consists of what McCrumb calls her Ballad series. These are set in the Appalachians and tell haunting stories of crime and punishment which reflect both modern, small-town America and the history of the struggle to put down roots. Steeped in the folk culture of the area and written with an unforced and lyrical sense of its landscape and people, the Ballad books are as much examples of regional American literature as they are of mystery fiction.

Sharyn McCrumb's second series features a forensic anthropologist called

Elizabeth MacPherson. Much lighter in tone than the Ballad books, these are easy-going, humorous mysteries with an engaging heroine. Thanks to Elizabeth MacPherson's profession, they do share with the Ballad books an interest in the interplay of past and present. Typical titles are *Lovely in Her Bones* about a dig at a Native American archaeological site which unearths more than was expected and *If I'd Killed Him When I Met Him . . .* in which a death in the present appears to have parallels with an unsolved murder from the time of the American Civil War.

She has also written two entertaining mixtures of sci-fi and crime with splendidly pulpy titles: *Bimbos of the Death Sun* and *Zombies of the Gene Pool*.

THE HANGMAN'S BEAUTIFUL DAUGHTER (1992)
In Dark Hollow, Tennessee, an old woman said to have the gift of glimpsing the future is sewing a funeral quilt with six graves on it. Four of the graves, it is soon clear, will be for members of the Underhill family – mother, father and two children – who are found killed in their farmstead. But which bodies are destined to occupy the remaining two? McCrumb weaves together a complex plot which involves the family tragedies of the Underhills, the tribulations of a preacher's wife whose husband is serving in the Gulf, the investigation of Sheriff Spencer Arrowood and the revenge plotted by a man dying of cancer.

Sharyn McCrumb's other Ballad books are If Ever I Return, Pretty Peggy-O, She Walks These Hills, The Rosewood Casket, The Ballad of Frankie Silver *and* The Songcatcher. *The other Elizabeth MacPherson books include* The Windsor Knot, MacPherson's Lament *and* Paying the Piper.

READ ON

- **She Walks These Hills** (set in the Appalachians past and present and featuring, among others, a historian retracing an eighteenth-century woman's flight from Indian captivity and an escaped prisoner with a curious illness).
- ▶ to the Ballad novels: ▷ James Lee Burke, *Heartwood*; Nevada Barr, *Deep South*; Deborah Adams, *All the Dirty Cowards*.
- ▶ to the Elizabeth MacPherson books: Elizabeth Peters, *The Deeds of the Disturber*; Carolyn Haines, *Them Bones*.

McDERMID, Val (born 1955)
British novelist

Val McDermid has written some of the best British crime fiction of the last ten years and has produced three series of books as well as a number of non-series titles. In her early career as a crime writer she created one of Britain's first lesbian investigators in Lindsay Gordon, a journalist drawn (often reluctantly) into webs of deceit and murder. In *Report for Murder* (1987), for example, Lindsay, working on an assignment at a private girls' school, takes on the investigation of the murder of one of the school's most famous old girls when it seems that the police have the wrong person. This first book, as well as introducing Lindsay to her lover in books to come, also introduced the reader to Lindsay's character as it was further revealed over five more titles – independent, principled and often bloody-minded.

In 1992 McDermid created her second series character, Kate Brannigan, a

Manchester-based private detective. The Brannigan books are very recognizably set in the real world of contemporary Manchester, with its big-city crimes, computer fraud and get-rich-quick schemes out to con the gullible. A good example is *Dead Beat* (1992), in which a friend of her rock journalist partner asks Kate to track down a missing songwriter, a trail which leads her into the seedier areas of several northern cities. In more recent years McDermid has published novels more complex in narrative and more willing to stretch the boundaries of the genre than either the Lindsay Gordon or Kate Brannigan books, which feature psychological profiler Tony Hill and his police colleague Carol Jordan. *Killing the Shadows* introduced Fiona Cameron, an academic psychologist reluctantly drawn into a murder investigation.

THE WIRE IN THE BLOOD (1997)
Appointed as head of the National Profiling Task Force, Tony Hill asks his newly formed team to undertake an exercise in which they try to find links between the unexplained disappearances of a group of teenagers nationwide. The exercise turns to tragedy when one of the team is murdered and mutilated. Is there an unsuspected connection between this death and the teenage runaways? McDermid's gradual unfolding of a deviant mind, and Hill's and Jordan's struggles to trap it, are powerfully and graphically portrayed in a novel of ever-escalating psychological intensity.

The Lindsay Gordon novels are Report for Murder, Common Murder, Final Edition, Union Jack *and* Booked for Murder. *The Kate Brannigan books are* Dead Beat, Kick Back, Crackdown, Clean Break, Blue Genes *and* Star Struck. *McDermid's novels featuring Tony Hill and Carol Jordan are* The Mermaids Singing, The Wire in the Blood *and* The Last Temptation.

| READ ON ▷

- **●** *A Place of Execution* (in the 1960s a schoolgirl disappears and a young detective is launched on an investigation that will shape his life).
- **▶** to the Lindsay Gordon novels: Mary Wings, *She Came Too Late*; Katherine V. Forrest, *Sleeping Bones*; Manda Scott, *Hen's Teeth*.
- **▶** to the Kate Brannigan novels: Cath Staincliffe, *Dead Wrong*.
- **▶** to McDermid's other fiction: ▷ Ian Rankin, *The Black Book*; ▷ Peter Robinson, *In a Dry Season*; Jane Adams, *The Greenway*; ▷ Patricia Cornwell, *Cruel and Unusual*.

MACDONALD, John D(ann) (1916–1986)
US novelist

Macdonald is best known for his novels featuring Travis McGee, a large, humorous ex-footballer who lives on a houseboat in Florida and comes out of 'retirement' to 'salvage' people in distress – to save them from crooks or avenge wrongs done to them. Although McGee's investigations are like those of a private eye, he sees himself as more like a knight errant of old, a Sir Galahad or Sir Lancelot, on the side of right against the evil in the world. Macdonald's plots are tortuous, the action is fast and tough, and McGee is as handy with one-liners as with his fists.

ONE FEARFUL YELLOW EYE (1966)

A famous surgeon, dying of a wasting disease, has squandered the $600,000 he was supposed to be leaving to his new young wife and his two bitter, grown-up children. Why? McGee sets out to help the wife (an old friend) recover the money and patch up the family quarrel – a quest which grows ever more complicated and life-threatening, until the final, least expected and potentially most deadly twist of all.

All Macdonald's McGee books have a colour in the title: The Deep Blue Goodbye, The Quick Red Fox, A Deadly Shade of Gold, The Girl in the Plain Brown Wrapper, The Empty Copper Sea, The Turquoise Lament *and so on. Macdonald was also the author of some fifty other crime novels, including* A Bullet for Cinderella, The Price of Murder, Soft Touch, The Executioners *(twice filmed as* Cape Fear, *by J. Lee Thompson in 1962 and Martin Scorsese in 1991) and* The Last One Left. *They are good, but miss the 'classic' status of the McGee books.*

> READ ON

▶ ▷ Carl Hiaasen, *Double Whammy*; ▷ James W. Hall, *Under Cover of Daylight*; Randy Wayne White, *Ten Thousand Islands* (one of a series featuring Doc Ford, a kind of Travis McGee for the present day).

MACDONALD, Ross (1915–1983)
US novelist

Ross Macdonald and John Ross Macdonald were pseudonyms used by the Californian writer Kenneth Millar. His Lew Archer books are atmospheric private-eye thrillers, with a hypnotic, leisurely pace, a likeable and human detective, tortuous plots and casts of marvellously eccentric secondary characters. Unlike Philip Marlowe or Sam Spade, to whom he is regularly compared, Lew Archer is an ordinary man, more likely to use psychology or simple patience to unmask the villains than to resort to violence or intrigue. One of Macdonald's greatest strengths is that he never resorts to melodramatic plotting or stagy dialogue.

THE UNDERGROUND MAN (1971)

The novel begins, in a low-key way that is typical of Macdonald, with Archer giving a small child peanuts to feed to jays on his front lawn. Almost at once he is called in to find the child's missing father, and begins to uncover a nest of lies, treachery and murder spreading back over fifteen years and taking in half a dozen families. The case is complicated first by a (non-accidental) forest fire and then, when the child is kidnapped, by two desperate deluded teenagers on a stolen boat.

Macdonald's Archer books include The Moving Target, The Drowning Pool, The Zebra-Striped Hearse, The Goodbye Look, Find a Victim *and* Sleeping Beauty.

> READ ON

▶ ▷ Raymond Chandler, *Farewell, My Lovely*; Jonathan Valin, *Day of Wrath* (Valin's Harry Stoner inhabits a bleaker world than Lew Archer but comes from the same tradition); Stephen Greenleaf; *False Conception*; Thomas B. Dewey, *A Sad Song Singing*.

McILVANNEY, William (born 1936)
Scottish novelist and poet

McIlvanney has written a number of non-crime novels which analyse the traditional values and beliefs of Scottish working-class men and look at the ways in which a changing economy and society have affected them. His crime fiction, featuring Inspector Jack Laidlaw of Glasgow CID, recasts the same themes into the forms of the police procedural – although McIlvanney is never averse to subverting conventions when it suits his purpose. The Glaswegian inspector, tough but with a highbrow taste in literature, first appeared in *Laidlaw* in 1977, the story of the aftermath of a brutal rape and murder. The killer is known to the reader from early in the novel but this doesn't prevent McIlvanney from ratcheting up the tension as Laidlaw and others attempt to track him down. As well as a crime thriller the book is a complex portrait of its central character and of the city in which he operates. One of McIlvanney's strengths as a writer is his ear for the rhythms and intonations of ordinary, everyday Scottish speech and he employs it to great effect in showing the layers and structures of Glaswegian society. McIlvanney has been sparing in his use of Jack Laidlaw – only three novels in more than twenty years – but his character is as memorable as any of those Scottish detectives who have made more frequent appearances in print.

The other two Laidlaw novels are The Papers of Tony Veitch *and* Strange Loyalties.

READ ON

▶ ▷ Ian Rankin, *Black and Blue*; ▷ Derek Raymond, *He Died With His Eyes Open*; Denise Mina, *Garnethill*.

MacLEOD, Charlotte (born 1922)
Canadian/US writer

MacLeod's breezy comedy mysteries centre on two groups of recurring characters. Her Professor Shandy books are set in Balaclava Agricultural College, Massachusetts, and draw on the teaching staff. Professor Shandy and his wife are quiet, rational individuals, whose placid domestic life is thrown into high relief by the extraordinary personalities about them. MacLeod has fun, just in passing, with people's names, no-nonsense Scandinavian American ladies who look like Botticelli angels, and the politics of education. The Sarah Kelling books are set among Boston's upper crust. Kelling and Max Bittersohn solve murder mysteries often connected with art and with the philanthropic, leisured world of the widespread Kelling clan.

Under the name Alisa Craig, Charlotte MacLeod has written two further series of whimsical whodunits, one featuring Canadian Mountie Madoc Rhys and the other the writer Osbert Monk and his wife Dittany.

The Shandy novels include Rest Ye Merry, The Curse of the Giant Hogweed, An Owl Too Many, Something in the Water *and* Exit the Milkman. *Kelling and Bittersohn appear in, among others*, The Family Vault, The Convivial Codfish, The Silver Ghost, The Resurrection Man *and* The Balloon Man.

READ ON >

▶ Carolyn G. Hart, *April Fool Dead*; Jill Churchill, *Grime and Punishment*; ▷
Elizabeth Peters, *Crocodile on the Sandbank*.

READ ON A THEME: MAFIA AND THE MOB

Richard Condon, *Prizzi's Honour*
▷ John Grisham, *The Client*
Mario Puzo, *The Godfather*
Leonardo Sciascia, *The Day of the Owl*
Nick Tosches, *Trinities*
Stuart Woods, *LA Dead*

MANKELL, Henning (born 1948)
Swedish novelist and dramatist

On mainland Europe Henning Mankell's books are enormous bestsellers and his
reputation in Britain and America is growing all the time. Viewed from one angle,
the extent of his success is rather surprising. The novels present a bleak view of
his native Sweden as a country where welfare-state idealism has been destroyed.
Immigrants are viewed with suspicion and even hatred; families are dislocated
and dysfunctional; the values of tolerance and social inclusiveness are under
permanent threat. Mankell gives a rawer picture of modern life than is usual in
books that regularly top bestseller charts. Viewed from another angle, his success
is not so surprising. The great strength of the books lies in his central character,
Inspector Kurt Wallander, one of the most rounded and sympathetic figures in
contemporary crime fiction.

SIDETRACKED (1999)
A teenage girl commits suicide by burning herself to death. A serial killer with a
taste for gruesome violence and an urge to scalp his victims is on the loose.
Inspector Kurt Wallander, who has been a horrified witness to the girl's self-
immolation, looks for a reason for her despair while also heading the police
search for the killer. Like Mankell's other Wallander novels this is not conventional detective fiction. We know the identity of the killer well before the
book's conclusion. The emphasis is not on mystery but on character and on
the contradictions and corruptions of the Swedish society in which Wallander
works.

READ ON >

▶ ▷ Nicolas Freeling, *Love in Amsterdam*; ▷ Maj Sjöwall and Per Wahlöö, *The
Laughing Policeman*; Jan Willem de Wetering, *The Amsterdam Cops*.

MARRIC, J. J., see John CREASEY

MARSH, Ngaio (1899–1982)
New Zealand novelist

Few authors handle the classic detective story as well as Marsh. The murder methods in her books are ingenious, unexpected and gruesome. The locations are unusual: during a village-hall concert, in the shearing-shed of a sheep farm, among Satanists in a villa in France, at a diplomatic reception and, above all – reflecting her own passionate interest in drama – backstage, in the wings and onstage at theatres. Her theatre books (*Enter a Murderer, Opening Night, Vintage Murder, Death at the Dolphin*) are among her wittiest. She was fond of exotic characters, especially artists, preening actors and the eccentric English upper classes. Her detection is scrupulously fair, with every clue appearing to the reader at the same time as to Roderick Alleyn, her urbane and hawk-eyed sleuth. Above all, her books move at a furious pace, fuelled by her glee at the fantasies and follies of humankind.

SURFEIT OF LAMPREYS (1947)
The Lampreys are a large upper-class English family, devoted to one another and fond of private jokes, charades and a self-consciously eccentric approach to life. They are also broke. They invite grim, unsmiling Uncle Gabriel to their flat to borrow money from him – and he is murdered in the lift. Alleyn's task is not just to work out how the murder was done (and who dunit), but also to pick his way through the maze of false clues, red herrings and downright lies which the Lampreys amuse themselves by telling him.

Apart from those mentioned, Marsh's more than thirty books include Death in Ecstasy, Overture to Death, Death and the Dancing Footman, Colour Scheme, Spinsters in Jeopardy, Hand in Glove *and* Clutch of Constables.

READ ON ▷

- ● *Artists in Crime* (a model is murdered while posing in an art class); *Final Curtain* (grand old man of theatre dies in suspicious circumstances).
- ▶ to *Surfeit of Lampreys*: ▷ Margery Allingham, *The Beckoning Lady*.
- ▶ to the theatrical novels: ▷ Michael Innes, *Hamlet, Revenge!*; ▷ Caroline Graham, *Death of a Hollow Man*.

MARTELL, Dominic, see Sam REAVES

READ ON A THEME: **MEDIA**
(newspapers, magazines, publishing, the advertising business)

Colin Bateman, *Divorcing Jack*
▷ Lilian Jackson Braun, *The Cat Who Could Read Backwards*
Ruth Dudley Edwards, *Publish and Be Murdered*
Kenneth Fearing, *The Big Clock*
Lesley Grant-Adamson, *Wild Justice*
▷ Peter Guttridge, *No Laughing Matter*
Tim Heald, *Brought to Book*
▷ P. D. James, *Original Sin*
Meg O'Brien, *The Daphne Decisions*

▷ Dorothy L. Sayers, *Murder Must Advertise*
▷ Donald E. Westlake, *Trust Me on This*

READ ON A THEME: **MEDIEVAL MYSTERY**

▷ Paul Doherty, *The Assassin in the Greenwood*
  Umberto Eco, *The Name of the Rose*
  Elizabeth Eyre, *Death of a Duchess* (one of a series set in late medieval/
    Renaissance Italy)
▷ Michael Jecks, *The Last Templar*
  Margaret Frazer, *The Reeve's Tale*
  A. E. Marston, *The Wolves of Savernake*
  Ian Morson, *Falconer's Crusade* (the Falconer books are set in medieval Oxford)
▷ Ellis Peters, *A Morbid Taste for Bones*
▷ Candace Robb, *The Apothecary Rose*
▷ Kate Sedley, *The Brothers of Glastonbury*
  Peter Tremayne, *The Monk Who Vanished*

MELVILLE, James (born 1931)
British novelist

James Melville is the pseudonym of Roy Peter Martin. His Commissioner Otani is the Maigret of Hyogo Prefecture in Japan – a placid, middle-aged man, happily married, solving crimes not by melodrama and violence but by gentle, patient probing. For the non-Japanese reader, the books have plenty of exotic detail – a great deal of sushi is consumed by people sitting on tatami mats – but the main interest is in the characters of Otani himself, his wife Hanae and his inspectors, man-about-town Kimura and bovine-seeming Noguchi. The clash between cultures caused by foreigners visiting Japan is a theme in many books, for example *The Wages of Zen* (1979), about a murder in a monastery, and *Kimono for a Corpse* (1987), about extortion and murder in a high-fashion business.

The other Otani novels include The Ninth Netsuke, Death of a Daimyo, A Haiku for Hanae, The Bogus Buddha *and* The Body Wore Brocade.

READ ON ▷

▶ ▷ H. R. F. Keating, *Inspector Ghote Trusts the Heart*; Shizuko Natsuki, *Murder at Mt Fuji*; Sujata Massey, *The Salaryman's Wife*.

MELVILLE, Jennie, see Gwendoline BUTLER

MILLAR, Margaret (1915–1994)
Canadian novelist

Millar is best known for psychological crime stories, usually set in small communities and among close-knit families or ethnic groups. She was fascinated by the way crime exposes the raw nerves and guts of people's characters and spends less time solving the mystery (though that is done) than in detailing how each member of a group only begins to reveal his or her true nature once the deed is done. To this onion-skinning psychological investigation she added the pleasure of satire – although her books are serious, she was happy to send up her characters if their obsessions or behaviour ask for it.

SPIDER'S WEB (1986)

In a California court, Cully King is on trial for murder. The judge is eccentric, the district attorney is a domestic tyrant, the defence attorney has a crazy wife – and as for the witnesses . . . As the trial proceeds, Millar shows us each person's obsessions in turn – and brings both trial and story to a surprise conclusion, a twist within a twist, which not even Perry Mason could have stage-managed.

Millar's other books include Wall of Eyes, Beast in View, The Fiend, Beyond This Point Are Monsters, The Murder of Miranda *and* Mermaid.

> READ ON

▶ ▷ Celia Fremlin, *Dangerous Thoughts*; ▷ Minette Walters, *The Ice House*.

READ ON A THEME: **MINDSICK**

  John Franklin Bardin, *Devil Take the Blue-Tail Fly*
  Stanley Ellin, *Mirror, Mirror on the Wall*
▷ Patricia Highsmith, *The Talented Mr Ripley*
  Dorothy Hughes, *In a Lonely Place*
▷ Francis Iles, *Malice Aforethought*
  Helen McCloy, *Through a Glass Darkly*
▷ Georges Simenon, *The Hatter's Ghosts*

See also Serial Killers

MITCHELL, Gladys (1901–1983)
British novelist

One of Gladys Mitchell's many admirers was the poet Philip Larkin, who once described her in a review as 'the great Gladys'. For more than fifty years she produced her own idiosyncratic and quite unmistakable versions of the classic English detective novel. Her detective, Mrs (later Dame) Beatrice Adela Lestrange Bradley, 'a pterodactyl with a Cheshire Cat smile', is psychiatric adviser to the Home Office. She appears in dozens of novels, beginning with *Speedy Death* (1929). She is as near a witch as anyone can be without being arrested, and solves bizarre crimes, many of which involve ghosts, skeletons and dark doings in ancient British burial grounds. In many books, she is assisted by Laura Menzies, a galumphing, slang-spouting, jolly-hockey-sticks Scottish girl who is forever striding purposefully over wild moorland or stripping off her clothes to swim across fast-flowing rivers. Mitchell plants every clue fairly, so that you can solve the mystery ahead of Dame Beatrice, if you dare.

THE TWENTY-THIRD MAN (1957)

A popular tourist site, of twenty-three embalmed kings sitting round a table, becomes even more macabre when a twenty-fourth body joins them just as one of the guests at the hotel where Dame Beatrice is staying disappears. On holiday in Capri, Dame Beatrice investigates means, motive and opportunity for murder in one of the strangest cases even she has encountered.

Gladys Mitchell's novels under her own name include The Saltmarsh Murders, Death at the Opera, Hangman's Curfew, Laurels Are Poison, Sunset Over Soho, The Rising of the Moon, The Devil's Elbow, Spotted Hemlock, Death of a Delft Blue, Skeleton Island, Gory Dew, Convent on Styx, Nest of Vipers, The Whispering Knights, The Death-Cap Dancers *and* Here Lies Gloria Mundy. *In the 1930s Gladys Mitchell also wrote a few novels under the pseudonym of Stephen Hockaby and, in the 1960s, she published novels under the name Malcolm Torrie.*

READ ON ▷

- ● *The Rising of the Moon* **(a serial killer stalks the streets of Brentford in what Larkin called 'Gladys Mitchell's** *tour de force***').**
- ▶ **H. C. Bailey,** *Shadow on the Wall* **(Bailey wrote a series of short stories and novels in the 1930s and 1940s featuring Reggie Fortune, who encounters crimes almost as strange as those confronting Dame Beatrice);** ▷ **John Dickson Carr,** *Below Suspicion*; **Colin Watson,** *Coffin, Scarcely Used.*

MONTALBAN, Manuel Vazquez (born 1939)
Spanish novelist

In some of the best *noir* series, the city in which the action is set is almost as important as the central character. Usually the city is an American one. In Manuel Vazquez Montalban's enjoyable sequence of novels, the city is Barcelona. Montalban's hero is private detective Pepe Carvalho, a former member of the Spanish Communist Party, who finds himself regularly drawn into the sleaze, corruption and crime that beset his native city. Although an ex-Communist, Carvalho is a lover of the good life, fine food and wine, and beautiful women. The thrillers in which Montalban involves his likeable hero work on several levels – as clever and unusual variants on the classic private eye novel, as unpretentious and subtle accounts of Spain's transition from Franco's dictatorship to democracy, and as fictional portraits of an individual and the city he loves.

MURDER IN THE CENTRAL COMMITTEE (1984)

The lights suddenly go out during a meeting of the central committee of the Spanish Communist Party and, when the power is switched back on, the general secretary Fernando Garrido is found murdered. As an ex-communist himself Pepe Carvalho is the obvious choice to investigate the murder and its background of political intrigue and corruption. As long as he's allowed to do things his own way Pepe is happy to try to unearth the truth. He's even prepared to leave his beloved Barcelona and spend time in the uncongenial surroundings of Madrid.

The other Carvalho novels include The Angst-Ridden Executive, An Olympic Death, Off Side *and* Southern Seas.

MOSLEY, Walter (born 1952)
US novelist

Mosley, reportedly Bill Clinton's favourite author, has written a series of books featuring Ezekiel 'Easy' Rawlins, a black detective/fixer and his good friend, the entertaining, if psychopathically violent, Mouse. The first to be published was *Devil in a Blue Dress* (1990), filmed in 1995 with a Mosley screenplay and Denzel Washington as Easy Rawlins. This debut was followed by *A Red Death* (1991), *White Butterfly* (1992), *Black Betty* (1994) and *Little Yellow Dog* (1996). In 1997, *Gone Fishin'*, a kind of prequel to the series originally written (and rejected by publishers) in 1988, finally appeared. This seemed to bring the Easy Rawlins books to a close (ironically by going back to its beginning), but Mosley has returned to the character in *Bad Boy Brawly Brown* (2002). In the Easy Rawlins books Mosley has created both a series of refreshingly different and entertaining crime stories and a portrait of black experience in America from the 1940s to the 1960s. Rawlins moves from the teenager of *Gone Fishin'* to a war-scarred private eye operating amid the racial tensions and moral ambiguities of the big city.

Mosley's other books include *RL's Dream*, a non-crime novel in which an old blues guitarist reminisces about his meeting with Robert Johnson, king of the Delta blues singers and a man notorious for having sold his soul to the Devil (presumably *sans* any kind of dress) in return for unrivalled musical talent and fame. Two books feature Socrates Fortlow, a tough, wise ex-con, trying to go straight and having a tricky time of it – *Always Outnumbered, Always Outgunned*, the first Socrates collection, appeared in 1998 and the sequel, *Walkin' the Dog*, in 2000.

DEVIL IN A BLUE DRESS (1990)
Although all the Easy Rawlins books are memorable, *Devil in a Blue Dress* remains the best. A racial inversion of Raymond Chandler's classic *noir* novel *Farewell, My Lovely*, Mosley's tale sees a white man going into a Negro bar and enlisting the aid of a black man (Rawlins) to help find a missing white woman.

MULLER, Marcia (born 1944)
US novelist

Marcia Muller has been described so frequently as 'the founding mother' of the modern female private eye novel that it has become almost a cliché. But it is certainly true that many other women writers have paid tribute to her example and that the first Sharon McCone novel, *Edwin of the Iron Shoes* (1977), was one of the first to use a recognizably street-smart, emotionally complex contemporary woman as its heroine. In the quarter of a century since that début, Muller has continued to produce mysteries that are satisfyingly complex and Sharon McCone has continued to develop as a character. Most of the stories are set in San Francisco, where Muller's heroine has had to deal with terrorist bombers (*A Wild and Lonely Place*), dot.com entrepreneurs (*Dead Midnight*), sinister antiques dealers (*Leave a Message for Willie*) and dark secrets in the country music business (*The Broken Promise Land*). Muller has varied the setting by sending McCone to more exotic locations (a Caribbean island, Hawaii) but it is on the streets of San Francisco that she always has seemed most at home and where the best of the mysteries have been played out.

LISTEN TO THE SILENCE (2000)
Sharon McCone's most personal investigation is triggered by her father's death. He has specified that only Sharon must go through his papers and, in doing so, she learns of her own adoption. The discovery propels her into a search for her Native American birth family and into a mystery where old secrets and contemporary disputes over land and development rights collide.

The other Sharon McCone novels include Edwin of the Iron Shoes, The Shape of Dread, Pennies on a Dead Woman's Eyes, Till the Butchers Cut Him Down, A Wild and Lonely Place, The Broken Promise Land, While Other People Sleep, A Walk Through Fire *and* Point Deception.

READ ON

▶ ▷ Sara Paretsky, *Hard Time*; Dana Stabenow, *Blood Will Tell*; ▷ Sue Grafton, *C is for Corpse*.

READ ON A THEME: MUSIC
(mostly classical but with a touch of country and rock)

  Delano Ames, *Murder, Maestro Please*
  John Franklin Bardin, *Devil Take the Blue-Tail Fly*
▷ Robert Barnard, *Death and the Chaste Apprentice*
▷ Liza Cody, *Under Contract*
▷ Edmund Crispin, *Swan Song*
▷ Stella Duffy, *Beneath the Blonde*
▷ Cyril Hare, *When the Wind Blows*
▷ Marcia Muller, *The Broken Promise Land*
▷ Ellis Peters, *Black is the Colour of My True Love's Heart*

N

NABB, Magdalen (born 1947)
British novelist

Nabb, who is also a writer of children's books, has lived in Florence for many years and her crime fiction takes the reader behind the tourist façade to reveal the city's dark side. Her chief protagonist in most of her novels is the stolid Marshal Guarnaccia, a Sicilian who works for Florence's *carabinieri*. Guarnaccia is a shrewd and unpretentious investigator who solves his cases with a mixture of persistence and psychological acuity, and Nabb provides him with enough background and depth to make him a likeable and believable character.

THE MARSHAL AND THE MURDERER (1987)
An art student visiting the area around Florence is found murdered and Marshal Guarnaccia finds that what might seem a simple killing has roots that go back to deadly feuds begun in the Second World War. Nabb shows once again that, in Guarnaccia, she has created a downbeat but convincing detective who can almost rank with ▷ Simenon's Maigret and that her evocation of the grimmer realities of Florentine life makes for a very satisfying read.

The other Marshal Guarnaccia books are Death of an Englishman, Death of a Dutchman, Death in Springtime, Death in Autumn, The Marshal and the Madwoman, The Marshal's Own Case, The Marshal Makes His Report, The Marshal at the Villa Torrini, The Marshal and the Forgery *and* Property of Blood.

> READ ON

▶ ▷ Donna Leon, *A Venetian Reckoning*; Timothy Holme, *The Devil and the Dolce Vita*; ▷ Nicolas Freeling, *What Are the Bugles Blowing For?*

NADELSON, Reggie
US novelist

In her first novel, *Red Mercury Blues*, Reggie Nadelson seemed to have created a classic New York detective in her protagonist, Artie Cohen. Even if he was originally Artemy Maximovich Otalsky, son of a KGB hero, Artie has re-invented himself since he arrived in America as a teenager. The killing of a Russian general on live TV, however, takes him back to the Moscow of his youth. In further Cohen novels Nadelson has sent her New York Russian just as far afield. *Hot Poppies* has Artie investigating a murder in New York that eventually leads to Hong Kong and a gang of very bad guys whose criminal tentacles stretch around the world. The Cohen series so far consists only of four books but they are all well written and Artie, a descendant of Philip Marlowe operating in a world of international crime, is a memorable creation.

The other Artie Cohen books are Bloody London *and* Sex Dolls.

READ ON ▷

▶ ▷ Stuart M. Kaminsky, *Fall of a Cosmonaut*; Martin Cruz Smith, *Gorky Park*; Stuart Woods, *The Short Forever*.

NEEL, Janet (born 1940)
British novelist

Janet Neel has worked in the Department of Trade and Industry and all her books show an insider's knowledge of the byzantine workings of both government bureaucracy and the City, which greatly adds to the authority and authenticity of her plots. Her novels feature Francesca Wilson of the DTI and Detective Inspector John McLeish of the London CID and the stories usually centre on the territory where her investigations of financial shenanigans and skulduggery meet with his search for a murderer. The relationship between these two strong characters is one of the many pleasures of this series of well-written, well-plotted novels that show a shrewd understanding of the way individuals can be trapped and destroyed in the web of high finance and big business.

DEATH'S BRIGHT ANGEL (1988)
A senior executive in a Yorkshire fabrics firm is found murdered in London. His company is already under investigation by the DTI and by Francesca Wilson, who are concerned that the firm is in difficulties and jobs are at risk. Inspector McLeish is interested in whether or not the financial troubles of the company have anything to do with the murder and finds Francesca both help and hindrance. In Janet Neel's first crime novel the breezy, witty interaction of the two chief protagonists, one of the strengths of her books, is already in evidence.

Janet Neel's other Inspector McLeish and Francesca Wilson books are Death on Site, Death of a Partner, Death Among the Dons, A Timely Death, To Die For *and* O Gentle Death. *She has also written books (e.g.* The Highest Bidder*) under her real name of Janet Cohen.*

READ ON ▷

▶ ▷ Emma Lathen, *Double, Double, Oil and Trouble* (for a similar knowledge of the workings of high finance); Kate Ellis, *An Unhallowed Grave*.

READ ON A THEME: NEW YORK

  Caleb Carr, *The Alienist* (New York in the 1890s)
▷ Jeffery Deaver, *Rune*
▷ Kinky Friedman, *Greenwich Killing Time*
▷ Dashiell Hammett, *The Thin Man*
▷ Sparkle Hayter, *The Chelsea Girl Murders*
▷ Chester Himes, *A Rage in Harlem*

▷ Sandra Scoppettone, *Everything You Have is Mine*
Jonathan Lethem, *Motherless Brooklyn*
K. J. A. Wishnia, *Soft Money*

READ ON A THEME: NONESUCH
(one-offs, crime novels like no other)

Marc Behm, *The Eye of the Beholder*
Paul Cain, *Fast One* (classic pulp *noir* by mysterious *Black Mask* writer)
Helen Eustis, *The Horizontal Man*
Davis Grubb, *The Night of the Hunter*
William Hjorstberg, *Falling Angel*
Richard Hull, *The Murder of My Aunt* (blackly comic British crime novel from
   the 1930s)
Ted Lewis, *Jack's Return Home* (the book on which the Michael Caine film
   Get Carter was based)
Cameron McCabe, *The Face on the Cutting Room Floor*

O

O'CONNELL, Carol (born 1947)
US novelist

The maverick cop, unwilling to abide by the rules and customs that confine his colleagues, is one of the clichés of the genre and has been for many years. Over the last decade the figure of the female detective, unwilling to abide by the rules and customs imposed by a male-dominated world, has threatened also to become a rather stale and lazy piece of characterization. Carol O'Connell's character Mallory is a maverick female detective in the New York police force and yet she is anything but a cliché. Mallory – she dislikes first names because they're too personal – is a genuinely unsettling and original creation. Chillingly obsessive about her job, exceptionally intelligent and self-contained, she is more comfortable with computers than people and harbours dark secrets in her past. The plots of O'Connell's novels are offbeat and subtly contrived but what really fuels the tension in her books, and what the reader remembers of them, is the enigmatic personality of her chief character.

MALLORY'S ORACLE (1994)
As a child Mallory was saved from a life of crime and deprivation on the streets of New York by the intervention of a police officer called Louis Markovitz and his wife, who took her into their home. Now, while investigating a serial killer who targets the elderly, Markovitz has himself been killed. Mallory enters the case determined as only she can be on unearthing the truth and avenging the death of her mentor. To do so she has to enter dangerous realms in both the city and her own psyche.

O'Connell's other Mallory books are The Man Who Lied to Women, Killing Critics, Flight of the Stone Angel, Shell Game *and* Crime School. Judas Child *is a non-Mallory novel but equally gripping and intense in its account of a man's search for the truth about the killing of his sister.*

> READ ON

▶ Shirley Kennett, *Chameleon*; ▷ Kathy Reichs, *Déjà Dead*; Jan Burke, *Good Night, Irene*; Mary Willis Walker, *The Red Scream*.

READ ON A THEME: OTHER LANDS, OTHER CUSTOMS

Margot Arnold, *The Menehune Murders* (Hawaii)
Jon Cleary, *Five-Ring Circus* (Australia)
Dan Fesperman, *Lie in the Dark* (Bosnia)

Carolina Garcia-Aguilera, *Bitter Sugar* (Cuba and the Cuban community in Miami)
Peter Hoeg, *Miss Smilla's Feeling for Snow* (Greenland)
▷ H. R. F. Keating, *Inspector Ghote Caught in Meshes* (India)
▷ Henning Mankell, *Faceless Killers* (Sweden)
Alexander McCall Smith, *The No. 1 Ladies' Detective Agency* (Botswana)
James McClure, *The Steam Pig* (South Africa)
Karin McQuillan, *The Cheetah Case* (a Kenyan safari)
Sujata Massey, *The Salaryman's Wife* (Japan)
Arthur W. Upfield, *Man of Two Tribes* (Australia)

READ ON A THEME: OXBRIDGE

▷ Gwendoline Butler, *A Coffin for Pandora*
▷ Edmund Crispin, *The Case of the Gilded Fly*
Glyn Daniel, *The Cambridge Murders*
▷ Antonia Fraser, *Oxford Blood*
▷ Elizabeth George, *For the Sake of Elena*
Patricia Hall, *Skeleton at the Feast*
▷ Michael Innes, *Death at the President's Lodging*
Robert Robinson, *Landscape with Dead Dons*
▷ Dorothy L. Sayers, *Gaudy Night*
Jill Paton Walsh, *The Wyndham Case*

See also: Higher Education

P

PARETSKY, Sara (born 1947)
US novelist

Sara Paretsky's V.I. Warshawski was one of the first of a new generation of independent and spirited female detectives to appear in the genre in the 1980s and, although many more have followed, she remains among the best. Set in Chicago, the plots of the Warshawski novels pitch their heroine into murky worlds of drug-trafficking, union corruption, high finance, medical fraud and, of course, murder. All V.I. has to sustain her are her determination, her talents as a crack shot, her martial arts expertise and an armoury of bruisingly unanswerable one-liners. Over more than twenty years, Paretsky has been remarkably successful in developing the character, making V.I. more complex and believable and avoiding the pitfalls of cliché and dull repetition that have affected other long-running series.

TOTAL RECALL (2001)
Lotty Herschel, V.I.'s friend and mentor, has been an important and regularly recurring character in the novels and she is at the centre of this intricate and cleverly constructed narrative. A man named Paul Radbuka emerges from Lotty's troubled past, claiming that he knows her from the Nazi-threatened Europe that she left behind as a teenager. Is Radbuka who he claims to be? Why is Lotty afraid of him? In investigating these questions on behalf of her friend V.I. also finds that her current case of insurance fraud is leading back to the corruptions and conspiracies of wartime Europe.

The other Warshawski novels are Indemnity Only, Deadlock, Killing Orders, Bitter Medicine, Toxic Shock, Burn Marks, Guardian Angel, Tunnel Vision *and* Hard Time. V.I. for Short *is a collection of short stories.* Ghost Country *is a non-Warshawski title but is set in the sort of Chicago streets that V.I. knows so well.*

> READ ON

▶ ▷ **Sue Grafton, *A is for Alibi*; Virginia Lanier, *Death in Bloodhound Red*; Margaret Maron, *Bootlegger's Daughter*; ▷ Marcia Muller, *The Cheshire Cat's Eye*.**

PARKER, Robert B(rown) (born 1932)
US novelist

Many crime writers have been described as the heir to ▷ Raymond Chandler's mantle. Most are clearly not up to the job. Since the publication of his first Spenser novel Robert B. Parker has been regularly acclaimed as Chandler's modern successor and he has a better claim to the title than most. Spenser is as tough as Philip Marlowe, as unafraid of walking the mean streets and as much a master of the wisecrack. Boston stands in for Los Angeles but the extortionists, the beautiful women and the filthy rich, stewing in the corruption of their wealth, are just the same. It seems appropriate that it was Parker who was chosen to complete Chandler's last, unfinished Marlowe novel, *Poodle Springs*. Parker continues to publish Spenser novels but he has started two new series, one featuring an ex-alcoholic cop, Jesse Stone, who retreats from the big city in search of peace but finds that murder and crime follow him, and one featuring a female private eye in Boston, Sunny Randall.

The Spenser novels include The Godwulf Manuscript, The Judas Goat, Looking for Rachel Wallace, The Widening Gyre, Taming a Sea-Horse, Pale Kings and Princes, Paper Doll, Small Vices, Sudden Mischief, Hugger Mugger *and* Potshot. *The Jesse Stone novels are* Night Passage, Trouble in Paradise *and* Death in Paradise. *The Sunny Randall novels are* Family Honour *and* Perish Twice.

> READ ON >

▶ to the Spenser novels: ▷ Raymond Chandler, *Farewell, My Lovely*;
▷ Lawrence Sanders, *McNally's Luck*; Jeremiah Healy, *Invasion of Privacy*.
▶ to the Jesse Stone novels: ▷ Lawrence Block, *Even the Wicked*.

READ ON A THEME: PARTNERS IN CRIME
(detective teams)

▷ Agatha Christie, *N or M?* (Tommy and Tuppence Beresford)
▷ Dashiell Hammett, *The Thin Man* (Nick and Nora Charles)
▷ Faye Kellerman, *The Forgotten* (Pete Decker and Rina Lazarus)
▷ Dennis Lehane, *A Drink Before the War* (Patrick Kenzie and Angela Gennaro)
▷ Dorothy L. Sayers, *Busman's Honeymoon* (Lord Peter Wimsey and Harriet Vane)

PATTERSON, James (born 1947)
US novelist

James Patterson won the Edgar Award for his novel *The Thomas Berryman Number* in 1976 but it was not until he created the character of Alex Cross, a black police officer and psychological profiler in Washington DC, that he achieved bestseller status. Cross first appeared in *Along Came a Spider* in 1993 and has since featured in seven more fast-paced thrillers. Patterson is not always a subtle writer. His dialogue is often unconvincing and his characterization, apart from that of Cross himself, strays frequently towards the clichéd. What he does superbly – better than almost any other contemporary thriller writer – is draw the reader into the narrative and move him or her swiftly and compellingly through it. In a series of short, sharp chapters – like a Hollywood director cutting rapidly from one scene to another – Patterson drives the narrative forward and leaves us with no chance to take breath as it moves, with constantly surprising twists and turns, to its gripping conclusion.

VIOLETS ARE BLUE (2001)

Two joggers are found killed in a brutally ritualistic fashion. The killings appear to be the work of someone who is, or believes he is, a vampire. The case is not unique and Cross plunges into a bizarre underworld of vampiric role-players and cultists as he searches desperately for information that will prevent further killings. Meanwhile his adversary from the previous book, *Roses Are Red*, is still teasing and tormenting him.

The other Alex Cross novels are Along Came a Spider, Kiss the Girls, Jack and Jill, Cat and Mouse, Pop Goes the Weasel, Roses Are Red *and* Four Blind Mice. *The non-series books include* The Jericho Commandment, The Midnight Club, Hide and Seek, See How They Run, When the Wind Blows, 1st to Die *and* 2nd Chance.

READ ON

- *1st to Die* (first in a new Patterson series about a female homicide inspector in San Francisco).
- ▷ Jeffery Deaver, *The Coffin Dancer*; Stuart Woods, *New York Dead*; William Diehl, *Primal Fear*.

PEARCE, Michael (born 1933)
British novelist

Drawing on his knowledge of the Anglo-Egyptian world in which he grew up, Michael Pearce has written one of the most unusual and entertaining series of historical mysteries published in the last twenty years. Set in Egypt in the years just prior to the First World War, the series features Gareth Owen, head of Cairo's secret police and known as the Mamur Zapt. Religious and political tensions abound in the melting pot of Cairo and the Mamur Zapt needs all his wit and diplomacy to unravel the problems that land on his desk. Often very funny, the books also draw on the tangled and colourful history of colonial Egypt to great effect.

THE MINGRELIAN CONSPIRACY (1995)

A new protection racket is threatening the café owners of Cairo and the identity of the racketeers remains a mystery. The Mamur Zapt hears of links with the city's Mingrelian community and of a wider conspiracy which may be aimed at the forthcoming visit of a Russian Grand Duke. As in all his Mamur Zapt novels, Pearce combines arcane erudition – how many other crime novelists know much of the Mingrelians, a Muslim people from Central Asia? – with a swiftly moving plot and lively, funny dialogue.

The other Mamur Zapt novels include The Mamur Zapt and the Return of the Carpet, The Mamur Zapt and the Donkey-Vous, The Mamur Zapt and the Spoils of Egypt, Death of an Effendi, A Cold Touch of Ice *and* The Face in the Cemetery. *Pearce has also written two books featuring a young lawyer in Tsarist Russia –* Dimitri and the Milk-Drinkers *and* Dimitri and the One-Legged Lady.

READ ON

▷ Elizabeth Peters, *Lord of the Silent*; ▷ Laurie King, *O Jerusalem.*
See also Read on a Theme: Egypt.

PEARS, Iain (born 1955)
British novelist

An art historian and author of a much-acclaimed historical novel set in seventeenth-century England (*An Instance of the Fingerpost*), Iain Pears has also written an erudite and engaging series of crime novels set in the Italian art world. His hero is the English art dealer Jonathan Argyll, who works in conjunction with General Bottando of Rome's art theft squad and his glamorous assistant (and Argyll's girlfriend) Flavia di Stefano. The books deftly combine Pears's expert knowledge of art history with clever plotting and a wry, ironic sense of humour. In *Death and Restoration* (1996), a typical entrant in the series, thieves break into a monastery and steal only one painting – an icon of the Madonna that seems of little value compared with what they left behind. Argyll and Flavia investigate the crime and its connection with the murder in Rome of a French art dealer.

Pears's other crime novels are The Raphael Affair, The Titian Committee, The Last Judgement, The Bernini Bust, Giotto's Hand *and* The Immaculate Deception.

READ ON

▶ Arturo Perez-Reverte, *The Flanders Panel*; Aaron Elkins, *Loot*; John Malcolm, *Into the Vortex*; Derek Wilson, *The Borgia Chalice*; Jane Langton, *The Dante Game*.

PELECANOS, George (born 1957)
US novelist

In his first three novels George Pelecanos wrote about a ferociously hard-drinking Greek-American, Nick Stefanos, who drifts into private investigation and finds that he is almost as suited to it as he is to boozing. Set in Washington DC, the books are fine examples of the most up-to-date hard-boiled fiction – fast-paced, violent excursions into the sleazier corners of contemporary culture. He followed these up by turning his eye on the history of the Greek and Italian immigrant communities in the city, delving back into earlier generations of the Stefanos family and introducing two compelling characters in Dimitri Karras and Marcus Clay. Pelecanos's most recent novels feature a black P.I., Derek Strange, and a disgraced white cop, Terry Quinn, who form an unlikely and uneasy alliance when Strange is hired to investigate Quinn's possible involvement in the killing of a fellow cop. All of Pelecanos's fiction, whether set in past or present and whether featuring Stefanos or other protagonists, feels like one part of a larger, on-going project to chart the darker side of America's capital.

DOWN BY THE RIVER WHERE THE DEAD MEN GO (1995)
Part-time private eye and full-time drunk Nick Stefanos wakes from a massive bender to find himself sprawled in a public park and unwilling witness to a murder. His search for the truth behind what he has heard and seen leads him into the dark heart of the Washington drugs and porn industries. Pelecanos weaves sleaze, corruption and popular culture into a very Nineties take on the hard-boiled crime novel.

The two earlier Nick Stefanos novels are A Firing Offense *and* Nick's Trip. The Big Blowdown, King Suckerman, The Sweet Forever *and* Shame the Devil *feature Karras and Clay.* Right as Rain *and* Hell to Pay *feature Strange and Quinn.*

READ ON ▷

▶ ▷ Dennis Lehane, *A Drink Before the War*; ▷ Sam Reaves, *Bury It Deep*; ▷ Michael Connelly, *City of Bones*; ▷ James Ellroy, *Brown's Requiem*.

PENNAC, Daniel (born 1944)
French novelist

Daniel Pennac is the current king of French crime fiction and his series of weird and wonderful novels featuring the professional scapegoat Benjamin Malaussène (he is so disarming that he is employed to deflect complaints and take the blame for errors in a department store and, later, a publishing house) is just about as offbeat as the genre gets. The books are set in the melting-pot that is the multi-racial Parisian *quartier* of Belleville, and Malaussène's bizarre extended family usually has at least one member in conflict with, or flight from, the police, drugs gangs or both. Played largely as engaging farce, the novels also have an undertow of radical social commentary which is the more effective because it is so underplayed.

THE FAIRY GUNMOTHER (1997)
Someone is killing the grannies of Belleville. Half a dozen female pensioners have been found dead but now the grannies appear to be turning murderous themselves. A policeman is shot dead by the old dear he is shepherding across a busy street. Into this awkward situation stumble Malaussène and his journalist lover, Julie. Hindered and helped by a bewildering array of drugs dealers, OAPs, a Vietnamese plainclothes man and his own family, Malaussène tries to make sense of a nonsensical situation.

The other Malaussène novels translated into English are The Scapegoat, Write to Kill *and* Passion Fruit.

READ ON ▷

▶ Delacorta, *Diva*; ▷ Jakob Arjouni, *Happy Birthday, Turk.*

PERRY, Anne (born 1938)
British novelist

Anne Perry has long been one of the most reliably entertaining writers of historical mysteries set in Victorian England. She has produced two series. The longest-running series, which began with *The Cater Street Hangman* in 1979, features Inspector (later Superintendent) Thomas Pitt of Bow Street police station and his wife Charlotte. Her other series stars the saturnine private investigator William Monk, a man with secrets in his past which are slowly uncovered as the series progresses, and is set some decades earlier in the nineteenth century than the Pitt books. Both series are characterized by Perry's feel for historical detail and her sense of the complex society, so different from our own, in which the crimes take place.

THE HYDE PARK HEADSMAN (1995)

It is 1890 and Thomas Pitt, newly promoted to Superintendent, is facing difficulties in his work. Not only are there resentments and petty intrigues among his colleagues but, more importantly, the discovery of a headless body in a boat on the Serpentine suggests that there may be a lunatic killer at large. As similar gruesome murders occur the pressure is on for Pitt to catch the perpetrator.

The other Thomas Pitt novels include The Cater Street Hangman, Resurrection Row, Death in the Devil's Acre, Brunswick Gardens *and* Half Moon Street. *The William Monk books include* The Face of a Stranger, The Sins of the Wolf, Cain His Brother, The Silent Cry *and* The Twisted Root.

READ ON

▶ ▷ **Peter Lovesey, *Wobble to Death*; Emily Brightwell, *Mrs Jeffries and the Missing Alibi*; John Buxton Hilton, *The Quiet Stranger*; Alanna Knight, *The Coffin Lane Murders*; Gillian Linscott, *Absent Friends*.**
See also Read on a Theme: London.

PETERS, Elizabeth (born 1927)
US novelist

Elizabeth Peters is the crime-writing pseudonym of Barbara Mertz, who also publishes historical and supernatural stories as Barbara Michaels. Her crime books are romantic mysteries, strong on humour and parody, and often using her interest in history and archaeology. A good example is *Street of the Five Moons*, in which medieval art expert Vicky Bliss travels to Rome where she promptly becomes mixed up with forgers and falls in love. Peters's liveliest comedies (beginning with *Crocodile on the Sandbank* in 1975) feature the late Victorian/Edwardian archaeologist and feminist Amelia Peabody and her husband Radcliffe Emerson. In each book husband and wife leave their home comforts to dig in Egypt, usually accompanied by their hyper-intelligent brat of a son, Ramses. As soon as they arrive, a wonderfully bizarre supporting cast appears, cross-purposes abound and murder or mystery ensue. In later entries in the series Ramses, grown up and married himself, works for British intelligence, which leads to even more trouble amid the Egyptian ruins.

The other Peabody novels are The Curse of the Pharaohs, The Mummy Case, Lion in the Valley, The Deeds of the Disturber, The Last Camel Died at Noon, The Snake, the Crocodile and the Dog, The Hippopotamus Pool, The Ape Who Guards the Balance, Seeing a Large Cat, The Falcon at the Portal, He Shall Thunder in the Sky, Lord of the Silent *and* The Golden One. *Elizabeth Peters's non-Peabody books include* Borrower of the Night, Trojan Gold, Silhouette in Scarlet, The Seventh Sinner, Naked Once More, The Dead Sea Cipher *and* The Copenhagen Connection.

READ ON

▶ ▷ **Michael Pearce, *Death of an Effendi*; ▷ Charlotte MacLeod, *The Silver Ghost*; Carolyn Hart, *April Fool Dead*.**
See also Read on a Theme: Egypt.

PETERS, Ellis (1913–1995)
British novelist

Romantic and historical novelist Edith Pargeter used the pseudonym Ellis Peters to publish her crime fiction. There are two series. Much the most famous, thanks to the TV series starring Derek Jacobi, centres on the twelfth-century monk Brother Cadfael. Cadfael works in the herb garden of Shrewsbury Abbey (although he has had a more adventurous past as a soldier and crusader) and each novel in the series includes, as well as murder and romance, fascinating and convincing detail of medieval life. Cadfael is a well-rounded and sympathetic character and his friendship with Hugh Beringar, the sheriff of the county, is cleverly developed through the series. Ellis Peters's other series features the family of police officer George Felse.

ONE CORPSE TOO MANY (1979)
The year is 1138 and England is torn apart by the civil war between the opposing supporters of two of William the Conqueror's grandchildren (Stephen and Matilda), rivals for the throne. Shrewsbury is a stronghold for Matilda but Stephen's forces attack the castle there and ninety-four of Matilda's soldiers die. Cadfael has the unpleasant duty of preparing the dead for burial but discovers that there is an extra corpse – a victim of murder that has little to do with the war. Ellis Peters neatly combines history and mystery in one of the best of the Cadfael novels.

The other Cadfael novels are A Morbid Taste for Bones, Monk's Hood, St Peter's Fair, The Leper of St Giles, The Virgin in the Ice, The Sanctuary Sparrow, The Devil's Novice, Dead Man's Ransom, The Pilgrim of Hate, An Excellent Mystery, The Raven in the Foregate, The Rose Rent, The Hermit of Eyton Forest, The Confession of Brother Haluin, The Heretic's Apprentice, The Potter's Field, The Summer of the Danes, The Holy Thief *and* Brother Cadfael's Penance. A Rare Benedictine *is a collection of Cadfael short stories. The George Felse novels include* Death and the Joyful Woman, A Nice Derangement of Epitaphs, Mourning Raga, City of Gold and Shadows *and* Rainbow's End.

> READ ON

- *A Nice Derangement of Epitaphs* (mystery follows the Felse family on holiday to Cornwall as an ancient grave yields up not so ancient corpses).
- ▶ to the Cadfael novels: ▷ Paul Doherty, *Murder Wears a Cowl*; ▷ Michael Jecks, *The Boy-Bishop's Glovemaker*; Ian Morson, *Falconer and the Face of God*; ▷ Candace Robb, *The Apothecary Rose*; ▷ Kate Sedley, *Death and the Chapman*.
- ▶ to the George Felse novels: ▷ Catherine Aird, *Some Die Eloquent*.
See also Read on a Theme: Medieval Mystery.

POE, Edgar Allan (1809–1849)
US poet and short story writer

Poe's handful of crime stories (for example *The Murders in the Rue Morgue, The Case of the Purloined Letter* and *The Mystery of Marie Roget*) mark the point, most historians of the genre agree, where detective fiction begins. First published in the 1840s, they star the first amateur sleuth in fiction: Chevalier C. Auguste Dupin, a brilliant eccentric who solves mysteries by a blend of investigation and laser-like brain-power. The stories are narrated by a friend of Dupin, slower-witted, dogged and full of admiration. Poe may be more widely remembered today for his supernatural and horror stories but his crime tales have influenced detective writers from ▷ Doyle to ▷ Stout, from ▷ Allingham to ▷ Carr – and they still work their particular magic in the twenty-first century.

Poe's Dupin stories, with other tales such as The Gold Bug, *are collected in* Tales of Mystery and Imagination.

| READ ON ▷ |

▶ ▷ Arthur Conan Doyle, *The Adventures of Sherlock Holmes*; Michael Harrison, *Murder in the Rue Royale* (stories of Dupin by a twentieth-century crime writer); Emile Gaboriau, *Monsieur Lecoq* (novel by the nineteenth-century inventor of the *roman policier*).

READ ON A THEME: **POLICE PROCEDURALS (BRITISH)**

Jo Bannister, *Broken Lines*
Judith Cutler, *Hidden Power*
▷ Colin Dexter, *Last Bus to Woodstock*
▷ John Harvey, *Still Water*
▷ Reginald Hill, *Exit Lines*
▷ Bill James, *The Detective is Dead*
J. J. Marric (▷ John Creasey), *Gideon's Day* (classic 1950s police procedural)
▷ Ruth Rendell, *Wolf to the Slaughter*
▷ Peter Robinson, *Past Reason Hated*
R. D. Wingfield, *Hard Frost*

READ ON A THEME: **POLICE PROCEDURALS (AMERICAN)**

▷ Michael Connelly, *The Black Echo*
Linda Fairstein, *The Deadhouse*
W. E. B. Griffin, *Men in Blue*
Michael Jahn, *Murder in Central Park*
▷ Stuart M. Kaminsky, *Lieberman's Law*
▷ Ed McBain, *Hail, Hail, the Gang's All Here*
Christopher Newman, *Precinct Command*
Lawrence Treat, *V as in Victim* (1940s novel often claimed as the first American police procedural)
▷ Joseph Wambaugh, *Finnegan's Week*
Hillary Waugh, *Last Seen Wearing*

READ ON A THEME: **PRIVATE EYES**
(the American P.I. out on the mean streets)

▷ Raymond Chandler, *Farewell, My Lovely* (Philip Marlowe)
Max Allan Collins, *True Detective* (Nate Heller)

Howard Engel, *Dead and Buried* (Benny Cooperman)
▷ Loren D. Estleman, *A Smile on the Face of the Tiger* (Amos Walker)
G. M. Ford, *The Bum's Rush* (Leo Waterman)
Stephen Greenleaf, *Flesh Wounds* (John Marshall Tanner)
▷ Dashiell Hammett, *The Maltese Falcon* (Sam Spade)
▷ Ross Macdonald, *The Drowning Pool* (Lew Archer)
▷ Robert B. Parker, *The Godwulf Manuscript* (Spenser)
Jonathan Valin, *Missing* (Harry Stoner)

Q

QUEEN, Ellery
US novelist and short story writer

Ellery Queen was the pseudonym of two cousins, Frederic Dannay (1905–1982) and Manfred Lee (1905–1971). Ellery Queen is also the name of their detective. The cousins wrote novels, plays and short stories, and edited several crime fiction weekly and monthly magazines including the *Ellery Queen Mystery Magazine*. Their stories are brilliant potboilers. Characterization and style take second place to plot and to the careful planting of clues and red herrings, which distract the reader until the very last line. Typically, Ellery Queen's father, Inspector Richard Queen, is faced by an apparently insoluble mystery and calls on his son, the dandyish crime writer Ellery Queen, to help him find the guilty person. The formula was unvaried, except for locations and murder methods, for forty-five years and produced some of the most reliably intriguing brainteasers in the genre.

Queen's best novels were written before 1935 and after 1942 – in between the authors concentrated more on plays and on editing their magazine. 'Great' Queen novels include, from the earlier period, The Greek Coffin Mystery, The Dutch Shoe Mystery, The French Powder Mystery *and* The Four of Hearts *(set in a believable Hollywood) and, from the later period,* Calamity Town, Ten Days' Wonder, The Finishing Stroke *and* A Fine and Private Place. The Case Book of Ellery Queen *is a good collection of short stories. Under the name of Barnaby Ross, the authors wrote a series of linked books featuring the actor-detective Drury Lane: the first is* The Tragedy of X.

READ ON ▷

▶ ▷ John Dickson Carr, *The Hollow Man*; ▷ George Harmon Coxe, *Murder with Pictures*; ▷ S. S. Van Dine, *The Bishop Murder Case*.

R

RADLEY, Sheila (born 1928)
British novelist

Sheila Radley is the pseudonym of Sheila Robinson, who has also written non-fiction under her own name and gothic romances as Hester Rowan. Radley's detective stories are set in a small (and magnificently evoked) country town. The main characters, led by Chief Inspector Quantrill, recur from book to book, developing as the series proceeds. Quantrill solves his cases by a mixture of procedural routine and his knowledge of human nature but he is no super-sleuth and makes all-too-human mistakes. Radley excels at showing relationships between the sexes: a happy marriage, for example, in *Who Saw Him Die?* or Quantrill's infatuation for his (female) sergeant in *Fate Worse Than Death*.

Radley's other novels include Death and the Maiden, The Chief Inspector's Daughter, Blood on the Happy Highway *and* Cross My Heart and Hope to Die.

> **READ ON**

▶ ▷ **Ruth Rendell, *A Guilty Thing Surprised*; Jill McGown, *A Shred of Evidence*; ▷ W. J. Burley, *Wycliffe and the Dunes Mystery*.**

RANKIN, Ian (born 1960)
Scottish novelist

So successful has Ian Rankin been as a crime writer in the last decade that he has established a whole new sub-genre. According to one critic Rankin, whose novels are set in Edinburgh, is 'the king of tartan *noir*'. Certainly he has been successful in portraying an image of Edinburgh very different from the traditional one. He shows the skull beneath the skin of the tourist façade. He takes us away from the Royal Mile and Prince's Street and into a bleak and gritty Edinburgh of junkie squats, gangland wars and corruption in high places. Our guide through this other, darker Edinburgh is the central character in most of Rankin's novels, Detective Inspector John Rebus. Rebus, although he owes something to crime fiction clichés of the lone wolf investigator tormented by his own inner demons, is a genuinely original creation and has a complexity not often encountered in characters in genre fiction. From the first novel, *Knots and Crosses* (1987), Rebus has been as interesting as the cases he investigates and, as the series has progressed, Rankin has developed the character with great skill. He has also shown increasing ambition in the subjects he covers. In *Dead Souls* (1999) the plot accommodates the human consequences of a paedophile scandal in a children's home, the return of a killer from the States to his native Scotland,

Rebus's own return to his home town and the party-filled world of Edinburgh's *jeunesse dorée*. All the threads of the narrative are effortlessly woven into a satisfying whole. Rankin is not only one of the best contemporary crime novelists, he is also one of the best of modern Scottish novelists.

BLACK AND BLUE (1997)

Bible John was the name given by the media to a serial killer in the 1970s. He was never caught. Now a copycat killer is at work. Rebus, struggling with a drink problem and unsympathetic superiors, has been sidelined. But, as another investigation takes him from Glasgow ganglands to Aberdeen and an offshore oilrig, he is drawn into the web of intrigue and corruption that surrounds the search for the killer dubbed by the media (with characteristic inventiveness) Johnny Bible.

The other Rebus novels are Hide and Seek, Tooth and Nail, Strip Jack, The Black Book, Mortal Causes, Let It Bleed, Death is Not the End, The Hanging Garden, Set in Darkness, The Falls *and* Resurrection Men. A Good Hanging *is a collection of Rebus short stories* and Beggars Banquet *also includes some Rebus stories. Rankin has also written three novels (*Witch Hunt, Bleeding Hearts *and* Cold Blood*) under the pseudonym Jack Harvey.*

> READ ON ▷

- *The Hanging Garden* (one of Rankin's most complicated and rewarding plots, in which war criminals, gang warfare and the importation of prostitutes from eastern Europe all have a part to play).
- ▶ ▷ Reginald Hill, *On Beulah Height*; ▷ John Harvey, *Cutting Edge*;
- ▷ Quintin Jardine, *Skinner's Rules* (the first in a series of Edinburgh-set police procedurals); Denise Mina, *Garnethill*.
See also Read on a Theme: Scotland.

RAYMOND, Derek (1931–1994)
British novelist

Raymond is best known for the five Factory novels (*The Devil's Home on Leave, He Died With His Eyes Open, How the Dead Live, I Was Dora Suarez* and *Dead Man Upright*), set in the Department of Unexplained Deaths (a.k.a. A14). Working from an unnamed London police station is a nameless protagonist known only as the Detective Sergeant. These are among the most brutal and bleakest crime novels ever written by an English novelist and are certainly not for the even mildly squeamish. In *I Was Dora Suarez* the Detective Sergeant is after a psychopath who cuts off the heads of his victims and takes them home to 'watch' him perform a strange ritual of sexual mutilation. It is very difficult to précis the Factory novels without making them sound like exercises in the pornography of violence, which they are not. They are all characterized by Raymond's offbeat, almost poetic prose style and by a strange tenderness that lurks beneath the surface of the hardened, damaged Detective Sergeant. He is moved by the bleakly meaningless, and brutally curtailed, lives of the victims and aware of the grim realities of a society in which their violent, lonely deaths are possible. Raymond's novels are most definitely not to everybody's taste but they are undeniably powerful and unsettling.

READ ON >

▶ David Peace, *Nineteen Seventy Four* (first of a series set in Yorkshire at the time of the Ripper murders and just as bleak as Raymond's Factory novels); ▷ Mark Timlin, *Paint It Black*; Ken Beven, *London Boulevard*.

READ ON A THEME: **REAL CRIMES FICTIONALIZED**

Max Allan Collins, *Stolen Away* (the Lindbergh kidnapping case)
Judith Cook, *The Slicing Edge of Death* (murder of Christopher Marlowe)
Ann Dukthas (▷ Paul Doherty), *A Time for the Death of a King* (the murder of Lord Darnley)
▷ James Ellroy, *The Black Dahlia* (the 1940s Black Dahlia murder)
Robert Graves, *They Hanged My Saintly Billy* (William Palmer poisoning case)
F. Tennyson Jesse, *A Pin to See the Peepshow* (Thompson/Bywaters murder case)
Meyer Levin, *Compulsion* (the Leopold/Loeb murder case)
▷ Josephine Tey, *The Daughter of Time* (Princes in the Tower)

REAVES, Sam (born 1954)
US novelist

In the early 1990s, Reaves published four tough thrillers, all set in the windy city of Chicago and featuring Vietnam veteran Cooper MacLeish, a cab-driving private eye. *A Long Cold Fall* saw Cooper investigating the suspicious death of an old flame, a woman with whom, unbeknown to him, he fathered a son. Witty, even charming, Cooper is also capable of immense courage and a kind of single-minded strength. There are scenes in this novel that are extremely violent, but in a realistic and down-to-earth way, displaying none of the cartoon brutality beloved of so many more celebrated authors. The three other novels, *Fear Will Do It*, *Bury It Deep* and *Get What's Coming*, are just as impressive, with Cooper marrying his girlfriend Diana and progressing from cabbying to being a chauffeur. Whatever or whoever he's driving, trouble, usually murder, always seems to be along for the ride.

Reaves has also produced three fine political thrillers, *Lying Crying Dying*, *The Republic of Night* and *Gitana*, all written under the name of Dominic Martell. Set in a superbly realized Barcelona – like Harry Lime's Vienna, all twisting side streets and treacherously dark alleys – the novels feature a very charismatic hero called Pascual, a former terrorist turned informer, trying to lead a quiet life as a translator. Always, his violent and dangerous past catches up with him and he is flushed from his simple existence, forced out into a world of danger where, invariably, only the past tense is spoken.

READ ON >

▶ to the Cooper MacLeish novels: ▷ Robert Campbell, *The Junkyard Dog*; David L. Walker, *Applaud the Hollow Ghost*.
▶ to his books as Dominic Martell: ▷ Manuel Vazquez Montalban, *An Olympic Death*; David Serafin, *Madrid Underground*.

REICHS, Kathy (born 1950)
US novelist

The forensic thriller has been one of the thriving sub-genres of crime fiction in the last ten years and Kathy Reichs, in her novels featuring Dr Temperance Brennan, has proved one of its best exponents. In some writers of these novels the expertise (or the research) can seem a little intrusive. In Reichs's books all the technical details of Brennan's investigations – the blood spatter patterns, the bone sample analysis, the skeletal reconstruction and so on – serve to move the narrative forward to a final solution: she succeeds in marrying the science with the story. And Tempe Brennan – bright, dedicated and compassionate – makes an attractive heroine.

DEJA DEAD (1997)
The first of the Temperance Brennan books set the pattern for the ones that have followed. When the bones of a woman are discovered in the grounds of an abandoned monastery in Montreal, the remains are too decomposed for a standard autopsy. Dr Brennan's expertise as director of forensic anthropology is required. Brennan decides that the woman is the victim of a serial killer but the detective in charge of the case is unconvinced. Brennan chooses to take matters into her own hands but the killer is aware that she is on to something.

Déjà Dead *has been followed by* Death du Jour, Deadly Decisions, Fatal Voyage *and* Grave Secrets, *all featuring Temperance Brennan.*

READ ON ▷

▶ ▷ Patricia Cornwell, *Postmortem*; Lisa Gardner, *The Next Accident*; Tess Gerritsen, *The Surgeon*; Beverly Connor, *Dressed to Die* (one of a series featuring a forensic archaeologist from the University of Georgia).

REID, Matthew, see Quintin JARDINE

READ ON A THEME: RELIGIOUS SLEUTHS

▷ G. K. Chesterton, *The Innocence of Father Brown*
Umberto Eco, *The Name of the Rose* (Brother William of Baskerville)
Andrew Greeley, *The Bishop in the West Wing* (Father Blackie Ryan)
▷ Harry Kemelman, *Friday the Rabbi Slept Late* (Rabbi Small)
William X. Kienzle, *The Rosary Murders* (Father Koesler, a Catholic priest in Illinois)
Arturo Perez-Reverte, *The Seville Communion* (Father Lorenzo Quart)
▷ Ellis Peters, *A Morbid Taste for Bones* (Brother Cadfael)
Peter Tremayne, *Hemlock at Vespers* (Sister Fidelma)

RENDELL, Ruth (born 1930)
British novelist

Rendell, one of the finest and most imaginative of contemporary crime novelists, writes books of three entirely different kinds. Her Chief Inspector Wexford novels are atmospheric police procedurals set largely in the imaginary Sussex town of Kingsmarkham and the leafy countryside and picturesque villages surrounding it. The stories depend greatly on the character of Wexford himself, a liberal and cultured man appalled at the psychological pressures which drive people to crime. Those pressures are the subject of Rendell's non-Wexford novels. They are stories of inadequacy, obsession and paranoia, told in a matter-of-fact style which enhances the unsettling effect of what Rendell has to say.

The novels published under the name Barbara Vine also show how remorse-less psychological pressure leads to mental collapse and crime. They often concentrate on the intricate relationships between groups of people – families, neighbours, friends – or analyse, with gripping intensity, the ways in which the past re-surfaces to haunt the present. In *The Brimstone Wedding*, for example, a carer at an old people's home gradually learns more about the past life of one of its inhabitants and how a doomed relationship in that past eerily foreshadowed her own experiences.

THE KEYS TO THE STREET (1996)

This is a typically complex and intelligent non-Wexford book in which Rendell weaves a series of narratives around the central character of Mary Jago and introduces a selection of lost souls with whom she comes into contact. The stories are centred on Regent's Park where a killer is targeting the homeless and impaling them on the park gates. As Mary is drawn into the search for the killer, her comfortable world is shaken to its core.

The Wexford novels include From Doon With Death, Wolf to the Slaughter, A Guilty Thing Surprised, Shake Hands Forever, The Speaker of Mandarin, An Unkindness of Ravens, Kissing the Gunner's Daughter, Road Rage *and* Harm Done. *The non-Wexford crime novels include* To Fear a Painted Devil, A Demon in my View, A Judgement in Stone, Master of the Moor, Live Flesh, Talking to Strange Men, Going Wrong, The Keys to the Street, A Sight for Sore Eyes *and* Adam and Eve and Pinch Me. *The Barbara Vine novels are* A Dark-Adapted Eye, A Fatal Inversion, The House of Stairs, Gallowglass, King Solomon's Carpet, Asta's Book, No Night is Too Long, The Brimstone Wedding, The Chimney Sweeper's Boy, Grasshopper *and* The Blood Doctor.

READ ON ▷

● *The Face of Trespass* (a writer in love with a rich woman resists her urgings to kill her husband and is driven to distraction and the extremes of experience).
▶ to the Wexford novels: ▷ Reginald Hill, *Deadheads*; ▷ Colin Dexter, *Last Seen Wearing*.
▶ to the psychological crime novels: Alison Taylor, *Child's Play*; Celia Dale, *Sheep's Clothing*.
▶ to the Barbara Vine novels: ▷ P. D. James, *Innocent Blood*; ▷ Minette Walters, *The Sculptress*.

RIPLEY, Mike (born 1952)
British novelist

▷ Val McDermid once wrote: 'If laughter is the best medicine, Mike Ripley's Angel novels should be on National Health prescription.' Certainly the stories of

Roy Angel, making his way through the dodgier areas of London life, are full of cherishable one-liners and comic set-pieces but they do have a harder edge to them as well. They are also full of a rueful acknowledgement of urban decay and an impatience with the cant that politicians and those who know what's best for us always use when prescribing solutions to London's problems. Ripley also manages a nice balance between comedy and a convincing unfolding of the thriller elements in the plot.

The Angel novels include Angel Touch, Angel in Arms, Angel Confidential, Angel City, Family of Angels, That Angel Look, Lights, Camera, Angel *and* Angel Underground.

READ ON ▷

▶ ▷ Peter Guttridge, *No Laughing Matter*; ▷ Lauren Henderson, *The Black Rubber Dress.*

READ ON A THEME: **RIVALS OF SHERLOCK HOLMES**

▷ Ernest Bramah, *Max Carrados*
▷ G. K. Chesterton, *The Innocence of Father Brown*
  R. Austin Freeman, *Dr Thorndyke's Casebook*
  Jacques Futrelle, *The Thinking Machine*
  Arthur Morrison, *The Chronicles of Martin Hewitt*
  Baroness Orczy, *The Old Man in the Corner*
▷ Edgar Wallace, *The Mind of Mr J. G. Reeder*

ROBB, Candace (born 1950)
US novelist

Since the remarkable success of ▷ Ellis Peters's Cadfael novels, the band of medieval sleuths has expanded rapidly. Candace Robb has created one of the most engaging in Owen Archer, a Welshman who works as spy and detective for the Archbishop in fourteenth-century York. As well as a likeable central character, the series has two great strengths. One is its setting. Robb brings medieval York back to life in convincing detail. The other is Robb's awareness that men and women of the period are not just you and me in fancy dress. She works hard to reconstruct a society based on very different assumptions about man and his place in the world than those of the present day. And the crimes Owen investigates have their place in that very different world.

THE APOTHECARY ROSE (1993)
A series of mysterious deaths in York persuades the Lord Chancellor to send Owen Archer to discover what's happening. Apprenticed to the Master Apothecary, Nicholas Wilton, as a cover for his investigations, Archer finds himself attracted to Wilton's beautiful wife Lucie and drawn into a complicated web of intrigue. Fans of Ellis Peters may notice some obvious similarities – Welsh hero, medieval cathedral town setting, herbalism – between Robb's first book and the Cadfael series but Robb is good enough to withstand the comparison.

The other Owen Archer novels are The Lady Chapel, The Nun's Tale, The King's Bishop, The Riddle of St Leonard's, A Gift of Sanctuary, A Spy for the Redeemer *and* The Cross-Legged Knight. A Trust Betrayed *is the first in a planned series featuring a female detective in medieval Scotland.*

READ ON >

▶ **Peter Tremayne,** *Absolution by Murder***;** ▷ **Paul Doherty,** *The Demon Archer***;** ▷ **Ellis Peters,** *One Corpse Too Many***; Alys Clare,** *Ashes of the Elements***.**
See also Read on a Theme: Medieval Mystery.

ROBINSON, Peter (born 1950)
British novelist

Since the publication of *Gallows View* in 1987, Peter Robinson has written a series of books featuring Inspector Alan Banks, all set in the Yorkshire Dales and all combining the charm of old-fashioned English mysteries (the largely rural setting is brilliantly evoked) with a very contemporary concern with the realities of violence, desire and greed. As the series has progressed Robinson's ambition and confidence have grown and the books are now among the most satisfying of all British police procedurals. Banks himself is a well-rounded character – decent and caring but sometimes oblivious of the effects of his job on his personal relationships – and the supporting cast (D.C. Susan Gay, the career-minded Chief Constable Jeremiah 'Jimmy' Riddle, Banks's wife Sandra) is well drawn. The plots, which often move between past and present, are complex but unfold smoothly towards convincing resolutions.

IN A DRY SEASON (1999)
The village of Hobb's End has been hidden beneath a reservoir for forty years. In the drought caused by an unusually hot summer, a secret from Hobb's End's history emerges in the shape of a human skeleton. Banks, in his chief constable's bad books, is sent by Riddle to head up what is assumed to be a dead-end investigation. Slowly Banks, aided by the unusually intelligent and attractive Detective Sergeant Annie Cabbott, edges towards the truth about a death in the past that is still affecting the present.

The other Inspector Banks novels are A Dedicated Man, A Necessary End, The Hanging Valley, Past Reason Hated, Wednesday's Child, Final Account, Innocent Graves, Dead Right, Cold is the Grave, Dry Bones That Dream *and* Aftermath.

READ ON >

▶ **Patricia Hall,** *In the Bleak Midwinter***; Barry Maitland,** *Silvermeadow***; Peter Turnbull,** *After the Flood***; Stephen Booth,** *Black Dog***.**

READ ON A THEME: ROME (MOSTLY ANCIENT)
    Kenneth Benton, *Death on the Appian Way*
    Ron Burns, *Roman Nights*
    Camilla Crespi, *The Trouble With Going Home*
▷ **Lindsey Davis,** *Three Hands in the Fountain*

▷ Michael Dibdin, *Cabal*
▷ Ngaio Marsh, *When in Rome*
▷ Steven Saylor, *Roman Blood*
  Marilyn Todd, *I, Claudia*
  David Wishart, *White Murder*

ROSS, Barnaby, see Ellery QUEEN

ROSS, Kate (1956–1998)
US novelist

The early death of Kate Ross brought to a sad and abrupt end a most entertaining and unusual series of historical mysteries. Set in the Regency, a period not as overpopulated by fictional detectives as some others, the books feature a society dandy called Julian Kestrel. This likeable Beau Brummell-like figure is drawn into investigating murder and mystery in high and low society in 1820s London (and, in the last book, *The Devil in Music*, in a disunited Italy of operatic plots and conspiracies). The Kestrel books are well plotted and researched and Ross wrote with a good deal of wit and charm. Because of her early death there are only four titles in the series but they are all well worth reading.

CUT TO THE QUICK (1993)
The book which introduced Kestrel and his ex-pickpocket valet, Dipper, *Cut to the Quick* shows how the dandy was first obliged, in self-defence, to turn his attention from his impeccable wardrobe to the investigation of crime. After rescuing a young man from a gaming hall, Kestrel is invited to stay at his estate and be best man at his wedding. Kestrel accepts but, no sooner do he and Dipper arrive at the country house than the body of an unknown young woman is discovered. The two newcomers are immediately suspected of murder and Kestrel must use his wits to find the true killer.

The other Julian Kestrel novels are Whom the Gods Love, A Broken Vessel *and* The Devil in Music.

READ ON ▷

▶ Bruce Alexander, *Murder in Grub Street*; Rosemary Stevens, *The Bloodied Cravat* (one of a series with Beau Brummell as detective); Stephanie Barron, *Jane and the Genius of the Place* (Jane Austen as detective).

S

SALLIS, James (born 1944)
US novelist

James Sallis began his writing career by publishing science fiction short stories in the 1960s, and he has always shown an interest in taking the conventions of genre fiction and pushing them beyond their limits. Nowhere is this more in evidence than in his Lew Griffin novels. The books bear some resemblance to ▷ Walter Mosley's Easy Rawlins novels, in that they follow a black character through several decades of American history, and they share with the work of several writers an interest in the dark vibrancy of New Orleans as a setting for crime fiction. Yet, ultimately, they defy comparison with other crime fiction. The books are self-consciously – sometimes too self-consciously – experimental, playing games with readers' expectations of the crime novels, subverting traditional notions of narrative and the reliability of the narrator. Those who like their crime fiction to start at the beginning and work logically through to the end will find Sallis's work infuriating but anyone with an interest in how the genre can be stretched and re-formulated will enjoy his challenging version of *noir*.

THE LONG-LEGGED FLY (1992)
Spanning nearly thirty years in the life of its protagonist, a black New Orleans private eye, the first of Sallis's Lew Griffin books is a daring exercise in literary experimentation in the shape of a crime novel. Four disappearances across the decades, and Griffin's investigations of them, provide the plot but Sallis's interest lies in character – the unfolding character of Griffin – and questions of identity and selfhood rather than the conventional working out of a mystery. Using the conventions of the genre for quite different purposes, Sallis produces a memorable and poetic book.

The other Lew Griffin novels are Moth, Black Hornet, Eye of the Cricket, Bluebottle *and* Ghost of a Flea. *Sallis has written a biography of* ▷ Chester Himes *and* Difficult Lives, *a study of pulp/noir writers of the 1940s and 1950s.*

> **READ ON** ▷

▶ James Lee Burke, *The Neon Rain* (for another take on New Orleans); ▷ Chester Himes, *A Rage in Harlem*; ▷ Walter Mosley, *Devil in a Blue Dress*; Jerome Charyn, *The Isaac Quartet*.

SANDERS, Lawrence (1920–1998)
US novelist

Sanders was a prolific writer of crime and suspense fiction who created several series characters. Edward X. Delaney, who appears in four books, all of which have the words 'Deadly Sin' in the title, is a retired cop who investigates crimes which have their origin in one of the seven deadly sins. The books are inventive and ingenious and a nice mix of the procedural and the private eye style. It is a pity that Sanders abandoned the series when he still had three sins remaining. Much the most entertaining, and best known, of Sanders's creations is the scapegrace playboy and private investigator Archie McNally. Set largely among the moneyed set of Palm Beach, the McNally books are amiable, funny mysteries in which the hero saunters nonchalantly through an unlikely plot, usually with a beautiful girl on his arm.

The McNally books written by Sanders are McNally's Secret, McNally's Luck, McNally's Risk, McNally's Caper, McNally's Trial, McNally's Puzzle *and* McNally's Gamble. *Since Sanders's death other titles have appeared, written by Vincent Lardo.*

> **READ ON** ▷

▶ ▷ Lawrence Block, *The Burglar Who Thought He Was Bogart*; ▷ Robert B. Parker, *Looking for Rachel Wallace*; ▷ Donald Westlake, *Bad News*.

SAYERS, Dorothy L(eigh) (1893–1957)
British novelist

Sayers's detective, Lord Peter Wimsey, is one of the giants of the genre, a creation to match Holmes himself. Sayers's plots are masterly and all her settings (from Oxford college to East Anglian village, from London advertising agency to the House of Lords) are painstakingly researched. Sometimes her 1930s social attitudes grate – a snobbishness that is always somewhere in the background, in particular – but her stories are ingenious, her characters are fascinating and her planting of clues is scrupulously fair. Some readers prefer the books in which Wimsey courts and marries Harriet Vane (a crime writer not unlike Sayers herself); others prefer the non-Vane books, uncluttered with arch or witty repartee.

THE NINE TAILORS (1934)
The story effortlessly blends such disparate ingredients as country working-class morality, a flood, an unworldly vicar, an emerald necklace, a peal of bells and skulduggery in northern France. Wimsey is on peak form, and the book has a wonderfully old-fashioned English atmosphere, compounded of wintry weather, fen countryside and the brooding churchyard and ancient bells of Fenchurch St Paul.

Sayers's books including Harriet Vane are Strong Poison, Gaudy Night, Have His Carcase *and* Busman's Honeymoon. *The non-Vane Wimsey books are* Whose Body?, Clouds of Witness, Unnatural Death, The Unpleasantness at the Bellona Club, The Five Red Herrings, Murder Must Advertise *and* The Nine Tailors. Lord Peter Views the Body *and* Hangman's Holiday *are short story collections.*

READ ON >

- *Murder Must Advertise* (Wimsey goes undercover at an advertising agency to investigate a killing in a story largely set in a world Sayers herself knew very well).
- ▷ Ngaio Marsh, *Enter a Murderer*; ▷ Margery Allingham, *Police at the Funeral*; ▷ E. C. Bentley, *Trent's Last Case*; H. C. Bailey, *The Bishop's Crime* (Bailey's hero, Dr Reggie Fortune, has some similarities to Wimsey).

SAYLOR, Steven (born 1956)
US novelist

Very few of the many series of historical mysteries that have appeared over the last thirty years have the unmistakable authority of Steven Saylor's books set in the last decades of the Roman Republic. Where other writers have a rather stagey sense of their historical settings, Saylor's descriptions – based on wide-ranging research – of the sights, smells and sounds of the crowded streets of ancient Rome carry immediate conviction. His central character, Gordianus the Finder ('the last honest man in Rome', as another character calls him), is a tough, unsentimental but sympathetic hero and we see him ageing and maturing as the series progresses and the dangerous politics of the period swirl around him, occasionally sweeping him up in conspiracy and murder. The real history of the dying days of the Roman Republic and the fictional narratives of Gordianus's casebook are brilliantly entwined.

ROMAN BLOOD (1991)
Based on a real case involving the Roman orator and politician Cicero, the first in the Gordianus series showed immediately Saylor's talent for blending real history with fictional mystery. The up-and-coming Cicero hires Gordianus to investigate the background to a murder case in which he is defending a man charged with killing his father. As Gordianus digs deeper, he finds that the case goes to the very heart of the political corruption and infighting in the Republic.

The other Gordianus the Finder books, best read in this order, are The House of the Vestals *(short stories),* Arms of Nemesis, Catalina's Riddle, The Venus Throw, A Murder on the Appian Way, Rubicon, Last Seen in Massilia *and* A Mist of Prophecies. A Twist at the End/Honour the Dead *is a novel set in late nineteenth-century Texas with the short story writer O. Henry as chief protagonist.*

READ ON >

▷ Lindsey Davis, *The Iron Hand of Mars*; Ron Burns, *Roman Nights*; Joan O'Hagan, *A Roman Death*.

READ ON A THEME: SCHOOLS
▷ Robert Barnard, *School for Murder*
▷ Nicholas Blake, *A Question of Proof*
▷ Elizabeth George, *Well-Schooled in Murder*
   Carolyn G. Hart, *The Rich Die Young*

▷ Val McDermid, *Report for Murder*
Jill McGown, *Death of a Dancer*
Jill Staynes & Margaret Storey, *A Knife at the Opera*

SCOPPETTONE, Sandra (born 1936)
US novelist

Sandra Scoppettone had been a writer for many years and had published, under a pseudonym, a number of well-received crime books before creating her best and most vivid character, the lesbian private eye Lauren Laurano, in 1991. Set in New York – largely Greenwich Village – the books not only succeed as mysteries but provide a likeable and engaging portrait of Lauren, her psychotherapist lover Kip and the circle of friends in which they move. Often it is from these friends that the mystery emerges. In *I'll Be Leaving You Always*, for example, the killing of one of her oldest friends in a jewellery heist leads Lauren to an investigation in which she realizes that she knew little about her friend's real self and true past. In *Let's Face the Music and Die*, a friend is suspected of the murder of an elderly relative from whom she stands to gain a large inheritance and it is up to Lauren to prove her innocence. The plots are not outstandingly original but the books show much wit in the writing and strength in the characterization, particularly that of the savvy, hip and up-to-date Lauren Laurano.

The other Lauren Laurano novels are Everything You Have is Mine, My Sweet Untraceable You *and* Gonna Take a Homicidal Journey. *In the 1980s, Scoppettone wrote several novels (e.g.* A Creative Kind of Killer *and* Razzamatazz*) under the name Jack Early.*

> READ ON ▷

▶ Elizabeth Pincus, *The Two-Bit Tango*; Jean M. Redmann, *Death by the Riverside*; Katherine V. Forrest, *The Beverley Malibu.*

READ ON A THEME: SCOTLAND

Margot Arnold, *Lament for a Lady Laird*
M. C. Beaton, *Death of a Snob*
▷ Antonia Fraser, *The Wild Island*
▷ Quintin Jardine, *Skinner's Rules*
Frederic Lindsay, *Kissing Judas*
▷ William McIlvanney, *Laidlaw*
Denise Mina, *Garnethill*
▷ Ian Rankin, *The Hanging Garden*

READ ON A THEME: SCOTLAND YARD

Rennie Airth, *River of Darkness*
▷ Robert Barnard, *Sheer Torture*
▷ John Creasey, *Inspector West at Home*

▷ Deborah Crombie, *Kissed a Sad Goodbye*
   Georgette Heyer, *They Found Him Dead*
   John Lawton, *Black Out*
▷ Ngaio Marsh, *Surfeit of Lampreys*
   Charles Todd, *Wings of Fire*

SEDLEY, Kate (born 1926)
British novelist

The chaos and conflicting loyalties of the Wars of the Roses is a good period in which to set a series of mystery novels, and Kate Sedley makes the most of the historical possibilities in her books about Roger the Chapman, a travelling pedlar who has a gift for stumbling into plots of murder and mayhem. Told by Roger himself, the books are filled with the detail of medieval life and are also cleverly plotted mysteries of a very traditional kind. Flitting through a number of the books is the enigmatic figure of the Duke of Gloucester, later to be the reviled Richard III.

DEATH AND THE CHAPMAN (1991)
In the first of the series, Roger leaves his comfortable place in a Benedictine monastery to embark on his career as a chapman (a wandering pedlar) and soon learns of a man's mysterious disappearance from a London inn. Later in his wanderings he finds evidence of other disappearances from the same inn. Are they connected and what can he do to solve the mystery?

Kate Sedley's other novels are The Plymouth Cloak, The Hanged Man, The Holy Innocents, The Eve of St Hyacinth, The Wicked Winter, The Brothers of Glastonbury, The Weaver's Inheritance, St John's Fern, The Goldsmith's Daughter *and* The Lammas Feast.

READ ON ▷

▶ Margaret Frazer, *The Novice's Tale*; Paul Harding (▷ Paul Doherty), *The Assassin's Riddle*; ▷ Michael Jecks, *The Last Templar*.

READ ON A THEME: SERIAL KILLERS
(not for the squeamish)

   Edna Buchanan, *Garden of Evil*
▷ Michael Connelly, *The Poet*
▷ Jeffery Deaver, *The Bone Collector*
   Tess Gerritsen, *The Surgeon*
   Thomas Harris, *The Silence of the Lambs*
   Mo Hayder, *Birdman*
▷ Val McDermid, *The Mermaids Singing*
▷ James Patterson, *Kiss the Girls*
▷ Kathy Reichs, *Déjà Dead*
   John Sandford, *Silent Prey*

See also: Mindsick

SHAMES, Laurence (born 1952)
US novelist

Florida is one of the most popular settings for contemporary American crime fiction, especially crime fiction with a comic edge to it. As a glance at Read on a Theme: Florida Crimes will show, there is something about the Sunshine State which brings out the wildest flights of farcical fantasy in those writers who choose to place their novels there. Laurence Shames is no exception. Set in Key West, his novels often feature Mafiosi from colder northern climes who are trying to leave their pasts behind them and embrace a new life of sun, sea and serenity. Unsurprisingly, their pasts tend to catch up with them. His plots are self-consciously skewed towards the farcical, his dialogue owes more, one suspects, to the movies than to gritty realism, and his characters are as eccentrically endearing as they are threatening. The result is a sequence of enjoyable, fast-paced entertainments.

SUNBURN (1995)
Joey Goldman has family troubles in plenty. His father, the last great Mafia godfather, has migrated south to join him in Florida and decided to tell his life story to a reporter. When they hear about the project, the New York mob are unimpressed by the idea and decide to do something about it. Also drawn to the sunshine is Joey's half-brother Gino – and where Gino goes, chaos follows. Joey's life is about to turn upside down.

Laurence Shames's other novels include Florida Straits, Scavenger Reef, Tropical Depression, Virgin Heat, Mangrove Squeeze, Welcome to Paradise *and* The Last Detective.

> READ ON

▶ ▷ **Carl Hiaasen,** *Tourist Season*; ▷ **Elmore Leonard,** *Pronto*; ▷ **Donald Westlake,** *Drowned Hopes.*

SIMENON, Georges (1903–1989)
Belgian novelist

Simenon is best known for his many crime stories featuring pipe-smoking, calvados-drinking Commissaire Maigret of the Paris police. The books are short, spare and dense with local atmosphere. They concentrate on Maigret's investigations in bars, lodging houses and rain-soaked Paris streets, and on his casual-seeming, fatherly conversations with suspects and witnesses. As well as the Maigret books, Simenon (who was inhumanly productive) wrote over 500 pulp books under a variety of pseudonyms and – under his own name – some 350 psychological thrillers: sinewy studies of people distracted by fear, obsession, despair or hate.

Simenon is one of the most consistent, as well as prolific, of authors. Each Maigret book is as good as the next; many of his thrillers are of equal quality – and some rank with the work of the finest psychological novelists of the twentieth century: Camus, say, or Graham Greene. Good Maigret novels to begin with are *Maigret's Pipe, Maigret Travels South, Maigret and the Killers, Maigret and the Burglar's Wife, My Friend Maigret, Maigret and the Reluctant Witnesses* and *Maigret Sets a Trap.* Among the best of the thrillers are *The Man Who Watched* the Trains Go By, Act of Passion, The Burgomaster of Furnes, Ticket of Leave and The Man with the Little Dog.

READ ON >

● **The Stain on the Snow (one of Simenon's best non-Maigret books – a chillingly brilliant portrait of a young criminal's psyche).**

▶ ▷ **Nicolas Freeling, Gun Before Butter; Friedrich Durrenmatt, The Pledge; Graham Greene, A Gun for Sale.**

SIMPSON, Dorothy (born 1933)
British writer

Dorothy Simpson's unfussy and unpretentious books featuring the Kent-based Inspector Thanet comprise one of the best and most readable series of traditional English crime stories of the last two decades. Thanet is not a poet, like ▷ P. D. James's Adam Dalgleish or a member of the aristocracy, like ▷ Elizabeth George's hero, but an ordinary family man who uses the mundane virtues of persistence and hard work to get at the solutions to the mysteries he confronts. Most of these take place in small village communities where the apparently civilized surface of life hides darker passions and desires. Typical titles are Dead by Morning (1989), in which a man returns to visit his family after a twenty-year absence, only to make a more permanent exit when he is found murdered, and Dead and Gone (1999), where Thanet and his regular partner, Mike Lineham, have to sort through complicated familial and marital entanglements when a barrister's wife is found murdered. Pitched somewhere between traditional cosy crime and modern police procedural, the Luke Thanet novels are unfailingly entertaining and well plotted.

The Inspector Thanet novels include The Night She Died, Six Feet Under, Last Seen Alive, Doomed to Die, Wake the Dead, A Day for Dying and Dead and Gone.

READ ON >

▶ ▷ **Elizabeth George, Deception on His Mind; ▷ Ann Granger, Say it With Poison; Barry Maitland, The Marx Sisters.**

SJÖWALL, Maj (born 1935) and WAHLÖÖ, Per (1926–1975)
Swedish novelists

Sjöwall and Wahlöö wrote police procedural novels starring the Stockholm detective Martin Beck. The authors were politically active on the left and wanted to use detective fiction to show some of the defects and dangers of Swedish society. But this is less apparent to the non-Swedish reader than the harshness of the stories, the tension of the investigations and the believability of characters and atmosphere (especially Beck's family life and the very Swedish mixture of banter and formality between him and his colleagues at the precinct). If Ingmar Bergman had written police procedural novels, they might have been like this.

The other novels featuring Martin Beck are Roseanna, The Man on the Balcony, The Man Who Went Up in Smoke, Murder at the Savoy, The Fire Engine That Disappeared, The Abominable Man, The Locked Room, Cop Killer and The Terrorists.

READ ON >

► ▷ Henning Mankell, *Faceless Killers* (Swedish society twenty years on); Jan Willem de Wetering, *Death of a Hawker*; Kirstin Ekman, *Blackwater*.

READ ON A THEME: **SMALL-TOWN AMERICA**
(some cosy, some bleak)

Deborah Adams, *All the Dirty Cowards*
Harold Adams, *No Badge, No Gun*
Margaret Maron, *Bootlegger's Daughter*
Katherine Hall Page, *The Body in the Belfry*
Denise Swanson, *Murder of a Small Town Honey*
Kathleen Taylor, *Foreign Body*
▷ Jim Thompson, *Pop. 1280*

SMITH, Joan (born 1953)
British writer

Joan Smith, who is also known as a journalist and cultural commentator, wrote five novels between 1987 and 1995 featuring the academic, Loretta Lawson. Although the same character appears in all the novels and although they are all imbued (not obtrusively) with Smith's social and political radicalism, the five books vary considerably in form and style. They range from the first novel, *A Masculine Ending*, which followed Loretta's investigation of the murder of a colleague at an academic conference and which stuck fairly closely to the conventions of the amateur detective sub-genre, to *Full Stop*, which, in its portrait of Loretta suffering the terror of being stalked, was more psychological thriller than mystery. The best of the series is probably *What Men Say* (1993). Bridget Bennett, Loretta's Oxford don friend and co-investigator in earlier books, has married and moved to a home in the country. At the housewarming party a body is found in one of the property's outhouses and, before long, the police have Bridget in the frame for murder. Loretta is outraged that the police have been so swift to cast her friend in the role of murderer but becomes aware that Bridget does indeed have some secrets she's not telling.

The five Loretta Lawson books are A Masculine Ending, Why Aren't They Screaming?, Don't Leave Me This Way, What Men Say *and* Full Stop.

READ ON >

► ▷ Sarah Dunant, *Under My Skin*; ▷ Val McDermid, *Dead Beat*; Veronica Stallwood, *Deathspell*.

SPILLANE, Mickey (born 1918)
US novelist

Spillane's Mike Hammer books are fast-moving pulp private eye adventures that constantly teeter on the edge of parody (and sometimes fall in). They pit his hero against drugs barons, Mafia bosses, crooked policemen, card sharps, international spies and straightforward thugs. Hammer punches and shoots his way to a solution, fending off busty blondes at every turn. The Hammer books are risible and ridiculous. They are fascist, macho, chauvinist – any censorious adjective you can think of. They have also been among the bestselling crime novels of all time and, to those who enjoy them, they are inexhaustibly entertaining, outranking countless imitations.

The Hammer books include I, the Jury, *My Gun is Quick,* Kiss Me, Deadly, *The Twisted Thing,* Survival . . . Zero, *The Killing Man and* Black Alley.

READ ON >

▶ Michael Avallone, *Lust is No Lady*; ▷ Peter Cheyney, *Your Deal, My Lovely*; Richard S. Prather, *Strip for Murder.*

STARK, Richard, see Donald E. WESTLAKE

STOUT, Rex (1886–1975)
US novelist

Stout's detective, Nero Wolfe, is an overweight, woman-hating eccentric who lives in a large old house with his cook, gardener, books, 10,000 orchids and his assistant and leg-man Archie Goodwin, the narrator of the stories. Archie is young, fond of excitement and high living. He goes out for Wolfe, using his photographic memory to retail scenes and conversations to the great man in exact detail, so that deductions can be made and plans set in motion. The plots of Stout's novels are bizarre and complicated; the dialogue is witty; above all, the characters of Wolfe and Archie, and the twists and turns of their partnership, are intriguing and unpredictable.

To counter (entirely justified) accusations of misogyny in the character of Nero Wolfe, Stout wrote a book (*Crime on Her Hands*) starring a wisecracking female sleuth called Dol Bonner. Set in a high society 1930s mansion full of disagreeable people, it fizzes with energy, like the 'screwball' Hollywood comedies of the period.

The Wolfe novels (over forty) begin with Fer-de-Lance *(one of the best) and include* Where There's a Will, Might As Well Be Dead, If Death Ever Slept, Murder by the Book, The League of Frightened Men *and* Death of a Dude. *After Stout's death the Nero Wolfe series was continued in a number of books by Robert Goldsborough. Some of these, most notably* Death on a Deadline, *were very nearly as inventive and entertaining as the originals.*

READ ON >

▶ ▷ Ellery Queen, *The Egyptian Cross Mystery*; ▷ Lawrence Block, *The Topless Tulip Caper*; Anthony Boucher, *The Case of the Crumpled Knave.*

SWANSON, Doug J. (born 1953)
US novelist

Doug J. Swanson has made his own contribution to the private eye genre in his series featuring the Dallas-based lawyer turned investigator Jack Flippo. Flippo – resourceful, sharp-witted and possessed of a nice talent for one-liners – is firmly in the great tradition of private eyes that runs from Chandler to Estleman and other contemporary novelists, but there is more than enough originality in the stories (and Flippo's wisecracks) to make them well worth reading. One of the best of Swanson's books is *Dreamboat* (1995) in which Flippo travels into east Texas redneck territory in search of information on a possible insurance scam and soon finds himself in a world of trouble. No one in Baggett County, from Sheriff Loyce Slapp to the pneumatic and improbably named bar waitress April Showers, is on the level and Flippo needs all his determination and wit to stay alive, let alone solve the mystery.

READ ON ▷

▶ Bill Crider, *When Old Men Die* (featuring another Texas private eye); ▷ Kinky Friedman, *Armadillos and Old Lace* (the Kinkster forsakes Greenwich Village briefly for Texas); Rick Riordan, *The Devil Went Down to Austin*.

SYMONS, Julian (1912–1994)
British novelist and critic

Julian Symons was a distinguished anthologist, critic and biographer as well as crime writer and wrote one of the best, if inevitably outdated, surveys of the genre: *Bloody Murder* (1972). He published two dozen novels of his own: fiendishly complicated murder plots, often involving swindles or family betrayals going back over a generation, and told in a relaxed, throwaway style distinctly at odds with the sinister obsessions of his characters. Few writers tease their readers quite so thoroughly – if you like crime stories which are intellectual Chinese boxes, bursting with red herrings, Symons is for you.

Symons's novels include The Thirty First of February, The Colour of Murder, The End of Solomon Grundy, The Man Who Killed Himself, The Plot Against Roger Ryder, The Blackheath Poisonings, The Detling Murders *and* The Name of Annabel Lee.

READ ON ▷

● *A Three Pipe Problem* (the first of several stories featuring Sheridan Haynes, a ham actor who specializes in playing Sherlock Holmes on stage and sometimes gets the chance to emulate him in real life).
▶ ▷ Michael Gilbert, *Smallbone Deceased*; ▷ H. R. F. Keating, *A Remarkable Case of Burglary*; ▷ Ruth Rendell, *Live Flesh*.

T

TAYLOR, Andrew (born 1951)
Scottish novelist

Andrew Taylor is a versatile and prolific writer who has written all kinds of fiction from children's books to espionage thrillers. His crime capers featuring William Dougal, an engaging young man whose ambition in life is to do the best he can – first for himself and then for others – are all thoroughly enjoyable. Dougal's willingness to accept what fate offers each day leads him into adventure, crime and (often) farce. A typical title is *Caroline Minuscule* (1982) in which Dougal and his latest girlfriend end up in a frantic chase after some precious diamonds, always one step ahead of an unscrupulous rival. Taylor has also written a series of books set in a fictional town, Lydmouth, on the Anglo-Welsh border in the decade after the Second World War, and a number of tense psychological thrillers. The best of the latter is *The Barred Window*, a subtle tale of a strange, symbiotic relationship between two cousins in which a seemingly guileless narrator slowly reveals dark secrets from the past. Taylor's most ambitious work – part crime fiction, part gothic melodrama – is the Roth trilogy (*The Four Last Things*, *The Judgement of Strangers* and *The Office of the Dead*), in which the history of a psychopath is unpeeled, layer by layer, back through time and through a cleverly interlocking series of narratives.

The Lydmouth books include An Air That Kills, The Suffocating Night, Where Roses Fade *and* Death's Own Door. *The other Dougal novels include* Our Father's Lies, An Old School Tie, Sleeping Policeman *and* Odd Man Out.

> **READ ON** ▷

▶ ▷ Frances Fyfield, *Perfectly Pure and Good*; Kate Ellis, *The Armada Boy*; Charles Todd, *Legacy of the Dead*; ▷ Reginald Hill; *Dialogues of the Dead*.

TEY, Josephine (1897–1952)
Scottish novelist

Josephine Tey was a pseudonym of Elizabeth Mackintosh, who also wrote plays under the name of Gordon Daviot. Her five mystery novels starring the urbane Inspector Grant include one of the best known of all crime-solving books, *The Daughter of Time* (1951). In this Grant, laid up in hospital, uses modern criminological methods (and persuades reluctant visitors to do his legwork) to solve the mystery of the 1480s murder of the Princes in the Tower. Tey's other Grant novels, and her non-series books, are about twentieth-century crime. Her stories often involve abnormal psychology, and she is known for her under-standing of human nature and for her meticulous background research.

THE FRANCHISE AFFAIR (1948)

Robert Blair, a country solicitor, is asked to represent Marion Sharpe who is accused of kidnapping, beating and imprisoning a young girl. The girl, Betty Kane, unerringly identifies the woman and the house, and Blair takes on the seemingly impossible task of showing that she is lying. A modern version of a real-life *cause célèbre* of the eighteenth century, *The Franchise Affair* is one of the few classic crime novels in which the crime is not murder.

Tey's Inspector Grant books are The Man in the Queue, A Shilling for Candles, To Love and Be Wise, The Daughter of Time *and* The Singing Sands. *Her non-series crime novels are* Miss Pym Disposes, The Franchise Affair *and* Brat Farrar.

READ ON >

- *Brat Farrar* (Is Brat Farrar who he claims to be? And if he isn't, where has this strange and plausible young man come from?).
- ▶ to *The Daughter of Time*: ▷ Colin Dexter, *The Wench is Dead* (Morse solves a 150-year-old murder from his hospital bed).
- ▶ to *The Franchise Affair*: Nina Bawden, *The Odd Flamingo*.
- ▶ to the novels in general: ▷ Margaret Millar, *A Stranger in My Grave*; Christianna Brand, *Fog of Doubt*; ▷ Francis Iles, *Malice Aforethought*.

READ ON A THEME: THEATRE

Marian Babson, *Break a Leg, Darlings*
Caryl Brahms and S. J. Simon, *A Bullet in the Ballet*
▷ Simon Brett, *Cast, In Order of Disappearance*
Ed Gorman, *Murder in the Wings*
▷ P. D. James, *The Skull Beneath the Skin*
Gillian Linscott, *Stage Fright*
▷ Ngaio Marsh, *Vintage Murder*
Susan Sussman and Sarajane Avidon, *Audition for Murder*

THOMAS, Ross (1926–1995)
US novelist

Ross Thomas wrote espionage thrillers, crime fiction and books that resist pigeon-holing in either category. All that his books have in common is that they are, almost without exception, wildly entertaining and inventive. His crime novels are as cynical as most hard-boiled writers' about the way US affairs are run. Every police officer, newspaper reporter, politician and lawyer is on the take, and there is little difference between business tycoons and crooks – the bigger they are, the worse they are. In this murky world Thomas's heroes move warily, taking pains to cover their backs, solving the mysteries, getting the girls but usually affecting the rottenness of the system as little as a pebble thrown into a churning sea. If all this were serious, it would be heavy going. But Thomas wrote in beautifully organized, wry prose, full of one-liners and acidly funny.

BRIARPATCH (1984)

Who blew up Ben Dill's policewoman sister and where had she been getting all her money from? In answering these questions, Dill takes the lid off his home city, somewhere in the South, and finds not only the writhing maggots of local politics but some very sleazy links with Washington and with international crime.

Thomas's other novels include Cast a Yellow Shadow, The Fools in Town Are On Our Side, The Pork Choppers, Chinaman's Chance, The Mordida Man, The Money Harvest, Missionary Stew, The Fourth Durango, Out on the Rim *and* Voodoo Ltd.

READ ON ▷

▶ ▷ Lawrence Block, *The Thief Who Couldn't Sleep*; ▷ Robert B. Parker, *Mortal Stakes*; Stephen Greenleaf, *Fatal Obsession*.

THOMPSON, Jim (1906–1977)
US novelist

During his lifetime Thompson was largely ignored by the critics. He wrote cheap paperback originals for the mass market and it was assumed that the contents of his books were as luridly simple-minded as their covers. There has now been a reaction in the other direction and, since the 1980s, he has been regularly acclaimed as a *noir* genius. The truth lies somewhere in the middle of the two extremes. He was not as extravagantly gifted as his most enthusiastic admirers claim – his writing can often be clumsy and unsubtle – but he had his own, dark vision of the world and he worked hard to realize it in his fiction. The typical Thompson novel is a descent into the soul of a doomed character, one of the hustlers, losers and small-time crooks who people his books. Caught in the coils of fate and circumstance, his characters struggle (usually unsuccessfully) to free themselves.

THE KILLER INSIDE ME (1952)

Lou Ford is the deputy sheriff of a small Texas town. Outwardly a respected and well-liked member of the community he carries a dark secret from his past and the sickness that overwhelmed him once before is about to return. Using a first-person narrative, Thompson transcends the limitations of his story to create a chilling portrait of a warped psyche lurking beneath an apparently ordinary surface.

Thompson's other novels include The Alcoholics, Savage Night, A Swell-Looking Babe, After Dark, My Sweet, Wild Town, The Getaway, Pop. 1280 *and* Texas by the Tail.

READ ON ▷

● *The Grifters* (compellingly sleazy account of small-time con artist, his Oedipal relationship with his mother and their doomed attempt to make it to the big time).
▶ ▷ James M. Cain, *The Postman Always Rings Twice*; ▷ David Goodis, *Dark Passage*; Peter Rabe, *Kill the Boss Goodbye*.

TIMLIN, Mark (born 1950)
British novelist

There are few British private eyes that have anything like the same hard-boiled street cred as the best of the Americans. Mark Timlin's south London investigator Nick Sharman is one of the best. The books are violent – the body count in any given title tends to be high and people often depart this life very messily – but they are laced with dark, dry humour and make good use of their London settings. As one reviewer put it, 'Sharman novels tend to divide people between those who think they're violent, gun-happy, fast action reads and those who don't like them.'

ALL THE EMPTY PLACES (2000)
Nick Sharman lands himself up to his neck in trouble once again as he romances the ex-girlfriend of a violent crook with no intention of letting the better man win, and sticks his nose into a meticulously planned multi-million-pound robbery. As always, Timlin keeps the pace cranked up to the maximum and the book culminates in one of the improbably body-littered shoot-outs that have always been a feature of the Sharman books.

The other Nick Sharman books include A Good Year for the Roses, Romeo's Tune, Gun Street Girl, Take the A-Train, Turnaround, Zip Gun Boogie, Hearts of Stone, Paint It Black, Dead Flowers *and* Quick Before They Catch Us.

READ ON

▶ Ken Bruen, *Her Last Call to Louis MacNeice*; Jerry Raine, *Frankie Bosser Comes Home*; John B. Spencer, *Stitch*.

READ ON A THEME: TINSELTOWN MURDERS

George Baxt, *The Fred Astaire and Ginger Rogers Murder Case*
Anthony Boucher, *The Case of Baker Street Irregulars* (murder on the set of a Sherlock Holmes film)
▷ Raymond Chandler, *The Little Sister*
Steve Fisher, *I Wake Up Screaming*
David Handler, *The Boy Who Never Grew Up*
▷ Stuart M. Kaminsky, *High Midnight*
▷ Jonathan Latimer, *Black is the Fashion for Dying*
▷ Elmore Leonard, *Get Shorty*

TUROW, Scott (born 1949)
US novelist

Together with ▷ John Grisham, Scott Turow is one of the masters of the sub-genre of the legal thriller and, like Grisham, he draws on his own legal expertise to give his fiction edge and authenticity. (He's a former US deputy attorney and a partner in an international law firm.) The courtroom is, inherently, a scene of drama, as so many crime writers have shown, but Turow is brilliant at extracting every last drop of tension from the ebb and flow of evidence and cross-examination. Unlike Grisham, whose gift is for high-paced, non-stop action, Turow is also interested in the moral and psychological subtleties of his characters and his narratives, which often twist back and forth between past and present, building slowly and nerve-wrackingly to their conclusions.

PRESUMED INNOCENT (1987)

Turow's first novel remains one of his best. Rusty Sabich is a deputy prosecuting attorney in charge of a rape and murder case. No one knows that he had a secret relationship with the victim but, as the investigation goes from bad to worse, secrets emerge and Sabich eventually finds himself charged with the crime. In a long but riveting sequence of chapters set in the courtroom, he has to defend himself and prove his innocence. Told in a first-person narrative that flits between flashback and the present, this is a long but consistently gripping story with a genuinely surprising twist in its tail.

Turow's other novels are The Burden of Proof, Pleading Guilty, The Laws of Our Fathers, Personal Injuries *and* Reversible Errors.

READ ON >

- *The Laws of Our Fathers* (a compelling narrative shifts back and forth in time as Turow investigates the conflict between the generations through the murder trial of a senator's son).
- ▷ John Grisham, *The Client*; Stephen L. Carter, *The Emperor of Ocean Park*; Steve Martini, *Undue Influence*; Philip Friedman, *Reasonable Doubt*.

U

READ ON A THEME: **UNUSUAL SETTINGS**

    Jasper Fforde, *The Eyre Affair* (in which reality and classic fiction interact)

    Eric Garcia, *Anonymous Rex* (an alternative reality in which dinosaurs still exist, in disguise, in modern society)

▷ Paul Johnston, *Body Politic* (a futuristic Edinburgh as an independent city-state)

    Laura Joh Rowland, *Shinju* (Japan in the seventeenth century)

    Katharine Kerr, *Polar City Blues* (murder and political intrigue in a future universe where a small human enclave sits uneasily between two giant alien confederations)

▷ Robert Van Gulik, *The Chinese Maze Murders* (mysteries from eighth-century China)

V

VACHSS, Andrew (born 1942)
US novelist

All of Andrew Vachss's novels focus on crimes involving the mistreatment and abuse of children and young people. Most of them feature Burke, a criminal and survivor in the urban jungle of New York (in more recent novels, Portland), who takes it upon himself to investigate cases of child abuse and mete out his own form of justice to the molesters and perverts. In *Flood* (1985), for example, Burke is drawn into the search for a disturbed Vietnam vet who rapes and murders young children. Some readers may feel slightly uncomfortable with Vachss's clear wish in his books to retain the moral high ground while still dwelling on the worst details of violence and abuse, but there is no doubting the sincerity behind his fiction or the raw power of his best writing. In his desire to use the dark, violent thriller as a form of social commentary and social campaigning (he is a lawyer deeply involved in the fight against child abuse), Vachss is unlike any other contemporary crime writer.

STREGA (1987)
Burke is offered money by a beautiful Mafiosa to delve into the world of child porn in New York and does so like an avenging angel, taking with him some of the strange dysfunctional allies (the Mole, Max the Silent) who re-appear in other novels. Vachss's vision is as dark as it always is and this journey through the Big Apple's underbelly is one of his best-plotted and dramatic novels.

Andrew Vachss's other novels include Blue Belle, Blossom, Down in the Zero, Choice of Evil, Dead and Gone *and* Pain Management.

> **READ ON**

▶ ▷ James Ellroy, *The Black Dahlia*; Ed Gorman, *Daughter of Darkness*; Benjamin Schutz, *Embrace the Wolf*.

VAN DINE, S. S. (1888–1939)
US novelist

S. S. Van Dine was the pseudonym of Willard Huntington Wright. He was a founding father of US detective fiction and his twelve Philo Vance books are classics. Vance is a 1920s man about town, an art critic, fond of his own voice and stupendously over-educated. In each book he pours out torrents of views on Beowulf, Ibsen, Tang China, Moselle wine, Egyptian scarabs – anything that the situation, or his passing whim, suggests to him. But, if Vance himself can be a pain, the mysteries are not. Van Dine was a stickler for the 'rules' of classic crime fiction, insisting that detective stories should be fair intellectual games, with no cheating between writer and reader. His books continue to delight any addict of 'Golden Age' detective fiction.

The Philo Vance books are The Benson Murder Case, The Canary Murder Case, The Greene Murder Case, The Bishop Murder Case, The Scarab Murder Case, The Kennel Murder Case, The Dragon Murder Case, The Casino Murder Case, The Garden Murder Case, The Kidnap Murder Case, The Gracie Allen Murder Case *and* The Winter Murder Case.

READ ON ▷

▶ ▷ Ellery Queen, *The Greek Coffin Mystery*; ▷ Rex Stout, *Fer-de-Lance*; ▷ Dorothy L. Sayers, *Clouds of Witness*; H. C. Bailey, *The Bishop's Crime.*

VAN GULIK, Robert (1910–1967)
Dutch novelist

Van Gulik was a Dutch diplomat who was posted to China in the 1930s and became fascinated by Chinese culture. He discovered that China has a long history of 'mystery' stories and published his own translations of some of these folk stories under the title of *Celebrated Cases of Judge Dee*. Dee was a real magistrate in eighth-century China and Van Gulik went on to use him as the central character in a sequence of books containing his own stories written in the style of the traditional Chinese tales. The mysteries, usually three interlinked cases, are unusual and unlike anything else in crime fiction. They are also fascinating because of the details about ancient Chinese life which Van Gulik includes. Typical titles are *The Chinese Maze Murders*, *The Chinese Gold Murders*, *The Chinese Lake Murders* and *The Chinese Nail Murders*.

READ ON ▷

▶ Laura Joh Rowland, *Shinju* (set in seventeenth-century Japan); Lauren Haney, *A Face Turned Backwards* (one of a series of historical mysteries featuring a law officer in another ancient civilization – Egyptian).

READ ON A THEME: VICTORIAN MURDER
Emily Brightwell, *Mrs Jeffries Takes the Stage*
▷ John Dickson Carr, *Scandal at High Chimneys*
▷ Michael Dibdin, *A Rich, Full Death* (the poet Robert Browning as detective)
Alanna Knight, *The Coffin Lane Murders* (one of a series set in Victorian Edinburgh)
▷ Peter Lovesey, *Wobble to Death*
Robin Paige, *Death at Devil's Bridge*
Charles Palliser, *The Unburied* (not a conventional detective story but a very powerful narrative of crime and mystery)
▷ Anne Perry, *The Hyde Park Headsman*
▷ Julian Symons, *The Blackheath Poisonings*

READ ON A THEME: VILLAGE LIFE
(murder and mystery in the traditional English village)

▷ Catherine Aird, *Passing Strange*
   M. C. Beaton, *Agatha Raisin and the Walkers of Dembley*
   Henry Cecil, *The Wanted Man*
▷ Agatha Christie, *The Murder at the Vicarage*
▷ Caroline Graham, *The Killings at Badger's Drift*
   John Sherwood, *Bouquet of Thorns*

VINE, Barbara, see Ruth RENDELL

W

WALLACE, Edgar (1875–1932)
British novelist and short story writer

Wallace's fertile mind and busy pen produced over a hundred novels, sixty books of short stories, fifty plays and a dozen volumes of journalism. Towards the end of his life he launched yet another career as a Hollywood screenwriter and died while at work on the script of *King Kong*. Wallace was a hack of genius and his best work (for example, the short stories in *The Mind of Mr J. G. Reeder*, about a private detective solving locked-room and other mysteries for the Prosecution Service) rivals ▷ Conan Doyle's for both ingenuity and atmosphere.

Wallace's best crime books include The Council of Justice, The Man Who Bought London, The Green Archer, The Clue of the Twisted Candle, The Man Who Knew, The Dark Eyes of London, Room 13 *and* The Squeaker.

> READ ON ▷

- ● *The Four Just Men* **(Wallace's first big success, about a group administering their own justice to criminals who evade the law).**
- ▶ **to the Reeder stories: ▷ G. K. Chesterton, *The Club of Queer Trades*; R. Austin Freeman, *The Singing Bone*.**
- ▶ **to his locked-room mysteries: Carter Dickson (▷ John Dickson Carr), *The Ten Teacups*.**

WALTERS, Minette (born 1949)
British novelist

Like so many of the best contemporary writers of crime fiction (▷ Ruth Rendell, ▷ Frances Fyfield, ▷ Andrew Taylor), Minette Walters produces books that are not so much whodunits as whydunits. Our interest is held not so much by the twists and turns of a convoluted, puzzle-like plot but by the way the narrative progressively reveals more and more about the psychology and hidden depths of her characters. This has been the case since her first novel, *The Ice House* (1992), about three women who may or may not have got away with murder ten years before the book opens. Her second novel, *The Sculptress* (1993), introduced the kind of pairing of disparate characters that has recurred in later books. The obese, unloved Olive Martin, imprisoned for the apparent murders of her mother and sister, represents a terrible enigma, affront almost, to the middle-class complacency of the woman intent on writing a book about her crimes. In her more recent novels Minette Walters has increasingly concentrated on stories which gradually unveil the hidden motivations of her characters. In *The Shape of*

Snakes (2000) a teacher refuses to accept that the death of an alcoholic neighbour is an accident. For twenty years she obsessively amasses evidence to prove that murder took place. Narrated by the teacher and reproducing many of the documents which constitute her evidence, the book moves relentlessly towards the revelation of dark, unsettling and moving truths about its characters. Retaining its tension and mystery until its last page, it is the best example yet of Minette Walters's ambition to press forward into territory not usually occupied by writers of crime fiction.

Minette Walters's other novels include The Scold's Bridle, The Echo, The Breaker, The Dark Room *and* Acid Row.

> READ ON

- *The Dark Room* (amnesiac after a terrible car crash, Jane Kingsley struggles to piece together her personality and prove herself no murderer).
- ▶ Barbara Vine (▷ Ruth Rendell), *A Fatal Inversion*; ▷ Nicci French, *The Safe House*; ▷ Val McDermid, *Killing the Shadows*; ▷ Andrew Taylor, *The Barred Window*; Joy Fielding, *Life Penalty*.

WAMBAUGH, Joseph (born 1937)
US novelist

The most important fact about Joseph Wambaugh's fiction is that he writes as an ex-cop. He served fourteen years with the Los Angeles police department. This experience gives his novels an authenticity and often bleak honesty that the work of similar novelists does not always have. Wambaugh's heroes are, unashamedly, the ordinary rank-and-file police officers of the LAPD but he does not sentimentalize them. These are men who are policing brutal streets and they have, often enough, become brutalized themselves. His best re-creation of the realities of police life in LA remains *The Choirboys*, but some of his other novels (*The New Centurions*, *The Delta Star*) are also well worth reading for those who like their crime fiction to be forthright and hard-hitting. *The Onion Field* (1973) is a true story told as fiction – somewhat in the mould of Capote's *In Cold Blood* – about the murder of a cop and the impact of the murder on his surviving partner. It is as powerful as any of Wambaugh's books.

THE CHOIRBOYS (1975)
Wambaugh has said in interviews that he was influenced in the writing of *The Choirboys* by his reading of Joseph Heller's black farce about the Second World War, *Catch-22*. It shows. Just as Heller's character Yossarian faces the insanity of war with his own crazy logic, the police protagonists of *The Choirboys* cope with the brutalities of their jobs through their 'choir practice', the after-hours sessions of booze, banter and (often) violence which keep them sane. Like all of Wambaugh's books – but more so – *The Choirboys* possesses a brutal authenticity.

Wambaugh's other novels include The Black Marble, Lines and Shadows, The Blooding, The Secrets of Harry Bright, Finnegan's Week *and* Floaters.

READ ON ▷

▶ Kent Anderson, *Night Dogs*; William Caunitz, *One Police Plaza*; Paul Bishop, *Citadel Run*.

WENTWORTH, Patricia (1878–1961)
British novelist

In 1928, at the height of the 'Golden Age' of English detective fiction, Patricia Wentworth introduced the spinster private detective Miss Maud Silver in the novel *Grey Mask* and she continued to produce Miss Silver novels until her death in 1961. Unpretentious and straightforward, the Miss Silver books are archetypal productions of the 'Golden Age' in which the crime and the puzzle are all and the characterization is largely secondary to the working out of the mystery. Miss Silver is a less individual character than the other great spinster detective (▷ Christie's Miss Marple) and it sometimes seems as if her only distinguishing feature is that she's forever knitting. However, unlike so many other writers of the era, Patricia Wentworth has retained a readership and many of the books remain in print. She deserves her place in the second tier below the greats like Christie, Sayers and Marsh.

The Miss Silver novels include The Chinese Shawl, Miss Silver Intervenes, Latter End, Miss Silver Comes to Stay, Ladies' Bane, The Silent Pool, Poison in the Pen, The Alington Inheritance *and* The Girl in the Cellar. *Patricia Wentworth's other novels include* The Dower House Mystery, Beggar's Choice, Fear by Night, The Blind Side *and* Unlawful Occasions.

READ ON ▷

▶ to the Miss Silver novels: ▷ Agatha Christie, *The Mirror Crack'd from Side to Side*; ▷ Simon Brett, *A Nice Class of Corpse*.
▶ to her crime fiction in general: ▷ Gladys Mitchell, *The Rising of the Moon*.

WESTLAKE, Donald E(dwin) (born 1933)
US novelist

One of the most prolific of American crime writers, Westlake began his career with *The Mercenaries*, a tough, no-nonsense tale of a hit man, and his next few novels confirmed his hard-boiled reputation. With *The Fugitive Pigeon* (1965), however, he began the kind of books for which he is now best known: comedy thrillers, among the funniest ever written. Many feature his most famous character, the incompetent, indolent but ever-optimistic burglar John Dortmunder and his gang of dysfunctional associates.

Under the name of Richard Stark, Westlake has written hard-boiled, fast-paced crime books in two series, one featuring the amoral, emotionless Parker, a professional thief and murderer, the other an unsuccessful actor called Alan Grofield who turns to theft. As Tucker Coe, Westlake has written a series of private-eye novels featuring a disgraced ex-policeman, Mitch Tobin, racked with guilt over the death of his partner. Each investigation forms part of Tobin's psychological rehabilitation and the books are best read in sequence.

The Dortmunder novels are The Hot Rock, Bank Shot, Jimmy the Kid, Nobody's Perfect, Why Me?, Good Behaviour, Drowned Hopes, Don't Ask, What's the Worst That Could Happen? *and* Bad News. *Westlake's other novels under his own name include* The Spy in the Ointment, God Save the Mark, Cops and Robbers, Brothers Keepers, Trust Me On This *and* The Hook. *Under the name of Tucker Coe he has published* Kinds of Love, Kinds of Death, Murder Among Children, Wax Apple, A Jade in Aries *and* Don't Lie to Me. *The novels under the name of Richard Stark include* Point Blank, The Outfit, The Black Ice Score, The Sour Lemon Score, Deadly Edge, Slayground, Backflash *and* Flashfire.

> **READ ON**

- ● **The Hot Rock** (the first Dortmunder novel, in which our hero hand picks a bunch of incompetents to assist and hinder him in the heist of a fabulously valuable emerald).
- ▶ to the Dortmunder novels: ▷ Lawrence Block, *Burglars Can't Be Choosers*; Joe Gores, *32 Cadillacs*.
- ▶ to the Richard Stark novels: Joe Gores, *Come Morning*; Max Allan Collins, *Primary Target.*

WILLEFORD, Charles (1919–1988)
US novelist

Before writing tough-guy fiction, Willeford had an archetypally tough-guy career as a US soldier. During the Second World War he fought in Europe as a tank commander and re-enlisted in the army after the end of the war. His first novel, *High Priest of California*, appeared in 1953 and he published several more hard-boiled stories, reminiscent of ▷ Jim Thompson in their bleak, unblinking pessimism, but shot through with a wry, unillusioned humour. *Cockfighter*, for example, is about a man so obsessed by winning at the brutal sport of cockfighting, still popular in the rural south at the time, that all else in his life is sacrificed to it. None of Willeford's early novels, published by cheap paperback firms, gained much attention and he was an unknown name in crime writing until his first book about the shabby, decidedly unheroic Miami detective Hoke Moseley, appeared in the 1980s. It was a surprise success, and was followed by three other Moseley books.

MIAMI BLUES (1984)
Willeford's low-life, seedy Miami detective Hoke Moseley, is on the receiving end of a beating which results in the loss of his gun, his badge and his false teeth as he investigates the death of a Hare Krishna follower. Clinging to what scraps of dignity remain to him, he sets about discovering the identity of his attacker. Willeford mixes hard-boiled realism with bizarre comedy in the Moseley sequence.

The other Hoke Moseley books are New Hope for the Dead, Sideswipe *and* The Way We Die Now. *Willeford's other books include* Pick-Up, High Priest of California, Cockfighter, The Burnt Orange Heresy *and* The Shark-Infested Custard.

READ ON ▷

- *The Burnt Orange Heresy* (a strange *noir* thriller about an art critic in search of a reclusive artist).
- ▶ ▷ Jim Thompson, *Savage Night*; ▷ David Goodis, *Down There*; ▷ James W. Hall, *Under Cover of Daylight.*

WILSON, Robert (born 1957)
British novelist

Robert Wilson began his career by inventing one of the most memorable anti-heroes of recent English crime fiction in Bruce Medway, a fixer and debt-collector working in the shadier areas of the West African commercial world. Not only was Medway himself an original creation but the African setting, the multinational supporting cast of rogues, chancers and deal-makers and Wilson's witty dialogue added their own particular pleasures. The best of the series is *Blood is Dirt* (1997) in which the gruesome killing of one of his clients leads Medway into a very dangerous world of oil and toxic-waste scams, money-laundering and corrupt politics.

Wilson's more recent novels have grown in ambition. *A Small Death in Lisbon*, for example, is a complex, multi-layered narrative in which the contemporary investigation of a young girl's murder leads back to a conspiracy that began in the Nazi-haunted Europe of 1941. Wilson handles the multiple threads of his story with great skill and introduces a compelling detective in the person of Inspector Zé Coelho.

The other Medway books are The Big Killing, Instruments of Darkness *and* A Darkening Stain.

READ ON ▷

- *The Company of Strangers* (more conspiracies and crimes with their roots in the past in a story largely set in wartime Lisbon; minor characters appear in both this and *A Small Death in Lisbon*)
- ▶ to the Medway books: Alexander McCall Smith, *Tears of the Giraffe* (for a very different view of Africa).
- ▶ to *A Small Death in Lisbon*; Alan Furst, *Night Soldiers*; John Lawton, *Blackout.*

WOODRELL, Daniel (born 1953)
US novelist

Daniel Woodrell writes dialogue and descriptive prose to die for. He has some claims to being the most offbeat and accomplished stylist in contemporary American crime fiction. If, that is, what he writes is crime fiction. Only the three St Bruno novels, featuring the Shade family, can truly be described as halfway conventional crime fiction, and even they are marked by Woodrell's determined originality. His more recent books are novels in which crime plays a leading role rather than crime fiction. In *The Death of Sweet Mister* (2002) the narrator Shug, an overweight teenager in the Ozark mountains of Missouri, is used by his brutish stepfather to carry out robberies that the stepfather, perilously close to a long jail sentence, no longer dares to do. Meanwhile Shug's mother, the desperately flirtatious Glenda, is trying to find a route out of the trap her life has become. There are no mysteries in *The Death of Sweet Mister* – beyond the permanent mysteries of human motivation – but Woodrell's unique prose and the acuteness of his characterization make the book unforgettable.

UNDER THE BRIGHT LIGHTS (1986)
A black councilman who has been rocking the boat of local politics is found shot after what seems like a failed burglary. The burglar, people assume, must be the killer. Detective René Shade is not convinced and his search for the real truth leads him into the violence of the Cajun and black quarters of St Bruno, Woodrell's imaginary Louisiana city, and the corruption of its city hall. Fast-moving and suspenseful, *Under the Bright Lights* is also full of Woodrell's wit and the unpretentious, offbeat lyricism of his language.

The other two St Bruno novels are The Ones You Do *and* Muscle for the Wing. *Woodrell's other books include* Tomato Red *and* Give Us a Kiss.

> READ ON

▶ ▷ Jim Thompson, *The Killer Inside Me*; William Faulkner, *Sanctuary*; Christopher Cook, *Robbers*.

WOOLRICH, Cornell (1903–1968)
US novelist and short story writer

Woolrich began his career as a writer of sub-Scott Fitzgerald Jazz Age romances. In the 1930s he wrote for pulp magazines like *Black Mask* and *Detective Fiction*, and then moved on to cheap paperbacks which were often the bases for movies in the 1940s and 50s. Woolrich has often been called the 'father of *noir* fiction'. It has even been claimed that his fondness for using the word 'black' in his titles (a reflection of his doom-laden view of the world) was the ultimate origin of the term '*film noir*'. Woolrich has also been called the 'Poe of the pulp stands' – certainly the miseries of his alcohol-haunted private life echo Poe – and his work has attracted much posthumous praise. By most standards he was an awful writer. His prose is often ridiculously overwrought and his plots tend to be a succession of variants on a few basic contrivances. Yet, pick up a Woolrich novel and you're hooked. He hauls you into his strange, warped universe and holds you there.

Woolrich's novels include The Black Curtain, Black Alibi, Rendezvous in Black, Savage Bride, Death is My Dancing Partner *and* Into the Night *(completed by ▷ Lawrence Block). He wrote a number of novels and short story collections under the name of William Irish including* Phantom Lady, If I should Die Before I Wake, I Married a Dead Man *and* Eyes That Watch You.

> READ ON

▶ ▷ David Goodis, *The Blonde on the Street Corner*; Fredric Brown, *The Screaming Mimi*; Bruno Fischer, *I'll Slay You in My Dreams*.

Y

YORKE, Margaret (born 1924)
British novelist

Margaret Yorke is the pseudonym of Margaret Nicholson. Her first successes were with a series of entertaining, but unexceptional books featuring Patrick Grant, an Oxford professor. However, in the mid-1970s, she took a new direction in her work and began to produce the psychological suspense thrillers for which she is now best known. She has an unnerving ability to escalate the fears and tensions of ordinary lives, and often shows us several apparently normal, apparently unconnected people who become enmeshed by the commission or effects of some ghastly crime. Her style is plain, even throwaway, but her vision that natural justice always prevails and her evocation of the thought processes of her characters (especially young women) make her books unique.

ACT OF VIOLENCE (1997)
In a small village a group of bored teenagers goes on a destructive rampage which ends in fighting and the death of an adult who intervenes. All the tensions that lurk beneath the apparently tranquil surface of the rural community emerge in the aftermath of the death. The schoolboys who witnessed it remain unprepared to say what they have seen. Marriages and relationships between parents and children suffer. And meanwhile someone else who once committed a murder is observing all that unfolds. This is a fine example of Yorke's ability (seen in a number of her books) to show, with great psychological acuity, how the ripples from one act of violence can slowly spread through a community.

The Patrick Grant novels are Dead in the Morning, Silent Witness, Grave Matters, Mortal Remains *and* Cast for Death. *Margaret Yorke's other novels include* Full Circle, The Apricot Bed, The Limbo Ladies, No Medals for the Major, The Hand of Death, Crime in Question, Almost the Truth, Serious Intent, A Question of Belief, False Pretences, The Price of Guilt *and* Case to Answer.

> READ ON

▶ to the psychological thrillers: ▷ Vera Caspary, *The Man Who Loved His Wife*; Barbara Vine (▷ Ruth Rendell), *The Brimstone Wedding*.

WHO'S WHO OF
INVESTIGATORS AND THEIR CREATORS

Character	Creator
Chief Inspector Roderick ALLEYN	Ngaio MARSH
AMEROTKE	Paul DOHERTY
Roy ANGEL	Mike RIPLEY
Inspector John APPLEBY	Michael INNES
Lew ARCHER	Ross MacDONALD
Owen ARCHER	Candace ROBB
Jacob ASCH	Arthur LYONS
Brother ATHELSTAN	Paul DOHERTY (as Paul Harding)
Detective Chief Superintendent Geoffrey BAILEY	Frances FYFIELD
Mario BALZIC	K. C. CONSTANTINE
Chief Inspector Alan BANKS	Peter ROBINSON
Inspector BARNABY	Caroline GRAHAM
Superintendent BATTLE	Agatha CHRISTIE
Inspector Martin BECK	Maj SJÖWALL and Per WAHLÖÖ
Tommy and Tuppence BERESFORD	Agatha CHRISTIE
Oz BLACKSTONE	Quintin JARDINE (as Matthew Reid)
Lew BLOODWORTH	Dick LOCHTE
Myron BOLITAR	Harlan COBEN
Dol BONNER	Rex STOUT
Harry BOSCH	Michael CONNELLY
Dame Beatrice Lestrange BRADLEY	Gladys MITCHELL
Charlie BRADSHAW	Stephen DOBYNS
Dave BRANDSTETTER	Joseph HANSEN
Kate BRANNIGAN	Val McDERMID
Dr Temperance BRENNAN	Kathy REICHS
Father BROWN	G. K. CHESTERTON
Commissario Guido BRUNETTI	Donna LEON
BURKE	Andrew VACHSS
Detective Inspector Kate BURROWS	Martina COLE
Brother CADFAEL	Ellis PETERS
Slim CALLAGHAN	Peter CHEYNEY
Albert CAMPION	Margery ALLINGHAM
Steve CARELLA	Ed McBAIN
Carlotta CARLYLE	Linda BARNES
Max CARRADOS	Ernest BRAMAH
Pepe CARVALHO	Manuel Vazquez MONTALBAN
Henri CASTANG	Nicolas FREELING
Lemmy CAUTION	Peter CHEYNEY
Roger the CHAPMAN	Kate SEDLEY
Nick and Nora CHARLES	Dashiell HAMMETT
Jim CHEE	Tony HILLERMAN
Inspector Zé COELHO	Robert WILSON
Inspector John COFFIN	Gwendoline BUTLER
Artie COHEN	Reggie NADELSON
Elvis COLE	Robert CRAIS
Hap COLLINS	Joe LANSDALE
Kat COLORADO	Karen KIJEWSKI
The CONTINENTAL OP	Dashiell HAMMETT
Bertha COOL	Erle Stanley GARDNER (as A. A. Fair)
Benny COOPERMAN	Howard ENGEL
Hugh CORBETT	Paul DOHERTY
Bill CRANE	Jonathan LATIMER

Sergeant CRIBB	Peter LOVESEY
Alex CROSS	James PATTERSON
Sergeant CUFF	Wilkie COLLINS
Commander Adam DALGLIESH	P. D. JAMES
Quint DALRYMPLE	Paul JOHNSTON
Detective Superintendent Andy DALZIEL	Reginald HILL
Charmian DANIELS	Gwendoline BUTLER
Pete DECKER	Faye KELLERMAN
Judge DEE	Robert VAN GULIK
Edward X. DELANEY	Lawrence SANDERS
Alex DELAWARE	Jonathan KELLERMAN
The DETECTIVE SERGEANT	Derek RAYMOND
Inspector Peter DIAMOND	Peter LOVESEY
John DORTMUNDER	Donald E. WESTLAKE
William DOUGAL	Andrew TAYLOR
Nick DUFFY	Dan KAVANAGH
Auguste DUPIN	Edgar Allan POE
Marcus Didius FALCO	Lindsey DAVIS
Kate FANSLER	Amanda CROSS
Dr Gideon FELL	John Dickson CARR
The FELSE FAMILY	Ellis PETERS
Professor Gervase FEN	Edmund CRISPIN
James FLANNERY	Robert CAMPBELL
Jack FLIPPO	Doug J. SWANSON
Inspector FRENCH	Freeman Wills CROFTS
Sheriff Matt GABRIEL	Paula GOSLING
Angela GENNARO	Dennis LEHANE
Inspector GHOTE	H. R. F. KEATING
Inspector GIDEON	John CREASEY (as J. J. Marric)
Archie GOODWIN	Rex STOUT
GORDIANUS the Finder	Steven SAYLOR
Lindsay GORDON	Val McDERMID
Inspector Alan GRANT	Josephine TEY
Dr Patrick GRANT	Margaret YORKE
Cordelia GRAY	P. D. JAMES
Lew GRIFFIN	James SALLIS
Marshal GUARNACCIA	Magdalen NABB
Bernie GUNTHER	Philip KERR
Mike HAMMER	Mickey SPILLANE
Det. Chief Superintendent Colin HARPUR	Bill JAMES
Inspector HAZELRIGG	Michael GILBERT
Nikki HILL	Dick LOCHTE
Dr Tony HILL	Val McDERMID
Sherlock HOLMES	Arthur Conan DOYLE
Charles HONEYBATH	Michael INNES
Matthew HOPE	Ed McBAIN
Robin HUDSON	Sparkle HAYTER
Assistant Commissioner Desmond ILES	Bill JAMES
Sergeant Gemma JAMES	Deborah CROMBIE
Coffin Ed JOHNSON	Chester HIMES
Grave Digger JONES	Chester HIMES
Sam JONES	Lauren HENDERSON
Detective Chief Inspector Carol JORDAN	Val McDERMID
Inspector Richard JURY	Martha GRIMES
Kemal KAYANKAYA	Jakob ARJOUNI
Sarah KELLY	Charlotte MacLEOD
Patrick KENZIE	Dennis LEHANE
Julian KESTREL	Kate ROSS
Superintendent Duncan KINCAID	Deborah CROMBIE
Willow KING	Natasha COOPER
Inspector Jack LAIDLAW	William McILVANNEY
Lauren LAURANO	Sandra SCOPPETTONE

Loretta LAWSON	Joan SMITH
Rina LAZARUS	Faye KELLERMAN
Joe LEAPHORN	Tony HILLERMAN
Anna LEE	Liza CODY
LIEBERMAN	Stuart M. KAMINSKY
LOVEJOY	Jonathan GASH
Detective Inspector LYNLEY	Elizabeth GEORGE
Sharon McCONE	Marcia MULLER
Travis McGEE	John D. MACDONALD
Cooper MacLEISH	Sam REAVES
Detective Inspector John McLEISH	Janet NEEL
Archy McNALLY	Lawrence SANDERS
Elizabeth MacPHERSON	Sharyn McCRUMB
Nick MADRID	Peter GUTTRIDGE
Trish MAGUIRE	Natasha COOPER
Inspector Jules MAIGRET	Georges SIMENON
Benjamin MALAUSSENE	Daniel PENNAC
Inspector MALLETT	Cyril HARE
MALLORY	Carol O'CONNELL
The MAMUR ZAPT	Michael PEARCE
Superintendent Alan MARKBY	Ann GRANGER
Philip MARLOWE	Raymond CHANDLER
Miss MARPLE	Agatha CHRISTIE
Terry MARRION	Dick LOCHTE
Saz MARTIN	Stella DUFFY
Kate MARTINELLI	Laurie KING
Perry MASON	Erle Stanley GARDNER
Alex MAVROS	Paul JOHNSTON
Bruce MEDWAY	Robert WILSON
Sir Henry MERRIVALE	John Dickson CARR (as Carter Dickson)
Kinsey MILLHONE	Sue GRAFTON
Milo MILOGRADOVITCH	James CRUMLEY
Tess MONAGHAN	Laura LIPPMAN
William MONK	Anne PERRY
Inspector MORSE	Colin DEXTER
Hon. Charles MORTDECAI	Kyril BONFIGLIOLI
Hoke MOSELEY	Charles WILLEFORD
Kent MURDOCK	George Harmon COXE
Commissioner OTANI	James MELVILLE
Mrs PARGETER	Simon BRETT
Charles PARIS	Simon BRETT
Jack PARLABANE	Christopher BROOKMYRE
Inspector Peter PASCOE	Reginald HILL
John PELLAM	Jeffery DEAVER
Toby PETERS	Stuart M. KAMINSKY
Francis PETTIGREW	Cyril HARE
Superintendent PIBBLE	Peter DICKINSON
Leonard PINE	Joe LANSDALE
Superintendent Thomas PITT	Anne PERRY
Stephanie PLUM	Janet EVANOVICH
Hercule POIROT	Agatha CHRISTIE
Chief Inspector QUANTRILL	Sheila RADLEY
Ellery QUEEN	Ellery QUEEN
Terry QUEEN	George PELECANOS
Qwill QWILLERAN	Lilian Jackson BRAUN
Sunny RANDALL	Robert B. PARKER
Ezekiel 'Easy' RAWLINS	Walter MOSLEY
Jack REACHER	Lee CHILD
Inspector John REBUS	Ian RANKIN
Detective Inspector Charlie RESNICK	John HARVEY
Bernie RHODENBARR	Lawrence BLOCK
Lincoln RHYME	Jeffery DEAVER

Dave ROBICHEAUX	James Lee BURKE
ROGER the Chapman	Kate SEDLEY
Porfiry ROSTNIKOV	Stuart M. KAMINSKY
Mary RUSSELL	Laurie KING
Congressman Ben SAFFORD	Emma LATHEN
The SAINT (Simon Templar)	Leslie CHARTERIS
Kay SCARPETTA	Patricia CORNWELL
Matt SCUDDER	Lawrence BLOCK
Nicholas SEGALLA	Paul DOHERTY (as Ann Dukthas)
Detective René SHADE	Daniel WOODRELL
Roger SHALLOT	Paul DOHERTY (as Michael Clynes)
Professor SHANDY	Charlotte MacLEOD
Nick SHARMAN	Mark TIMLIN
Roger SHERINGHAM	Francis ILES (as Anthony Berkeley)
Jemima SHORE	Antonia FRASER
Miss SILVER	Patricia WENTWORTH
Joe SIXSMITH	Reginald HILL
Deputy Chief Constable Bob SKINNER	Quintin JARDINE
Inspector SLOAN	Catherine AIRD
Rabbi David SMALL	Harry KEMELMAN
Sam SPADE	Dashiell HAMMETT
SPENSER	Robert B. PARKER
Michael SPRAGGUE	Linda BARNES
Nick STEFANOS	George PELECANOS
Jesse STONE	Robert B. PARKER
Serge STORMS	Tim DORSEY
Derek STRANGE	George PELECANOS
Nigel STRANGEWAYS	Nicholas BLAKE
C. W. SUGHRUE	James CRUMLEY
Evan TANNER	Lawrence BLOCK
Constable THACKERAY	Peter LOVESEY
Inspector Luke THANET	Dorothy SIMPSON
John Puttnam THATCHER	Emma LATHEN
THORN	James HALL
Mitch TOBIN	Donald E. WESTLAKE (as Tucker Coe)
Philip TRENT	E. C. BENTLEY
Inspector Perry TRETHOWAN	Robert BARNARD
Philo VANCE	S. S. VAN DINE
Inspector Piet VAN DER VALK	Nicolas FREELING
Harriet VANE	Dorothy L. SAYERS
Fran VARADY	Ann GRANGER
Amos WALKER	Loren D. ESTLEMAN
Inspector Kurt WALLANDER	Henning MANKELL
V. I. WARSHAWSKI	Sara PARETSKY
Inspector WEST	John CREASEY
Inspector WEXFORD	Ruth RENDELL
WHISTLER	Robert CAMPBELL
Francesca WILSON	Janet NEEL
Lord Peter WIMSEY	Dorothy L. SAYERS
Hannah WOLFE	Sarah DUNANT
Nero WOLFE	Rex STOUT
Superintendent WYCLIFFE	W. J. BURLEY
Helen WEST	Frances FYFIELD
Eva WYLIE	Liza CODY
Aurelio ZEN	Michael DIBDIN

THE CWA GOLD DAGGER AWARD

1960	Lionel Davidson	*The Night of Wenceslas*
1961	Mary Kelly	*The Spoilt Kill*
1962	Joan Fleming	*When I Grow Rich*
1963	John Le Carré	*The Spy Who Came in From the Cold*
1964	H. R. F. Keating	*The Perfect Murder*
1965	Ross Macdonald	*The Far Side of the Dollar*
1966	Lionel Davidson	*A Long Way to Shiloh*
1967	Emma Lathen	*Murder Against the Grain*
1968	Peter Dickinson	*Skin Deep*
1969	Peter Dickinson	*A Pride of Heroes*
1970	Joan Fleming	*Young Man, I Think You're Dying*
1971	James McClure	*The Steam Pig*
1972	Eric Ambler	*The Levanter*
1973	Robert Littell	*The Defection of A. J. Lewinter*
1974	Anthony Price	*Other Paths to Glory*
1975	Nicholas Meyer	*The Seven-Per-Cent Solution*
1976	Ruth Rendell	*A Demon in My View*
1977	John Le Carré	*The Honourable Schoolboy*
1978	Lionel Davidson	*The Chelsea Murders*
1979	Dick Francis	*Whip Hand*
1980	H. R. F. Keating	*The Murder of the Maharajah*
1981	Martin Cruz Smith	*Gorky Park*
1982	Peter Lovesey	*The False Inspector Dew*
1983	John Hutton	*Accidental Crimes*
1984	B. M. Gill	*The Twelfth Juror*
1985	Paula Gosling	*Monkey Puzzle*
1986	Ruth Rendell	*Live Flesh*
1987	Barbara Vine	*A Fatal Inversion*
1988	Michael Dibdin	*Ratking*
1989	Colin Dexter	*The Wench is Dead*
1990	Reginald Hill	*Bones and Silence*
1991	Barbara Vine	*King Solomon's Carpet*
1992	Colin Dexter	*The Way Through the Woods*
1993	Patricia Cornwell	*Cruel and Unusual*
1994	Minette Walters	*The Scold's Bridle*
1995	Val McDermid	*The Mermaids Singing*
1996	Ben Elton	*Popcorn*
1997	Ian Rankin	*Black and Blue*
1998	James Lee Burke	*Sunset Limited*
1999	Robert Wilson	*A Small Death in Lisbon*
2000	Jonathan Lethem	*Motherless Brooklyn*
2001	Henning Mankell	*Sidetracked*
2002	José Carlos Samoza	*The Athenian Murders*

THE EDGAR AWARD

(awarded by the Mystery Writers of America for Best Mystery of the Year)

1954	Charlotte Jay	*Beat Not the Bones*
1955	Raymond Chandler	*The Long Goodbye*
1956	Margaret Millar	*Beast in View*
1957	Charlotte Armstrong	*A Dram of Poison*
1958	Ed Lacy	*Room to Swing*
1959	Stanley Ellin	*The Eighth Circle*
1960	Celia Fremlin	*The Hours Before Dawn*
1961	Julian Symons	*The Progress of a Crime*
1962	J. J. Marric	*Gideon's Fire*
1963	Ellis Peters	*Death and the Joyful Woman*
1964	Eric Ambler	*The Light of Day*
1965	John Le Carré	*The Spy Who Came in From the Cold*
1966	Adam Hall	*The Quiller Memorandum*
1967	Nicolas Freeling	*King of the Rainy Country*
1968	Donald E. Westlake	*God Save the Mark*
1969	Jeffery Hudson	*A Case of Need*
1970	Dick Francis	*Forfeit*
1971	Sjöwall & Wahlöö	*The Laughing Policeman*
1972	Frederick Forsyth	*The Day of the Jackal*
1973	Warren Kiefer	*The Lingala Code*
1974	Tony Hillerman	*Dance Hall of the Dead*
1975	Jon Cleary	*Peter's Pence*
1976	Brian Garfield	*Hopscotch*
1977	Robert B. Parker	*Promised Land*
1978	William H. Hallahan	*Catch Me, Kill Me*
1979	Ken Follett	*The Eye of the Needle*
1980	Arthur Maling	*The Rhinegold Route*
1981	Dick Francis	*Whip Hand*
1982	William Bayer	*Peregrine*
1983	Rick Boyer	*Billingsgate Shoal*
1984	Elmore Leonard	*La Brava*
1985	Ross Thomas	*Briarpatch*
1986	L. R. Wright	*The Suspect*
1987	Barbara Vine	*A Dark-Adapted Eye*
1988	Aaron Elkins	*Old Bones*
1989	Stuart M. Kaminsky	*A Cold Red Sunrise*
1990	James Lee Burke	*Black Cherry Blues*
1991	Julie Smith	*New Orleans Mourning*
1992	Lawrence Block	*A Dance at the Slaughterhouse*
1993	Margaret Maron	*Bootlegger's Daughter*
1994	Minette Walters	*The Sculptress*
1995	Mary Willis Walker	*The Red Scream*
1996	Dick Francis	*Come to Grief*
1997	Thomas H. Cook	*The Chatham School Affair*
1998	James Lee Burke	*Cimarron Rose*
1999	Robert Clark	*Mr White's Confession*
2000	Jan Burke	*Bones*
2001	Joe Lansdale	*The Bottoms*
2002	T. Jefferson Parker	*Silent Joe*

INDEX

Bold page numbers indicate main references